SOMETHING
VERY
WICKED

SOMETHING VERY WICKED

MARY ZELINSKY

W🌐RLDWIDE®

TORONTO • NEW YORK • LONDON
AMSTERDAM • PARIS • SYDNEY • HAMBURG
STOCKHOLM • ATHENS • TOKYO • MILAN
MADRID • WARSAW • BUDAPEST • AUCKLAND

Recycling programs
for this product may
not exist in your area.

Something Very Wicked

A Worldwide Mystery/February 2016

First published by Five Star Publishing

ISBN-13: 978-0-373-26981-5

Printed in U.S.A.

SOMETHING VERY WICKED

ONE

CHLOE GALEN, NINETEEN-YEAR-OLD granddaughter of the late Etienne Gustave Galen, one of New Orleans' oldest and most respected families, was arrested last night for drunk-and-disorderly conduct and resisting arrest at a sorority house on the main campus of the University of Mississippi. This was not the first time Miss Galen had been arrested since transferring to Ole Miss following her expulsion from the prestigious Henderson College, where it is reported she was a gifted art student.

"Damn," Ethan Galen muttered and threw the newspaper down on the table. He downed the last of the amber contents of the snifter and signaled the waiter to bring another. He stared into the streaky glass trying to shut out the stares of the other patrons. Black Orchids was a favorite dining spot for locals and seldom discovered by tourists, thus many of the diners recognized him through family acquaintance.

The waiter returned with both another glass of cognac and the bottle. Ethan looked up with surprise. "Mr. Jerome instructed me to leave the bottle, Mr. Galen. Compliments of the house, sir." The waiter glanced briefly at the newspaper that had been cast aside before executing a small bow and disappearing. Ethan tossed back the next drink with a grimace. Partly from the fire that burned his throat as he swallowed the aged spirits, but mainly from the fact that everyone in town seemed to read the sensationalized rag, and, he assumed, believed the contents.

"Well, I see you've started without me, you old dog."

Ethan frowned at the cheery face of Nathan Price who had slouched down in the opposite chair, refilling the empty snifter from the bottle.

"Get your own glass," Ethan snarled.

"Can't wait that long. I've got to catch up." He polished off the contents in one long swallow. Almost magically the waiter returned with two fresh glasses and removed the dirty one. Nate's eyes registered surprise at the expedient service. "I'll never get used to the speed of service you get, old buddy. Orleans has two tempos—one for the cherished French Old Guard, and one for everybody else."

"Tip more than a buck, and you'll get better service, too," Ethan retorted without rancor. He had no heart for their usual sparring and resumed his blank stare above the heads of the other patrons.

"I'll take that under consideration." Nate's gaze landed on the newspaper. "I see you've read the story." His voice dropped so they wouldn't be overheard. "Did you get a call from little Chloe?"

"Of course. She's innocent, as usual." Ethan spat the word irritably. "I called our best criminal lawyer; he's there right now trying to get the charges dropped, or at least, encourage Chloe to plead no contest with a stipulation of community service instead of jail time."

"Oh, I don't know. I think a few weeks doing hurricane restoration, chained to husband-beaters and prostitutes while scrubbing black mold from the courthouse foundation, might do her good. She'd look good in stripes."

Ethan flashed a warning look, then relaxed and refilled his glass. "You know," he said softly, "you might be right. Nothing else has worked so far. No matter what I threaten her with, or how my mother begs, Chloe continues to do whatever she wants, whenever she wishes.

She'll just charm her by attending Mass in a starched pinafore, then accompany her to Brennan's for Sunday brunch so the blue-hairs can see what a dutiful daughter she is. Afterwards she'll beat it back to Ole Miss with a trunk load of wine and beer stolen from the cellar while mom packs her a hamper of food."

"The girl is creative; you must admit." Nate settled back in the chair, enjoying his second cognac at a slower pace.

"That she is. When I threaten to cut off access to her trust fund money, she just smiles sweetly, turns those soulful brown eyes on me, and promises to straighten up. She even crosses her heart. When was the last time anybody did that to prove their sincerity?"

"It still works on you, big brother, so why abandon a proven winner? She always did have you wrapped firmly around her purple-nailed finger." Nate laughed heartily.

"They were painted black the last time I saw her. And she's back to being a redhead." Ethan exhaled a sigh of fatigue and exasperation, stretching out his long legs under the table. "There's not much I can do anymore in the intimidation department. She'll be twenty-one in less than two years. Then no one can restrict her access to the trust. That's how my father set up his will. He was sure Chloe would mature by then. That certainly hasn't happened."

Ethan took another swallow, his face clouding with an unpleasant memory. "Of course, when my father set up his estate, Chloe wasn't the only Galen out of control. I'm afraid I didn't give him much to be proud of either. Neither did my brother." Deep creases furrowed his forehead, his face twisting into a mask of regret and shame.

"Hey, don't beat yourself up, man. You're definitely the best of the bunch. You were the only one never arrested." Nate poured them both another drink and drew a pack of cigarettes from his pocket. He lit up, then passed the pack to Ethan. "At least, not to my knowledge."

"No thanks. You know I quit awhile ago."

"Just checking. It's been about three years, hasn't it?" He blew smoke up into the thick, humid night air, the relentless cacophony of power saws, nail guns and jackhammers finally quiet for the evening. "About the time you quit all your fun-loving bad habits and vowed to save the family reputation."

Ethan studied his friend dispassionately, trying to gauge whether he was being mocked. It would be so easy to pull him out of that chair and wipe the smug look off his face. Price grinned back like a pet trying to amuse the master with its antics. Ethan decided the man's humor may stray left of center, but Price wouldn't purposely ridicule him.

"Yeah, for all the good my efforts have done. I've spent three years taking an active part in the family businesses, sitting on countless redevelopment boards since Katrina, attending enough community service functions to hate the smell of Lysol forever, while our reputation still resides in the crumbling sewers. If I overhear one more old bat say, 'He may throw his money around, but he's still no Etienne Galen, Junior or Senior,' I'm going to wring a dowager's neck. The opinions of those walking cadavers count little with me, but they mean a lot to my mother. They say that stuff while she's in earshot. And they mean even more to my grandmother." He slammed the snifter down on the table, causing a tiny hairline fracture to snake up the side.

"Take it easy, man. We can plot their comeuppance later. Maybe we'll lace their lattes with laxative, or doctor their denture adhesive with Superglue. First, let's figure out how to keep Chloe in college. You sure don't need her back in the Quarter if you're still bent on this mission to resurrect the revered Galen name from the ashes."

Ethan raked a hand through his long hair and managed a smile. "I can always rely on you for the mature, respectable solution to life's injustice. That's why we get along so well." He picked up the newspaper again and continued reading.

"And I hang with you because you get the broads flocking around with your expensive duds, hot car, and all that aristocratic charm. Chicks just eat that crap up. I watch women from fifteen to eighty turn their heads when you arrive anywhere."

"Maybe the fact you're the last man in America still using the term 'broads' has something to do with your lack of success with the ladies," Ethan said from behind the newspaper. His grip tightened as he continued with the story, squeezing all the blood from his fingers.

"According to the police report, Miss Galen was arrested in the early morning hours at the Chi Omega Sorority House after neighbors complained about blaring music, loud voices, and partial nudity. When police responded, approximately one dozen women were perched on the porch rail engaged in singing lewd drinking songs. Galen broke from the arresting officer's grasp, thus provoking the resisting arrest complaint, proclaiming that she had to retrieve her wrap if she was making a social call."

"Damn," Ethan muttered. "She was drunk, for crying out loud. That's her brand of humor when she's half-in-the-bag."

"She was probably more than half in the bag."

"No doubt, but since twelve girls were arrested, why am I only seeing Chloe's name printed in the paper?"

Ethan's voice rose despite his intentions, drawing looks from several curious diners.

"Maybe because the other girls' parents aren't rich, so their disgrace won't sell more newspapers? Just a wild guess."

That drew an angry response from Ethan, who straightened in his chair and cast a withering glare at the patrons who obviously enjoyed eavesdropping. The offenders quickly pivoted back to their suppers.

"That's exactly right. And I've just about had enough of it." His voice took on a deadly tone as he continued reading aloud.

"Chloe Galen is the daughter of Cotilde Galen of New Orleans and the late Etienne Galen, Jr. Cotilde Galen is the fundraising chairwoman of the Council of Performing Arts and director of the Mercy Hospital Auxiliary."

Ethan threw down the paper a second time.

"What? *Grandmère* didn't even get a mention this time?" asked Nate.

"Someone must be slipping." Ethan stared off through the open doorway where the convivial crowds of the Quarter could be glimpsed as they scurried by searching for the next watering hole. Even a category five couldn't keep the party lovers and drunks away for long.

"What're you going to do?" Nate's voice had lost its acerbic edge. He looked genuinely concerned for his friend.

"Same as always. I'll just work a little harder at damage control this time. Chloe doesn't realize it and neither does my dear brother Hunter, but what I'm trying to do is for them. They'll grow up and marry some day, wishing to live in the same city as their venerable ancestors. They won't like it if their offspring aren't accepted at the good schools, or if the other kids aren't allowed to come over to play."

Ethan's voice dripped with sarcasm, knowing the pain of banishment.

"Not to mention, never getting good tables at Three Sisters and Brennan's, or having to stand in the parish confessional line en masse."

Ethan's face softened into a smile. "Exactly." He laughed, then looked at his trusted confidant with determination. "My great, great grandfather made a name for the Galen family back when we were still a French colony. That legacy was nurtured and upheld by seven generations through hard work, commitment to the family and a sense of honor. It's taken my siblings and myself only a dozen years to trounce that into the river mud. I mean to get it back. For them, and for myself. And I won't let anyone or any tabloid rag stand in my way."

"Whoa. I haven't seen you this fired up since a protest march at college. Now, I can't even remember what we were protesting."

"This is the sort of journalism I can use right now," Ethan said, pulling a colorful magazine insert from beneath the paper. He tapped his index finger on the cover story. It featured two sweet-looking elderly women surrounded by children in a newly rebuilt Head Start facility. All faces smiled brightly at the camera.

Nate leaned closer to look, then scoffed. "The Sunday Magazine. Not the usual reading matter for he-men."

"When people arrive as late as you do for appointments, other people get desperate and will read anything. Turns out, I'm glad I ventured into journalism for the light-at-heart. These two women and their humanitarian deeds have been venerated for all posterity by this feature writer. And they didn't do anything more than my grandmother does on a daily basis." Anger ebbed from his voice, leaving only sad resignation. "She's spent years volunteering countless hours to local charities, besides donating huge sums of money, and gets no recognition beyond a plaque on the wall of the new library wing."

"She's storing up her riches in Heaven, my friend. That's where it counts."

"Yeah, but I'd like her to get some appreciation while still on Earth." Ethan pulled the magazine back from Nate to peruse the byline. "What I need is a....Cora Dearing on my side. She could go a long way to right a few wrongs. Create some good press for a change. Not only did this writer's story shine a rosy light on the city, but made these two ladies sound like incarnations of Mother Theresa in New Orleans."

"I believe I smell the fumes of wheels turning in your head. Is a plot to resurrect the family name hatching while we sit getting drunk?"

"Maybe. Find out what you can about this Cora Dearing at *The Times*. How long she's been there. What kind of stories she works on. Anything and everything."

"And if she's single...and available...and easily charmed?" Nate asked, wiggling his brows ridiculously.

"I refuse to prostitute myself," Ethan said, leaning back in his chair. "Not even to save the family name. But I would like to meet this Ms. Dearing." His eyes crinkled into a network of tiny lines.

Then the smile faded, replaced by a serious bent in an instant. "Anyway, I've got more pressing matters. A big, nasty fish to fry." Ethan finished his drink. "Keep your cell phone turned on. I'm going to need your help very soon."

"You goin' to work, boss?" Nate's voice relaxed into a soft drawl.

"I am. Just how well can you chauffeur a Town Car?"

"No, YOU ARE NOT going to work on the neighborhood restoration story and that's final. You are not a reporter, and I don't want you butting your nose in, Cora. It's a political powder keg. Folks have lived in those neighborhoods for generations, with a powerful sense of community and don't like that everything isn't being rebuilt as it was. You'll piss people off and blow the investigation for the real reporters." Jim Matthews slammed his coffee cup down on the desktop, sloshing coffee onto the fresh copy for tomorrow's front page. "Damn," he muttered. "Now see what you've done?" His blotchy face flushed a deeper hue, indicating the man's blood pressure had headed into dangerous territory.

"Real reporters?" Cora Dearing said, trying to control her temper. "I am a real reporter the last time I looked, just not for The Times. And that is your loss. All you ever let me write are endless stories about historical rehabilitation, the tourist impact on local economy, and the fund-raising success of tea-drinking, hat-wearing matrons from the Garden District. With the sole exception of Katrina, those stories have stayed pretty much the same for the past sixty years." Cora gritted her teeth and flattened both palms on his desk, ready for the fight. It was the third time they had danced this particular number in as many months.

"Those stories sell newspapers. The locals love seeing their names and faces in print, and tourists buy the paper for an insight into the phoenix rising from the ashes. Or shall we say from the Pontchartrain mud." He blotted at the coffee stain with his handkerchief, doing little good with the thin swatch of linen.

"Fine. Let someone else write them. When you hired me, Jim, you promised me a shot at reporting. I reported when I worked in Columbia." She didn't enjoy begging, but she was fresh out of alternatives.

"Cora, Cora." He muttered her name like a father admonishing a surly child.

She rolled her eyes. He may have been old enough to be her dad, but she didn't appreciate being patronized.

"Like I've told you before, New Orleans is not Columbia, South Carolina," he continued. "Not by a long shot. How long have you been here, eight months? That still puts you in the visitor category with the born-and-breds. Hell, I've lived here twenty years and I'm still looked at with a jaundiced eye." He stuffed the sodden handkerchief into his trouser pocket, then poured another cup of coffee from the carafe. "And you weren't here during the Big One," his tone implied some deficiency on her part.

"What does the fact that I wasn't baptized at St. Louis Cathedral and didn't ride out Katrina in Baton Rouge or the Superdome have to do with good reporting? You've seen the work I did for the Columbia Free Times. I can be an investigative reporter. I'm learning my way around the city, plus I've got a special knack with people." Cora fluttered her eyelashes in jest.

"Is that so? I must have missed that. All I ever see is a pushy woman who's always complaining about something. Hell, you nag me worse than my wife. And if my wife didn't rave so much about your feature stories, I'd fire you on the spot." He resettled his substantial bulk in the chair, perched his glasses on the bridge of his nose, and starting reading the stained copy.

Cora knew that her meeting with His Highness, editor of the *New Orleans Times,* was rapidly drawing to a close. She chose her words carefully, icing them with sugar. "Jim, everybody deserves a chance," she drawled. "Give me an assignment, just a lit'l assignment." She batted her lashes again, but to no avail. He never looked up from the papers.

"I've got an assignment for you," he said. "Something we can run a two-page in the Sunday Living section." He glanced at her briefly, then stared up at the ceiling. He leaned so far back in the chair, she feared his girth would tip him over backwards. "Something light for a change, nothing politically charged. How about 'Romance and Intrigue in the Big Easy'? Five, no ten places, guaranteed to tweak passions. You know, intimate restaurants, out-of-the-way bars, classy hotels that cater to non-business diversions. Women eat that stuff up."

"Ugh. It's been done. Many times. To death, as far as I'm concerned." She enunciated each word slowly as though talking to a child.

Jim glared over his half glasses. "The last time I checked, Ms. Dearing, I was still the boss around here. I may have hired you because your daddy was an old Army buddy of mine, but that doesn't mean I can't replace you with an employee who knows how to say, 'Yes, sir, Mr. Matthews. I'll get right on that story.'" His voice rose in increments along with the color in his cheeks.

"You hired me because you were impressed with my credentials, liked my work, and got me for a song. My salary is little more than *lagniappe*."

The editor folded his hands against his girth and laughed, his belly straining the starched shirt under his suit jacket. All he needed was a cigar and a glass of bourbon to complete a visage from an old, Southern melodrama. "That is the truth, I'll admit it." The deep lines around his mouth softened. "But the romantic spots story hasn't been done in a long while, with everything that's happened. Why don't you just write it from another angle? Find a new slant. If you're such a good investigator, maybe you can scare up some ghosts or vampires to help it along. Take a date. You do date, don't you? Go undercover to get the feature story, I don't care. But get the story, and get out of my office."

Cora opened her mouth for another retort, but the look on the editor's face curtailed the notion. "Oh, and get that piece on the library reopening on my desk by tomorrow morning, or you're fired," he shouted. The fleeting softness in his demeanor drained away.

Cora walked to her cubicle of an office, effectively ignoring the commiserating glances and nods from her coworkers. People were threatened with termination on a regular basis; that was just Jim Matthews' bluster. Whenever he did fire anybody, it wasn't on a whim during a heated argument.

Cora booted up her computer and stared at the floating screen saver without a single idea. You do date, don't you? It wasn't the fact that her career was going nowhere that made her wordless in New Orleans that afternoon. It was Jim's reminder that in the two years since her divorce and moving to the Big Easy, she'd gone on exactly three dates. All three had been fix-ups from her friend Lara in accounting, and all three had been disasters. Major disasters. Only one had even bothered to call her back a second time, and he hadn't sounded devastated when she'd politely recited a string of excuses.

What had happened to the perky girl destined-to-break-hearts-everywhere? The old sorority moniker still haunted her. It certainly turned out to be vastly over estimated. She'd never broken any hearts that she could remember. And hers had been broken twice. Not exactly a record to qualify her to check out romantic eateries and get-away trysting spots. She knew she'd write the piece; she didn't have much choice. The balance in her checking account wouldn't allow for an early retirement. And thirty years old was too young to retire anyway.

What she needed was a break. A big story that would make Jim Matthews sit up and take notice. A story that would get her out of temporary housing updates and into serious investigative reporting. She knew she could handle the work. After all, she could be cunning and devious with the best of them to ferret out information, and still remain cool under fire.

Cool, cunning Cora. Nobody's sweetheart anymore. Nobody's fool. All she had to do was prove it.

By evening, all Cora wanted was a glass of inexpensive wine, a good dinner, and to have enough money to pay the tab. Some peace and quiet would be nice, too, so she could plot her course of action. It wasn't easy making deadlines on drivel while trying to scoop the story that would put her career on track. Cora broke off another piece of crusty French bread and dipped it into the superb chicken and sausage gumbo. It was just how she liked it: not too spicy, lots of garlic and onion, and thickened with okra, not filé. The rice wasn't lumpy, while the parsley sprinkled on top was fresh, not dried. Perfect. Maybe she'd have a second bowl, she thought, while pouring the last of the house carafe into her glass.

"It's not my fault Claudette quit, and I haven't been able to replace her yet."

"She wouldn't have quit if you hadn't tried to turn her into your own personal maid."

"I don't see why a woman can't push the sweeper or run the dust cloth over the furniture while the children are napping."

Cora smiled into her Chablis as she eavesdropped on

the couple at the next table, stealing tiny glances at the protesting woman. Perfect skin: no crow's feet or an enlarged pore to be found anywhere. Laser peel, Cora concluded. Well-cut hair, bottle blond, the style a bit dated. Expensive suit. Jonathan Brooks? It had been a long time since Cora had been shopping, although it certainly wouldn't be to the same shops this woman frequented.

"Well, this dropping the children off at my mother's while you cavort with your friends all day long will stop now." The man's voice had risen a notch with added emphasis on the last word of his diatribe.

My, this is getting interesting, Cora mused, tipping her bowl to scrape the last of the gumbo with her bread. She stole a glance at the husband under scrutiny. His jaw jutted unattractively in anger, and Cora noticed damp stains on his perfectly starched white shirt. The sleeves had been rolled to his elbows, exposing tanned, strong forearms. About fifty, Cora guessed. Great hair—thick, wavy, graying at the temples. Very white teeth. Bleaching? Bonding? Too bad about his nasty, overbearing temperament.

"Cavort! Cavort?" The woman repeated the word with a laugh that held no humor. "An odd choice of words coming from you, Charles. I believe you're just afraid the children will tell your parents that you're seldom home before they're asleep. Or perhaps, that you're two months behind on their school tuition. Mommy and Daddy might just wonder what you do with the money they send every month. Or who you spend it on." The color in the woman's flawless cheeks rose to an unattractive flush.

The raucous street sounds from the Quarter were barely heard in this courtyard refuge. Hidden behind two-hundred-year-old buildings and lushly padded with dense foliage, Black Orchids was a serene oasis within the once liveliest and still noisiest city in the world. Sunlight never touched the mossy flagstones due to the huge magnolia that grew in the center. The tree had withstood hundred mile-per-hour winds to keep the courtyard cool even in the sultriest weather.

Cora often listened in on other people's conversations, and this was her favorite eavesdropping place. You never knew when you might overhear the perfect fodder for a breakthrough story. But she was no longer enjoying this dialogue. The malevolent look flashed by the husband frightened Cora, even while the wife remained steadfast, returning the glare with bravado. The scenario struck a little too close to home for Cora's comfort. She preferred problems she could empathize with, not personally identify with.

She reached under the bistro table for her bag and saw him, a man who made her breath catch in her chest and the blood halt in her veins. Her fingers hovered in midair, inches from her forgotten purse. He was sitting across the courtyard and staring at her. A faint smile creased his face when their eyes met. She knew instantly he'd observed her shameless eavesdropping. A blush rose up her neck and deepened across her cheeks, despite her thirty years of committing far worse social errors than this. The man, partly obscured by the overhanging gallery, lifted his wineglass in salute.

Cora did not return the gesture. She looked away and retrieved her bag, then began rummaging. When their gazes locked a second time, a lump formed in her throat while her stomach somersaulted, threatening the gumbo. If eyes were windows to the soul, then his were a portal to a rarefied world. A clear crystalline blue, magnetic in their intensity, they contrasted sharply with his pale complexion and black hair. A fine network of lines webbed his eyes, while silver liberally flecked his thick hair.

Startling, rather than handsome, he had a strong jaw and prominent cheekbones that demanded attention and lent a potent power. Aristocratic, that was the word to describe his looks. And she'd had a belly full of aristocrats in Columbia, starting with her ex-husband and ending with every member of his arrogant, blueblood family.

She looked away, feeling like Ulysses entrapped by the Sirens. The magnetism of his gaze shot adrenaline through her veins, and assailed her with feelings she didn't want to acknowledge. With her past track record with charismatic men, this wasn't one she should mess with.

Excitement flooded through her, warming an already overheated state to a dangerous level. A fleeting memory of the last time she'd felt these sensations brought her backed to reality, tamping down the hormones zinging through her blood. She glanced back to see him turn his attention to the bill on the table. He was dressed in a starched white linen suit with a wide-brimmed straw hat. The man was a cliché in the ancient city of ghosts and vampires, haunted cemeteries, and other macabre devices to separate the tourist from his dollar. Where was Tennessee Williams when you needed him? If the man wasn't a local actor, he was taking life in the Quarter far too seriously.

She realized she was staring again and pushed her chair back from the table. Something she couldn't quite put her finger on unsettled her. This man wasn't an actor. Suave and polished, he radiated something more dangerous than the charm of a thespian. Even half hidden in the shadows, he filled the courtyard with an aura of power.

"Madam?" The waiter looming at her elbow startled her.

"Yes?" Cora answered, looking into the young man's fresh-scrubbed face.

"The gentlemen there," the waiter said, motioning discretely to the man across the courtyard, "asked me to say that he thought you might enjoy this during your listening pleasures."

He held out a bottle of Dom Pérignon. Already opened. *A bit presumptuous*, she thought.

"Thank the gentleman, please, but tell him I must decline," she answered and dug for her wallet.

"He anticipated that response, madam, and begs you to reconsider." The boy sounded rehearsed, but plodded along animatedly.

The tip must have been generous.

"He said that since the bottle is already opened, it would be a shame for it to go to waste."

"And it wouldn't be opened, if he hadn't instructed you to open it," Cora retorted.

"He said that if you accept his gift, he won't trouble you further and will keep your nasty little secret for eternity," the waiter finished in a rush, flashing a charming smile.

"My nasty little—" Cora stopped herself. She had no desire to argue with a waiter. She turned toward the table where the man had been seated.

Empty. He was gone. Only the red ember of a cigarette dying in the crystal ashtray remained.

She extracted a twenty from her wallet and laid it on the table. "I'll take the bottle to go, please," she said. The look on his face indicated few patrons took a bottle of Dom home in a brown paper sack, but that's exactly what Cora had in mind. She knew how good the stuff tasted and wasn't leaving it for the kitchen staff to quaff.

"My glass is pathetically empty and you have so much." A disembodied voice seemed to radiate from the potted palm, then the stranger stepped from the shadows.

Cora jumped an inch off the flagstones. "Good grief," she hissed. "Don't sneak up on a person like that." One hand went to her throat while the other clutched her purse protectively to her chest.

"Have no fear of me, Miss," he drawled. "I'm not after your money. I'm merely thirsty." He set his glass on the edge of the table.

Her composure along with a hearty dose of pique returned. "If you were that thirsty, then you should have bought the bottle for yourself and not for a perfect stranger."

"Am I to assume that you are perfect? It's what I suspected, actually." His grin deepened the lines near his mouth.

"No, I am not perfect. If I were, we would not be having this conversation. Good evening, sir." Cora attempted to exit around the table, but the returning waiter blocked her path.

"Your take-out, madam, in brown paper. Sorry I wasn't able to get the stopper back in the bottle," the waiter said, holding out the bag. The cheeky man had twisted the paper around the neck, giving the distinct appearance of a hobo's purchase.

"Thank you so much," she said, grabbing the bottle from him, and hoisting her purse up her shoulder.

"Wait. What about my empty glass?" The stranger slipped into the spot vacated by the disappearing waiter. "And my desperate, incredible thirst?" His deep, honeyed voice drawled the last words with flair.

Cora narrowed her eyes and glared menacingly. "You must not be a man of your word." She took a step toward him.

"I beg your pardon?"

The question perplexed him as she'd intended. "You told the waiter if I accepted your gift, you would trouble me no further. And here you are—troubling me."

He threw back his head in a hearty laugh, revealing enviously perfect teeth. "Give me a chance to prove that that is the only promise I'll ever break to you, including my pledge to never divulge your nasty, little secret." His long fingered hand rose to a position above his heart. As he leaned dangerously closer, his aftershave mingled with the overhanging flowers in an intoxicating scent.

Cora stepped back, clenching her fists. "And what nasty little secret would that be?"

"Why, the fact that you are an eavesdropper, a voyeur, an interloper in life," he said. "Why don't we sit here, share a glass of the bubbly, and discuss how you can become more proactive in the world?" He pulled out the nearest chair.

Cora stared for a moment with wide eyes and a mouth that could've caught a circling moth, but recovered quickly. She pulled the bottle from its wrapper, picked up his glass and filled it, glancing between it and the man's smirking face. When the bubbles reached the top, she set the glass carefully back on the table. "There you go, Mister-whoever-you-are, your share of the champagne. The rest is mine for putting up with your insults." She stuffed the bottle back into the bag. "Now sit by yourself to drink it and ponder your methods for making new friends. This one is a total wash."

"Galen. My name is Galen. But please, you may call me Ethan."

His voice trailed after her, turning heads in their direction, but Cora had already pushed past him and disappeared, not looking back at the man who stared long after she was gone.

WITHIN MINUTES, CORA was back inside her suite of rooms in the renowned, heavy humidity of New Orleans with a two-hundred-dollar bottle of wine to drink alone. Isn't life strange? And all she had wanted was a quiet meal to plot her course of action, because if she didn't get a raise soon, she'd find herself at the local shelter instead of sipping Dom on her balcony.

Looking down on the Rue Chartres from her third-floor perch, she watched the street scene below. The rain had ceased battering the tile roof and brought a cool break in the late-spring warmth. Young couples strolled with linked arms and whispered endearments, refreshed from dinners of jambalaya and pralines. Rowdy, college-aged boys pushed and shoved each other along the street, swilling vast quantities of beer and hurricanes until the wee hours. Sage white-haired matrons led their husbands, exhausted from tromping through galleries and antique shops in search of the perfect treasure, back to expensive hotel rooms. And the male tourists probably hoped to get one more flash of young skin in exchange for beads before they called it a night.

Cora observed them all from her perch, feeling empty. That annoying man was right. *I am just an observer of life from the fringe. The safe, benign fringe.* She had thought that staying in the notoriously touristy French Quarter with its boisterous, convivial crowds would be too distracting to find solace, but it had proven to be a pleasant diversion. She had accomplished what she had set out. She'd lost herself in a sea of humanity who'd come to rebuild, had relocated from destroyed sections, or had come from out-of-town to gawk. None cared who she was, or where she came from as she walked the old streets of the Quarter for hours—alone in a city bulging with people.

She pulled back from the balustrade and padded back into the cool confines of her sitting room. Lusciously appointed in nineteenth-century reproductions, the gracious room had none of the cloying sweetness that often accompanied provincial decor. While her balconies overhung the street below, French doors opened onto a narrow walkway ringing the inner courtyard—a lush tropical garden surrounding two pools that were nearly hidden by the foliage. The sweet fragrance of bougainvillea and magnolia wafted in with the breeze. At night she could smell jasmine while she drifted to sleep along with the tinkling sound of porcelain wind chimes. The proprietress had hung them just outside her door to provide the necessary diversion from the street noise. It had worked magically. Cora had slept better than she had in years—deep and dreamless.

She sank into the upholstered chair before her vanity and scrutinized her reflected image. At least her skin breakouts had cleared up before the serious wrinkles arrived, she thought with wry satisfaction. Pulling her hair back from her face, she stared into her vivid green eyes with cool detachment. Her olive skin was still unlined; her hair a thick mass of loose curls when the heat and humidity allowed her to let it down from its requisite chignon. Her figure was still supple and slim thanks to her passion for long evening walks. She smiled in self-acceptance—she would not be the consummate modern woman if she allowed herself to fall apart over a little thing like a divorce.

He cannot hurt me anymore. He is nothing. He has

no power over me. No one will get close enough to hurt me again.

Comforted by her daily litany of affirmation, she settled back to peruse the classifieds. Rentals were in very short supply, but she had to find somewhere permanent to live. Her rooms in the hostel, Maison de Chartres, were too expensive for a long-term basis and the shared bathroom was inconvenient at best.

Despite the protests from her mom and sisters, Cora had decided to stay. What had begun as a freelance assignment on the heroic feats of the volunteer rescuers, followed by an article detailing the incredible resilience of the community, rapidly changed into something much more. She had fallen in love with the old city, lying like Atlantis waiting to be reborn.

"It's too hot, too steamy, too haunted," her sister Peg had wailed.

"Too dangerous, too decadent—filled with murder, suicides, crime and voodoo. No decent people ever move to New Orleans by choice," her mother had cajoled in her quiet, cultured voice. "And what if there's another hurricane?"

"Except for the hurricane part, you're both making the place sound absolutely irresistible," she had answered, much to their chagrin. It was their loving attempts to influence her that had made up her mind. She had spent seven years being controlled, being the exemplary wife, and living a perfect life in a fishbowl. She had taken a leave of absence from *The Free Times* and found the job at *The Times* in short order. Living on her income once her divorce settlement ran out would prove interesting, but worth the effort.

"Oh, please," her sister had teased. "You've never lived on your own in your life. You've always been taken care of by somebody. You'll probably write checks until the pad runs out, not realizing you were out of money a long time ago." Everyone had laughed, except her.

"I don't want to be taken care of anymore. That comes with too high a price. I want to be the woman who scoops every other news service and doesn't have to be home by a certain time to get dinner on the table. I want to be Laura Dern in *Wild at Heart*."

Peg had looked at her like she had lost her mind. Apparently her sister hadn't seen the movie. Cora sadly remembered her last encounter with Peg. She loved her, but was very glad to be away from home.

She thought about the bizarre, but undeniably attractive man she had seen in the restaurant. How about a feature story about New Orleans' sexy, powerful, single men? She certainly hoped no married man would squander two hundred bucks on a whim like that.

Something icy crept up her spine with the memory of his eyes flitting over her. An interloper in life. She laughed at how correct he was upon so short an acquaintance. Truth was, she had no desire to be part of what she watched, preferring to view human interaction from a safe distance. Until tonight, that was. Something unexplainable, something alien flickered in her soft, woman soul that had been long ignored.

"You don't sit back and watch and listen, do you, Mr. Personality?" she whispered to no one. What did he say his name was? She couldn't remember, but it didn't matter. She'd never see him again.

And that made her relieved and bitterly disappointed at the same time.

"IF MADAM WOULD step this way, I'll show her to the rental cottage," Emil Vacherie said in his clipped Cajun accent.

He walked another two paces and turned back to find
Cora rooted to the spot where he'd left her. He patiently
waited a few moments while she continued to gaze at
the immense, gnarly live oak that stood as sentinel in
the manicured back garden of the largest mansion on
Ursulines. Spanish Moss hung nearly to the ground giving the benches beneath perfect privacy. Flagstone paths
radiated in several directions from the center to encircle
dogwood trees, gardenias, azaleas, and jasmine, each
surrounded by raised beds of lilies and iris. The effect
was an organized riot of blooms.

"Mrs. Dearing? Mrs. Dearing?" the man drawled, not
regaining her attention until they were nearly face-to-
face.

Cora turned her head from studying the wisteria covering nearly every inch of the backside of the stucco
house. "The smell from the wisteria must be intoxicating in the back rooms when it's in bloom."

"Yes, it is. I'm afraid we've lived here so long we
take the beauty of this garden for granted." He let his
own eyes roam up the lush vines, then rest back on her
with unsettling boldness. "If you'd follow me, I'll show
you the rental house. It's on the back property line, but
there's a short alley to the side street through that gate."
He pointed towards an almost hidden opening through
the privacy fence. "That way you can leave your car at
the end of the alley and not have so far to walk with
your groceries."

"I don't own a car right now. Isn't there a market in the
Quarter that delivers, Mr. Vacherie?" Cora questioned.

"Well, yes, but shopping in our open air market is
something that most ladies…" His voice trailed off when
Cora's clear green eyes fastened on him in a frosty fashion.

"Jack's on Decatur delivers, I believe," he said, stepping onto the front porch of the most charming stone-and-tabby house Cora had ever seen. The stone had been sun-bleached to near white, while an old-fashioned tin roof overhung the house by several feet, casting welcome shade on twin porch rockers. The mansion's back garden was the cottage's front yard—no home in the Quarter could possibly have more seclusion than this.

Emil swung open the heavy, carved door. Cora stepped into the home she knew she couldn't refuse, no matter what the price.

A center hall opened on the left to a living room with high ceilings, pale green walls, glossy hardwood floors, Turkish area rugs and a fireplace. She didn't wait for the caretaker to lead the way, but stepped past a leaded glass door into a paneled library. It apparently doubled as the dining room since a drop-leaf table flanked by four upholstered chairs reposed in the center.

A matching door led Cora and the trailing Emil into an airy, ceramic-tiled kitchen that stretched across the back of the house. Ivy trailed from pots on the sills and from baskets hanging on thin silver chains.

Cora pushed out the casement windows, letting in the heady fragrance of honeysuckle. French doors opened onto a flagstone patio, completely secluded by a tall hedge. She ignored Vacherie's litany of conveniences the house offered and hurried back down the center hall, acting like a youngster escaping from a harness. Off to the right she found a guest room and bath.

"The rooms, as you can see, are not large, Mrs. Dearing, yet they're quite comfortable. This house was servants' quarters for the big house, ma'am, before the war, but finely built nonetheless."

"Yes, I see that," Cora answered when it occurred to her what war he obliquely referred to. Columbia had almost no antebellum architecture left. "And the upstairs, Mr. Vacherie?" she asked, cutting off any further historical explanation.

"You go on up, ma'am, and look around. I'm gonna have a smoke in the garden if you don't mind. Take as much time as you like." With that he turned and left, acting a bit miffed.

Perhaps his attempts at polite conversation would have been better received had he not kept staring at Cora's chest. She recoiled under his assessing gaze but gave him no further thought once she reached the second floor. The high ceilings of the first floor created a steep flight of steps, but the view was worth the climb. The landing opened into a sitting area containing a desk beneath the bay window that overlooked the garden. The upper branches of the oak reached the casement windows lending the atmosphere of a tree house.

But it was the view from the bedroom that captured her heart. French doors led to a wrought-iron balcony where she could look over the hedge onto the street below. She wouldn't have to forgo her pleasant observance of life undetected that she so enjoyed at her former suite of rooms. People milled back and forth even in this quieter end of the Quarter. She strained to overhear the dialogue between two quarrelling people below. Apparently they hadn't brought enough money with them on the vacation.

Cora smiled to herself. Perfect. This place was perfect for her. She hurried downstairs to find the caretaker leaning against the oak in the front garden. He exhaled a blue cloud of smoke as she approached.

"I'll take it, Mr. Vacherie," Cora said, digging in her handbag for her checkbook.

He ground out his cigarette, then stepped so close that she could detect the faint smell of whiskey. "But I haven't told you the price yet, and it wasn't printed in the paper," he drawled with lips turning up in a sneer. "The owners in the front house are very selective. They want one quiet person, preferably a woman, living behind them. Some of these contractors, architects, and engineers are a pack of carpetbaggers—raisin' all kind of racket when the workday's done. No respect for people trying to get a good night's sleep."

"Yes, well, I'm one quiet woman. What's the price?" she asked impatiently. She wanted this place even if she had to sell her plasma to augment her pittance of a salary. It would go a long way toward feeling successful and independent, after what a failure her marriage turned out to be.

"It's fifteen hundred dollars a month, but that includes the utilities. Now there ain't no central air, but the stone keeps the downstairs fairly cool. I've got a good window unit to cool off the second floor. I didn't set that price, the owners did." The man grinned at her, scratching absently at a scab. "I don't want you to think I'm trying to take advantage of you, being that you was ready to rent before I told you the price."

"I'd never think such a thing," Cora lied, then pretended to mull over the price. But her mind was made up. If there ever existed a perfect spot to get some writing done, this was it. "Will that be first month, last, and security, Mr. Vacherie?"

He looked surprised, then nodded, while giving her appearance another once-over. Apparently her outfit didn't coincide with having forty-five hundred dollars, part of her dwindling divorce settlement, sitting in a checking account.

Cora wrote the check, then pressed it into the man's hand before he regained his composure. "I assume I can move in immediately? I'd like to sign a one year lease and move some of my things tomorrow, if that's all right." She paused for a few moments, while he closed his gaping mouth. When he didn't argue, she murmured a soft, "Good, then it's all settled," and started down the walk, glad to be away from the man whose eyes rested on her breasts more often than her face.

"I'll be happy to keep a close eye on things for you. You know, like a watch dog." He issued a low, raspy laugh. "I live on the property, too, over the garage." His voice rose in steady increments as she increased the distance between them.

Cora kept walking, then breathed a sigh of relief when she reached the street. Every rose must have its thorns, she thought, and made a silent note to keep her blinds closed at night on the front side of the cottage.

Emil Vacherie gazed down on the check in his hand looking at the former address. "Columbia, South Carolina," he whispered disdainfully. The owner wasn't going to like the fact he'd taken an out-of-town check for the deposit. Too many people moved in, spent a week, and skedaddled in the dead of night before the bank notified that the check was no good. A free week's vacation in the Quarter.

"Well, Miz Columbia, that better not be the case with you. New Orleans has a way of bringing ladies like you to their knees."

"WILL YOU BE having breakfast on the terrace, *M'sieu* Galen?" The melodic voice of his housekeeper cut through the fog in his brain. Ethan looked up, the sudden action sending shards of pain shooting behind his eyes.

"I beg your pardon, Jeanette?" Ethan said, placing two fingers on his throbbing temples.

"I said, sir, would you like to have your breakfast outdoors? It's a beautiful day, already sunny and clear."

"No, thank you. And I don't care for anything this morning."

The aging Creole woman wore a smile that could rival a beauty queen's, tinged with a bit of wry humor. She knew very well her employer had no desire to subject himself to the brightness of day unless the house was on fire. She set down the tray on the edge of the desk where Ethan sat ignoring the stack of reports and correspondence before him.

"See here," she persisted, pointing a long finger at a glass. "I brought you a tall tomato juice with lots of hot sauce, and a shot of…what do you call it…fur of the dog in it."

Ethan cocked his eyebrow at the woman who knew him better than his own family. "It's called 'hair of the dog', madam, and I thank you. Now if you'd be so kind—"

"I made a pot of Espresso with lots of sugar and here are some warm beignets. I brought you both marmalade and cream cheese. And those kiwis are fresh. I bought them yesterday." She pointed at a plate of sliced fruit before placing her fine-boned hands on her hips. She dared him to argue with both her posture and expression.

Today Ethan was not up to the challenge. He looked at the shriveled green fruit and felt his stomach turn over. "I'm sure they're at their peak, Jeanette." He closed his eyes, tipped his head back, and downed the contents of the tall glass in three swallows.

"I do not understand why every time you see M'sieu Nathan Price, you end up in this condition." Her voice betrayed her pique. "You need a wife. A good wife this time. A lady who'll fascinate you and allow you no time to run around with friends like M'sieu Price."

Ethan groaned. As much as he loved this woman who'd worked for his family since he was a child, at thirty-eight he didn't need or want any castigation for his behavior. He had a mother and grandmother still up to the formidable task, and even they couldn't censure him as well as he censured himself. He straightened in the chair and poured steaming coffee from the carafe. "Thank you, Mrs. Peteriere. I will take your judgments of my friends under consideration," he said in a voice too loud to his own ears. "If you will excuse me, please, I'll be happy to report to *grandmère* that you've been diligent in her absence."

Jeanette narrowed her almond-shaped eyes and glared down an aquiline nose before delivering the customary exhale of exasperation. "There's something else for you, *cher p'tit*, in the corner of the tray."

Her aristocratic face framed by high cheekbones and swanlike neck softened with compassion and tenderness before she walked from the room. A waft of bougainvillea assailed Ethan as she left. She belonged in another era, another world, much like his grandmother. He spotted three aspirin tablets in a crystal bowl and downed them with a mouthful of coffee before pushing away the tray.

This is why I don't fire you, Jeanette.

But Ethan Galen had more serious concerns than his overly maternal housekeeper. He had gotten drunk again last night. In a very public place. Whenever they tied one on together, Nate Price had a habit of speaking about whatever social injustice happened to be on his mind. Loudly speaking his mind. In past years, Nate's expostulations had humored Ethan. He'd often joined in on the verbal quartering of crooked local politicians or social climbing do-gooders. It hadn't been quite so entertaining after Ethan observed first-hand the shame his mother endured whenever tales of her children's excesses reached her. He might not be the worst offender among his siblings, but as the eldest, he'd been first to recognize the consequences of such behavior.

He wracked his brain trying to remember if he'd known any of the other diners in Black Orchids, before he had become too drunk to recognize anyone. He vaguely remembered categorizing newspaper reporters a few notches below lawyers who defended child molesters or loan sharks who opened storefronts across from casinos.

"That's all I need," he muttered. It wasn't bad enough his mother had to listen to pseudo sympathetic phone calls all day regarding the newspaper story about Chloe. Hopefully, none of her friends had been dining at Orchids last night, or his efforts to mend the tarnished name of Galen had just been set back a decade.

Ethan stood abruptly, nearly upsetting the rattan breakfast tray and began to pace the room. Large and airy, the apartment above an art and antique shop on Rue de Royal had been exactly what he had been looking for when he moved out of the palatial family residence. Elegant and well appointed, four of the six rooms had balconies that either overlooked the secluded garden in back or Rue de Royal in front, a street of expensive galleries and shops. It stood a world apart from the rowdy, raucous Bourbon Street only a block away, filled with tourists and party-loving drunks.

But it also was only a block away when Ethan's carnal stirrings demanded a warm, willing female to pass the long hours before daybreak. He simply didn't want the annoying observance by family or staff whenever he brought women home to continue festivities after hours.

He hadn't appreciated his father's glare when he closed the library door as Ethan and a lady tripped up the stairs. A man needed space. A man needed anonymity, and this apartment provided that with a measure of aesthetic charm. After all, hadn't he been schooled in classical architecture and interior space? Not that he found time to produce any of his award-winning designs lately. He hadn't seen the need to earn a living as his father and grandfather had. Good investments generated a cash flow better than any career possibly could. What was the point of working if you didn't need the money? There was skiing in the Alps, Formula One racing in Europe, diving off the Great Barrier Reef, and sailing regattas in the blue waters of the Gulf. Not to mention the noble pastimes of drinking, gambling, and general carousing.

Picking up tipsy secretaries on vacation from Baton Rouge had finally lost its appeal about the time he decided it was time to improve the Galen standing in the Quarter. Waking up one morning to find a naked redhead in his bed finally changed his perspective in that regard. Especially since he couldn't remember how she'd gotten there or even her name.

It had been time to grow up.

It had been time to regain what he had lost. But it had been too late.

What is the matter with you, Ethan? I expect that behavior from Chloe, or from Hunter. They still see themselves as children. But not you, Ethan. You know you're a man and still you act like you have no dignity.

His father's words still cut through him like a blade after all these years. He thought he would have time to prove his father wrong, to show him he possessed as much honor as any Galen.

But he had been wrong.

Ethan stopped pacing long enough to pour more coffee. Hangover or not, he had plenty of work to do. If his friend followed his instructions, he might have a lovely diversion to soften the repugnance of what he had to do. Kill two birds with one stone, as the old adage so vilely suggests.

The image of Cora Dearing in Orchids floated back, driving some of the pain in his head away. She possessed an almost tangible independence. He admired her self-assurance and confidence. This wasn't a woman who worried about what others were thinking. His attraction to her was powerful, disturbing, and unwelcome, since he didn't need that kind of complication with what he had to do. Yet he felt drawn to pursue her.

Keep your mind on what you need her for. Good press. A sweet story about *Grandmère*. That's all.

Cora Dearing. He repeated the name he'd read on the magazine insert. The feature writer who knew how to turn a phrase and heap praise where it was due. Price had done his homework through a friend at the newspaper. He'd learned that the Columbia transplant partook of a meager dinner at Black Orchids every Wednesday, a place that should've been out of her price range on her salary. Being in the right place at the right time had been easy. Finding her to be so appealing was not.

Despite the fact he was no teenager with raging hormones, a physical reaction washed over his body like a wave with her memory. She wouldn't be like the others, he was sure of that. Her warm smile and sparkling eyes possessed none of the artifice he had grown accustomed to seeing in his lovers. She was pure, fresh and unspoiled. When she had licked her finger after eating the last of the gumbo soaked bread, he had longed to put her fingertip into his own mouth. To taste and savor skin still sweet and unsullied. Her lower lip, full and sensuous, just begged to be kissed. Her entire ripe, full body had him thinking of sex—something he'd blocked out for too long to remember.

Stop. Stop it now.

What he could offer a woman like her, he wasn't sure. Money, yes. Women always liked money, but her refusal of the champagne was adamant, not a coy ploy to appear seductive. If she wasn't impressed with wealth, Ethan feared he had little else to offer.

The phone rang, jarring him from his reverie. "Yes?" he asked into the receiver.

"I think I've got the information you wanted, Mr. Galen."

The voice brought Ethan back into the real world. Pleasant, sensuous visions vanished instantly. "Go on, I'm listening."

"It's a mother and a daughter team. They've done this sort of thing before. Twice to be exact. They're very good, so you'll have to be careful."

The voice on the other end waited for a response, but with the pounding in his head, Ethan said nothing.

"They're spending money like water in your neck of the woods, as a matter of fact. They don't have a care in the world."

"Is that right? Maybe we can change that."

There was a laugh on the other end, then a pause. "Well, if you can, it's worth ten million dollars to you."

The headache that had awakened him, then deviled Ethan all morning vanished like mist rising off the Mississippi.

TWO

"COME, WITNESS FOR YOURSELF, the locales of the famous New Orleans vampires. Hear the tales of their treacherous deeds that still haunt the city today." Or perhaps, "Tour the lanes of the 'Cities of the Dead'—ancient, above-ground tombs, many holding a story you'll remember always. Included on this tour is Marie Laveau's tomb, the high priestess of Voodoo of the Nineteenth Century." Then a third offered, "Hauntings of the French Quarter—ghost stories of murder, suicide and tragedy in America's most haunted city."

"My goodness. How does one pick from such a plethora of feature story fodder?" Cora mused sardonically, scanning the brochures she'd picked up from a restaurant's windowsill. In the end, she settled on the *Tour of the Garden District, including the largest collection of antebellum mansions and Lafayette Cemetery with its unique architecture and fascinating vignettes of those who repose for eternity.* "That should offer a little something for all my readers."

She rode the St. Charles Streetcar to Washington, then walked another block to meet the tour group. They stood bright-eyed and eager with tickets in hand and umbrellas clutched firmly under their arms. Cora smiled amiably as she paid her fourteen dollars and joined the group. All had apparently read the brochure's dire warning regarding New Orleans' frequent showers, and the warning that the tour would continue despite any sudden downpours.

She had brought nothing so practical, only her notepad and several free pens advertising the local casino.

The brochure didn't exaggerate the splendor of the antebellum mansions in the Garden District. Each was lovelier than the next with their intricately wrought iron-work, wrapping galleries, and cool pastel facades, amid lush, riotous blooms of every color and size. Growing up in Columbia, South Carolina, which had burned to the ground during the Civil War, she had seen few preserved mansions from the nineteenth century. And none that possessed the elegance and cool reserve of these homes. Sadly, several blackened empty lots scarred the neighborhood, too, still strewn with rubble where grand homes once stood. Some say the fires were from natural gas leaks, but most believe they'd been set by arsonist-looters traveling by boat, adding anarchy to the chaos in Katrina's wake.

Although many of the remaining homes weren't as large as one might expect, each exuded a sleek integrity that defied time, the climate's insidious heat and humidity, and the burrowing vermin of various species. Definitively female in their persona, each house was like a grand old lady, outdoing her friends in wardrobe and refreshments when it was her turn to host the bridge luncheon. Cora felt a tiny twinge of envy for the lucky few who'd been born-to-the-manor here.

You can barely keep your own four rooms dusted and presentable, she laughed and hurried to catch up with the queue of tourists entering Lafayette Cemetery. Inside the thick brick fence lay the walled city of the dead. Each aboveground tomb resembled a miniature house, architecturally unique. Marble obelisks, tall monuments and statuary interspersed the rows of tombs and lent a surreal effect. Cora was fascinated and repelled at the same time.

She'd seen the news photos of the people scrubbing muck and debris from the tombs once the floodwaters receded and a lump of emotion rose in her throat.

Their guide looked quintessentially perfect to dispense tales of the dissipated, broken lives of the rich and infamous. Tall and angular, his long unfettered hair reached halfway down his back. The man moved fluidly through the cobbled pathways of vaults, often walking backwards without missing a step. Cora tripped over several broken flagstones even while watching where she was going. His voice, low and raspy, imbued each vignette with romantic illusion, even those centering on poison, bludgeoning and chained starvation. That was truly a talent, she thought.

"The fact that we're below sea level and the soil is very sandy necessitates above ground burials. Each of these tombs is still owned by individual families. When a death occurs in the family, the recently deceased is respectfully interred on the highest level of the crypt. The previous inhabitant is moved one position lower—"

"Gives new meaning to the term 'top shelf,'" one tour patron muttered to his friends.

The guide paid no attention. "—local regulation prohibits opening the tomb before a year and a day has elapsed. In our climate, there is little left but fragments and dust at that point."

"—a poor man's method of cremation," the same tourist chided.

This time the guide turned a raised black eyebrow towards the young man, accompanied by a look that brooked little argument. The tourist's girlfriend poked him in the ribs.

"The majority of crypts contain only two burial shelves, under which the ashes of the deceased are mingled with their antecedents from hundreds of years before."

The gaping mouths and wide eyes of the visitors revealed their surprise at such an idea.

"This is a very old, very confined city where space has always been a premium," he continued. "By now, everyone knows we're below sea level and sinking lower every year. Our culture sees nothing wrong with a person's mortal remains mingled for eternity with that of his ancestors."

A shiver ran down Cora's spine. That particular information was rather interesting, but not exactly what her editor was looking for in *Romantic Retreats in America's Most Haunted City*.

The guide sought eye contact with Cora as they moved through the rows of crypts in the beautiful Lafayette Cemetery. Twice he offered a shy smile at the end of his rehearsed paragraph. Cora scratched off prodigious notes that she may or may not be able to weave into a feature story. *Fine background for a fourteen-dollar tariff*, she thought, scribbling until her hand cramped.

She hadn't noticed the group had moved on. Nor did she sense the young man standing in front of her until she glanced up to turn the page of her notebook. She shrieked like a banshee and jumped back a foot.

"Relax," the guide soothed. "I won't bite your neck or keep you captive in my attic...unless you demand your money back for the tour. I just wanted you to stay with the rest of the tour." He winked, then flourished his hand in the desired direction.

"All right," she said, glancing up at him. Maybe it was his height, at least six-foot-three, but more likely it was his gothic facade that made her patently uncomfortable. Sweat dampened her cotton dress as she stepped past him and hurried towards the group.

Cora resumed taking notes as the guide picked up his

narrative where he'd left off. Then something moved in the periphery on her left. She glanced quickly and saw, or thought she saw, a man in a white linen suit with a wide-brimmed straw hat. He appeared like a wraith behind a row of ornately decorated crypts.

The man from the café.

Cora stared, then walked quickly to the next lane. No one moved in the shadow-draped heat of midday. Not in that long row of tombs nor in the next. Only her own exhaled breath broke the stillness as she watched for him to show himself. The sharp caw of a crow perched on the Graconierre tomb nearly startled her from her shoes. She ran like a child to catch up with the group.

You're being stupid. No one was there. Not the man who bought the champagne in Black Orchids. No one. And there're lots of crows back in Columbia as well as everywhere else in the world. They're hardly rare birds seen only in graveyards, carrying the souls of the recently departed to the doorway of hell.

Cora hoped her feature story would affect her readers as profoundly as the guide's tales had affected her. No longer able to concentrate on the remaining lecture, she bobbed and jumped with every rustling branch or unidentified sound. Once again the group had moved off, leaving her alone and staring down an aisle for the phantom to reappear.

Despite every rational explanation, relief washed over her as she followed the walkway back to Prytania Street. The guide was animatedly answering questions of a well-dressed matron with two teenagers in tow. She had missed the final summation of the tour, except for his cryptic warnings and admonition not to return alone. Cora relaxed in the sunshine, away from the imagination provoking aura of Lafayette. There hadn't been anyone spying on her in the cemetery. She had just gotten caught up with the canned performance. Discretely dropping a ten spot into the upturned top hat, she walked towards the streetcar stop while the group headed into a shop selling souvenirs and ice cream.

"I was curious about all the note taking," the guide's familiar voice said over her shoulder. At least this time she didn't jump with overreaction. The hat that had been collecting tips only moments ago rested atop his head.

"I'm a writer. And someday I hope to be a famous, well-paid writer," she answered, offering her brightest smile.

"Planning on giving Anne Rice a little competition?" he drawled.

"No, she has nothing to fear from me. I'm into reality. I don't do Gothic, and I'm not into steamy sex." As soon as the words were out, she flushed a deep shade of scarlet.

"Sex never goes out of style with the fickle reading public."

"I'm a reporter…and a feature writer, not novels," she said, wiping her brow with the back of her hand. "I'm doing a spot on romantic places to eat, drink, or stay in. Places that aren't overrun with tourists that might tempt the locals to part with a little money."

"Is that right?" he asked as they arrived at the streetcar stop. He apparently was headed back to the Quarter, too, on her choice of transportation. "What about a plantation bed-and-breakfast on the bayou? Would that fit your story?" He leaned against a live oak and lit a cigarette from an ornate silver case.

"It might. Is it the real McCoy? Any haunted rooms or attractive apparitions? If it could provide even half the intrigue you have today, it would be lovely, Mr.—"

"Frederick. Just Frederick. No Mr. anybody. And I'll

give you the outstanding recommendation if you promise never to refer to me as 'Freddie', or worse, 'Freddie-the-tour-guide' when you're drunk on hurricanes with your friends and see me crawl by on Bourbon Street." He took a long drag on the cigarette, squinting his eyes in the slanting sun.

"I promise," she murmured, making an "X" motion across her chest. "Anyway, I have no friends," she added with an exaggeratedly sad expression.

"I'll bet that's about to change," he said with a wink. "Okay, the place is called Water Lilies, and it's a jewel. They don't advertise. Strictly word-of-mouth, so only the most industrious tourists find out and make their way up there. It was a real plantation at one time and has been in their family for two hundred years or so. They still own almost a hundred surrounding acres to keep the real world from intruding. Men love to take their mistresses there, after they dutifully take the wife and kiddies to Disney World. It's a lovely spot for...love."

"Sounds like a wonderful place to eavesdrop," she said.

He thought about that for a moment. "Absolutely. It's run as an inn, serving both breakfast and dinner. There's no McDonald's or much of anything else in the area. They'll pack a hamper if you want to go swamp exploring and give you a tour of the house along with its history, if you ask. Otherwise they'll just leave you alone. This is no tourist trap. Make no mistake about it. There's no gift shop to buy souvenirs for hubby and the kids back home."

"No hubby, Frederick. And no kids," she answered as they boarded the antique streetcar and slipped into a seat together. "Don't worry. I won't embarrass you and make you regret your recommendation by demanding twenty-four hour room service or satellite TV," she teased.

"Man, aren't these old girls great?" He patted the waxed paneling lovingly. "I glad they were parked uptown when the big one hit and they didn't get wasted like the Canal Street line."

"Took long enough to get the power system restored," she said over the clatter.

"Time is relative in the punch bowl." He gave her an appraising once-over. "Okay, then. If you swear I won't regret it, I'll give you their phone number." He jotted it down on a matchbook cover, then pressed it into her palm, squeezing her fingers tightly closed around it. "Guard this with your life."

Cora had no further opportunity to ask more questions about the inn or anything else. Frederick abruptly pulled the cord, shot her a smile and jumped off the streetcar before they'd even gone four blocks. She watched him head back in the same direction they came from, carrying the theatrical top hat tucked beneath his arm.

She took the streetcar back to Canal, then walked the endless blocks home to her cottage. Her shirt stuck to her back, while her hair turned wet and stringy by the time she turned the key in the lock and stepped into the cool, dim interior. Amazing how eighteen-inch walls can keep out the heat, she thought, pouring herself a glass of champagne from the other day's unfinished bottle. Despite her successful effort to jam a stopper into the bottle, it tasted slightly flat, but still refreshing. Pulling off her sodden shirt, she headed for her chaise under the back gallery clad only in chino capris and a sports bra. She brought her notebook along to finalize her thoughts about the tour for the story. Hopefully her readers would find historic mansions and a gothic cemetery romantic, but somehow she doubted it.

Images of the man from the restaurant, emanating raw

power that only serious money could buy, flitted through her head as she sipped the wine. Thoughts and ideas from the tour ebbed as memories of their encounter returned. His eyes had looked right through her, jolting her with a thrill as powerful as electricity. Naked—that's how she felt when she realized he'd been watching her.

Had it been he—slinking between the tombs and stalking her in Lafayette Cemetery? She closed her eyes, lulled into drowsiness by the hot afternoon. She was being silly. You are supposed to report stories, not invent them. The hideaway recommended by the guide enticed her. It sounded exactly like the sort of place Jim Matthews would eat up. And it would get her out of the hot city for a few days. She pulled the matchbook with its scribbled writing from her pocket and punched in the number to make reservations. After she'd booked a room and secured directions, she punched in her sister's number before her imagination could run all the way to Borneo and back.

After the usual pleasantries, Cora got down to the point of her call. She'd made a promise when she'd moved away to keep her sister informed of her whereabouts. Peg could point the bloodhounds or scuba divers in the right direction, if she ever turned up missing.

"I'm on my way into the bayou for the weekend. I'm being whisked to a romantic hideaway by a rich, mysterious man I met the other night," she teased. "He promises nothing but rivers of champagne, exquisite cuisine and marathon lovemaking. No meals to prepare. No dishes to wash. He promises to find me witty and intelligent, to hang onto my every word, and make me the center of his universe for the entire two days."

Her sister's uproarious laughter sounded good to Cora's ears. It had been too long since Peg had found anything she'd said or done very amusing. "Afterwards, he swears he won't bother me again until I'm ready for a repeat performance," Cora finished.

"Whew. For a minute there, you had me going. I was starting to curdle with envy."

"At what point did I give myself away? Do you think it impossible for a man to find me witty and intelligent?"

"I only find it unlikely for a man to stop talking about himself long enough to listen." The laughter increased on both ends. "And the center of the universe was a dead giveaway unless this hideaway is without ESPN, computer modems, and out of range for cell phones."

"This place might actually qualify, but unfortunately I'm going alone to research a story on romantic rendezvous spots. Talk about writing something you know nothing about."

"You'll probably appreciate the ambience more solo. If you get lonely, just remember James Dearing and sanity will return."

"That's the truth. Anyway, what I really need is a promotion to news reporter with a raise in salary, not a lover."

"Exactly. Who needs a man when you can have chic, expensive clothes paid for with the fruits of your own endeavors?"

Cora gave Peg the address and phone number of Water Lilies, promising to check in with her as soon as she returned to town. It felt good to share a few laughs with her sister. They spent too much time defending their own life choices and shoving them down the other's throat. Peg usually longed to hear that Cora was engaged and on her way back to Columbia.

She hung up the phone heartened by her sister's merriment, until memories of her own failed marriage returned. She imagined the breezy fantasy in context of her marriage to James Dearing:

Scads of political contributors to impress.

Back-stabbing party cronies to entertain.

Relaxation and renewal on the bottom of the list. No fun allowed for Cora Dearing, wife of the District Attorney being groomed for State Attorney at the very minimum.

Cora had been an accomplished role-player, who existed solely to further his personal dreams and aspirations. She padded out to her balcony with the last of the champagne. Lighting a candle to keep away the mosquitoes and mask the ever-present scent of bleach, she used the book of matches from Frederick-don't-call-him-Freddie.

A cold tightness gripped her heart when she closed the cover and read the lettering. The matchbook had come from Black Orchids, and it wasn't like that was the only restaurant in town.

I'll bet that's about to change. Frederick's words in response to her assertion of having no friends rushed back with a vengeance.

She closed her eyes, allowing the man from the restaurant to etch across her eyelids. She couldn't say why, but she felt certain the phantom in the graveyard had been real. He hadn't been a figment stimulated by an overactive imagination. Galen. Ethan Galen. The name floated back to her like a haunting blues melody from a club several blocks away. She could hear his enchanting accent enunciate syllables in her head.

He had been there in Lafayette. The only question in her mind was why.

Frederick waited only until the sound of the streetcar died before pulling his cell phone from his coat. The other party answered on the first ring.

"It's me. The faithful tour guide at your service, sir."

"What did you find out?"

"She'll be there. I'd stake my Christmas gift on it."

"Good work. I owe you one."

"More than one, my friend. But don't you think this idea of many birds, same rock might prove dangerous? She might throw a monkey wrench into what you need to do."

"You let me worry about that. I can handle it. You just make sure she's there."

"She will be. And I'm not worried 'bout a thing."

THE DRIVE INTO Lafourche Parish soothed Cora's spirit like a sauna and a massage. She had picked up a decent map from the car rental clerk and stayed off the freeways. Cora tried to ignore the abandoned cars still in the medium and parked under every bridge and piles of junked appliances everywhere as she left the metro area. The back roads showcased more waterfront property than the California coastline if one counted all the inlets of the meandering bayous. She fell in love with the dense, overgrown swamps of Louisiana, not fully recovered from their beating but making progress. Every now and then she glimpsed a house on high ground tucked beneath old cypresses, dripping with Spanish moss. She turned off the air conditioner, rolled down the windows, and breathed in the thick humid air.

She couldn't believe her good fortune. The owners of Water Lilies had said they received a cancellation for the weekend allowing her to come up on short notice. She jumped at the chance. Without time to catch up on laundry, she shopped for extra underwear and cool, gauzy sundresses, then stocked up on bug repellent and sunblock. She was headed towards the bayou in two days.

This impetuous behavior was unlike her. The old Cora planned everything for months ahead to make sure no contingency had been overlooked. She could grow to like the new, improved Cora.

The proprietors had explained that Water Lilies rented four guest rooms. After several pesky questions Cora learned that a newlywed couple from Baton Rouge was expected, along with a vacationing woman and daughter from New York. The way the heavily accented proprietress pronounced "New York", it sounded like a foreign land. Compared to the remote wilderness she viewed along the drive, it definitely was.

She hadn't mentioned who'd be staying in the fourth room. Cora hoped for an amorous couple escaping the city for a romantic tryst. Otherwise she'd have to rely on the newlyweds for juicy story details.

The trip took longer than the three hours prophesized on the phone due to her scenic route. When she finally pulled down the shady drive, three cars were already lined up under the trees: an SUV, a Cadillac with a rental agency plate holder, and a Jaguar. Her mind sorted the details, trying to match the guests with the vehicles as she crunched across the oyster shell parking lot.

She slung her garment bag over her shoulder and marched up the steps onto a broad verandah, wrapping the house on three sides. Inside, the center hall ran from back to front, allowing breezes from the water to move through the house. The grand foyer wall held enlarged photos of the damage to the house and grounds courtesy of the two nasty girls, Katrina and Rita, no doubt to circumvent the guests' inevitable questions. Uprooted trees, broken branches, missing shingles, shutters blown away, and some first-floor water damage. But nothing too serious, nothing permanent. No matter how many similar pictures she viewed of the devastation, she could never comprehend the awesome power of a hurricane.

"Ms. Dearing? I'm Mrs. Roussard. Welcome to Water Lilies."

Cora turned to see a cheerful woman smiling beside a marble-topped highboy that doubled as a check-in desk. She matched her lyrical name and charming accent. Around sixty or so, with silver hair and pale porcelain skin, the gracious Madame Roussard appeared the type Cora's mother would describe as "one who wouldn't raise her voice above a murmur even if her dress was on fire."

"How do you do?" Cora said, setting down her bag.

"Never better. The sun is shining. The breeze is light. Nothing nasty in the forecast." She nodded slightly at the montage on the wall then walked toward an open doorway. "May I offer you some refreshments in the parlor?"

Stiff from the drive, Cora politely declined the offer. She was anxious to start exploring and headed out the back patio door once her bags were sent up. She wandered the well-tended formal garden first, then followed a pebble path towards the swamp. Markedly cooler under the cypresses, she stayed on the trodden course into an overgrown area somewhere between tillable land and a watery bog. Birds and insects chattered at her intrusion as though guests seldom ventured into the humid, buggy woods.

Cora spotted a fallen log, checked it thoroughly for crawlies, then sat down to soak in the utter peace of a swamp. Although not quiet due to the insect hum, the din here served to soothe the nerves. As just reward for those patient enough to sit waiting for life to happen, Cora's attention caught on something moving in the black water in front of her. An alligator. A real, live alligator cut silently through the bayou, revealing only eyes and a portion of his back. It headed in the other direction, but she pulled back her outstretched legs just the same. Oddly, she felt no fear since it apparently sought tastier prey than her.

Cora kept to her log outpost until the afternoon drizzle turned into a downpour. She was soaked to the skin by the time she emerged from the woods and headed across the lawn. Having no desire to encounter other guests looking like a drowned rat, she set her course for the back door, hoping to slip up the stairs to her room before running into anyone. Such was not her luck.

With her head bent against the slanting rain, she didn't see him until she stepped up on the patio, then she froze like a deer caught in the glare of headlights. A man peered down from an upper gallery sheltered from the rain by the roof overhang. The corners of his mouth turned up in a smile as he politely tipped his hat to her. She stared back with water dripping from her eyelids and nose.

It was the man from the café. The one who'd bought a two-hundred-dollar gift for a complete stranger.

The same man she'd seen in Lafayette Cemetery. What did he say his name was?

Now he was here at a remote inn on the bayou. Two shivers shot up her spine, the first stemmed from excitement, the second from fear.

Cora pulled her eyes from his hypnotic stare and looked down at herself. Her white cotton shirt had turned transparent in the rain, while the thin silk of her bra concealed nothing. Her nipples stood out like tight knots in their brown pools. Cora felt exposed with a vulnerability that went beyond the sheerness of her blouse. She fled up the steps into the house.

This was no coincidence. Somehow he knew she'd be here. Her mind flew over every event that had taken place since he'd witnessed her eavesdropping in Black Orchids and sent over the bottle of champagne.

The laughing eyes of the tour guide flooded back. I'll bet that'll change soon. The name of the place is Water Lilies.

Okay, Cora Dearing, mystery sleuth, you've got an inkling on how, but the big question is…why? She wasn't the sexy, plaything type, sent to earth to break men's hearts and cause them to do foolish things. Men seldom hit on her, due to what her sister described as a transparent wall she'd erected around herself.

She let herself in her room, threw the bolt, and stripped off the soggy clothes. Was she in the middle of nowhere with a mad stalker who buys women bottles of Dom before having his way with them? No cheap stuff for his victims.

A knot of dread settled in the pit of her stomach as the warm shower water beat on her back and shoulders. There had to be a logical explanation, or it was just a bizarre coincidence. Coincidence, that's all. She hadn't known she would take the cemetery tour until the day before. You're letting your imagination carry you way downriver. This is not *House on Haunted Hill*, for Heaven's sake.

The story of the romantic rendezvous, invented to amuse her sister, flitted across her mind. She grinned remembering the dashing man secreting her away in the secluded hideaway to make passionate love all night long. Had she created a Twilight Zone type reality for herself in the bayou?

At least I won't wait long to find out, she thought as she toweled her hair before the dressing table mirror. A vellum note card had been left on the mirrored tray during her shower. It announced dinner would be served at seven. It was now half past six, but the pangs in her stomach had nothing to do with hunger. She laughed at her silly imaginings while she worked the tangles from her long hair. She needed to get a grip and do the job she'd come here for.

Tonight she'd meet the other guests—the possible research subjects for her story—and wanted to make a good impression. She carefully applied powder to her shiny nose, brushed some copper shadow on her lids and blusher to her cheekbones, finishing off with some bronze lipstick.

She sucked in a deep breath and took a final glance in the antique mirror. Not bad. Let the games on Haunted Hill begin.

"THERE YOU ARE, Mrs. Dearing," said Marie Roussard as Cora paused in the doorway.

"I hope I haven't kept you all waiting," Cora said, in her best attempt at contrition.

A man to the left rose to his feet smoothly as she entered the room. Cora knew without looking who it would be. Mr. Roussard stood also with only a moment's hesitation, followed by a tanned man of about thirty in golf shirt and chinos.

"No, not at all. You are right on time, my dear," said Mrs. Roussard. "I've put you there." She indicated with a wave of her hand the place next to the mystery man.

He moved quickly to pull out her chair. It was a polite gesture long absent from her life. She slipped into the chair and stole a glance at him as he sat back down. It was him, all right, even though the white linen had been replaced by a lightweight wool suit, expensive and well-tailored. The straw hat was nowhere to be seen. But she would remember those piercing blue eyes and that accent anywhere. His hair curled over his collar in the back, lending an artistic look to his otherwise perfect grooming. Silver highlights made him a great candidate for hair color for men—as the "before" picture—although she had to admit she liked it.

"Thank you," she murmured, shaking out her napkin.

"Not at all. I have much bad behavior to make up for."

"And even more to explain," she said under her breath.

"I look forward to that."

"May I make introductions?" said Mrs. Roussard. "Everyone, this is Mrs. Cora Dearing."

Cora glanced around the table at polite smiles and nods.

"This is Mr. and Mrs. Brian Guierre of Baton Rouge." The proprietress indicated the golf-shirted man and a young woman. The newlyweds, Cora supposed. Definitely the SUV owners.

"Susan," the woman corrected, with a cheerleader's stunning smile.

"They have honored us by selecting Water Lilies as their honeymoon destination."

"On your honeymoon? Congratulations," Cora said.

"Best wishes," said the man on her left almost simultaneously.

"I'm surprised that you'd want to come here. I would think that young people wanted more action these days," said a woman with bright auburn hair and prune-wrinkled skin. The accent was comically, quintessentially, New York. The largest diamond Cora had ever seen flashed on the woman's left hand. The rented Cadillac had to be theirs. This woman would never bother with a stick shift found in the Jaguar.

"Mother, this is a lovely place to spend a honeymoon," said a thirty-five-ish woman in washed silk and lots of jewelry. She stole a glance at Mr. and Mrs. Roussard to gauge their offense over her mother's remark.

The daughter, Cora mused.

"Not at all, ma'am," Brian Guierre responded. "This place is perfect. Now that I've found Susan, my action days are over." He punctuated his remark with a kiss on the back of the hand of his bride.

Susan blushed demurely. "Mine, too, darlin'."

What a sweet couple they were. Cora liked them instantly. They might just provide all the romance she needed for her story.

"And this is Mrs. William Rothman of New York City and her daughter, April," Mrs. Roussard continued.

"Of Manhattan," Mrs. Rothman corrected. "No place else in that city is worth the city services to keep it from falling into the East River. And good riddance, if it goes."

April Rothman looked mildly uncomfortable. She's danced this dance with mama before. Twenty or so pounds on the wrong side of perfection, April was not bad looking, in a haughty, austere way. The dinner suit she wore had to cost four hundred dollars, but it didn't fit well, hanging sack-like and unflattering.

"And this is Monsieur Ethan Auxier of New Orleans." Mrs. Roussard motioned with her hand to the gentleman on Cora's left. Finally, she was able to take a good long look at him without being obvious.

"I believe Mr. Auxier and I have already met." Cora extended her hand to him.

"Yes, but we were never properly introduced. I'm a firm believer in doing things right." He flashed her an unnerving smile as he clasped her hand tightly.

"Is that so? Is that a new resolution? Perhaps a new leaf you're overturning?"

"That's my fondest hope," he said in a voice intended

for only her ears. His smile deepened the lines and furrows around his eyes and mouth. It wasn't fair the way
wrinkles made men look distinguished.

She glanced at him surreptitiously while she reached
for her water glass and drank. He was even more attractive than she remembered. Like a silly schoolgirl,
she wished she'd have spent a bit more time on her hair
and makeup, feeling slightly disheveled next to him. He
exuded an aura of authority and power. Wealth seemed
to do that to people—imbue them with intelligence and
competence. She wondered what aura she emanated—
proficiency with gardening and floor washing?

"Monsieur Auxier? A Frenchman from New Orleans?"
Mrs. Rothman inquired with disdain in her voice.

Mr. Auxier turned his head slowly from Cora's direction to Mrs. Rothman's. His smile faded. "Yes, madam."

"A Cajun Frenchman?" she asked.

"No, madam. To my knowledge, there was no inter-
mediary stop in Canada during my ancestors' migration
to Louisiana."

His accent was half French, half southern, and wholly
charming. *I can listen to this man talk all day long. He
must be the lucky dog driving the twelve-cylinder Jag,*
Cora thought, matching the last vehicle in the parking
lot to a face.

Mrs. Rothman made a small, confused grimace.
"What's that?" The history lesson had apparently been
lost on her.

"The Cajuns first settled in Nova Scotia, before mi-
grating to the Louisiana Territory," he said to Mrs. Rothman, then pivoted slightly in his chair. "We have not
heard from where you hail, Mrs. Dearing."

"I recently moved here from Columbia, South Carolina. The fine capital of the palmetto state," she added. She felt like an idiot schoolteacher on sabbatical.

"A veritable jewel in the crown of the South," he said, and lifted his glass in salute.

"Oh, brother. The War is over, you two," screeched Mrs. Rothman. "And by the way, you all lost."

Cora knew it had been an attempt at humor by the woman, but no one laughed. Mr. Roussard looked shocked.

"How recently? Did you miss all the hurricane excitement?" April asked.

For a moment no one spoke, then Mr. Auxier drained his glass and stared at the woman. "We'd be hard pressed to describe the tragic loss of life and property as excitement, Miss Rothman." The temperature in the room seemed to drop several degrees.

Marie Roussard had just returned from the kitchen carrying two bottles of champagne and thought it a good time for the hostess to intervene. "M'sieu Auxier ordered these to toast Mr. and Mrs. Guierre on their nuptials. Emil, would you help me pour, please?"

Mrs. Roussard adeptly opened one bottle and handed it to her husband, then the next. The champagne was vintage Rothschild. Cora didn't catch the year, but either M'sieu Auxier thought a great deal of the institution of marriage or still had more money to burn. And something told her he'd never laid eyes on the young couple before this evening.

"Thank you, M'sieu Auxier," said Brian. "That was very kind of you, sir."

"It's my pleasure, I assure you." He lifted his glass in toast as soon as the last flute had been filled. "May every one of life's pleasures visit your doorstep, but disappointments only call when you're not home."

The pretty Susan Guierre nodded thanks, clinking her glass first with her husband, then with all within reach.

"Yeah, good luck, kids. Don't waste your money on rent. Buy a house right away to build equity. That's my advice for you," Mrs. Rothman offered, then clinked glasses with her daughter.

Cora barely heard the woman; she still stared at Auxier, impressed with the sweet sentiments of his toast. "What beautiful words. You must be happily married yourself, sir."

"No, I'm afraid not, Mrs. Dearing, but thank you for your compliment. I would never have been so forward in Black Orchids had that been the case." He gently clinked the glass she still held aloft. "And will the fortunate Mr. Dearing be joining us this weekend?" he asked softly, so that the others would have to strain to hear.

Cora lowered her eyes and flushed at his blatant charm. Only the French could get away with saying that sort of thing.

"Mr. Dearing is probably with his political aide-de-camp and soon-to-be-new-wife this weekend, and therefore, is not expected," she said. She earnestly hoped it didn't sound as bitter as it did to her own ears.

"He'll no doubt live to regret his mistake," he said, taking a long drink of champagne. "What about you? What kind of work do you do?"

"Oh, do you really believe that, Mr. Auxier?" interrupted Mrs. Rothman. "That her husband will live to regret his mistake? Men cease thinking with their brains when they reach a certain age."

"Present company excepted, of course," April added quickly, then drained her flute.

My, you are very good at damage control, Cora thought. She was getting a headache from Ethan's attempt to talk to her while the main conversation at the table continued around them. She didn't answer his query about her work. There'd be time to chitchat during the weekend. She had a few questions of her own to ask when Mrs. Rothman wasn't ready to swoop down like a circling hawk. He had been in Lafayette Cemetery. She was certain of it.

Ethan didn't look at Mrs. Rothman when he answered, but kept his gaze fastened on Cora. "Yes, madam. I do indeed. Men usually see the folly of their mistakes if they're lucky to live long enough." Then in a low voice that only Cora should have been able to hear, he added, "And all good things come to those who wait."

"Well, we've waited long enough to eat," said Mrs. Rothman.

Just at that moment, the Roussards reentered the dining room carrying large platters and bowls. She looked crestfallen. He looked piqued. They had heard the comment.

"Forgive us, everyone. Our cook is a bit of a perfectionist. I do hope the dinner will prove worth the wait," Mrs. Roussard apologized.

"Oh, April and I are accustomed to waiting. We're from Manhattan. We have to wait for the service industry to finish their English lessons before serving the next course."

Cora attempted to hand the serving bowl of snap beans almandine to Ethan, but halted with the bowl in midair. He was staring at Mrs. Rothman with undisguised contempt, then he said something to the Roussards in French as they passed behind his chair. Since Cora had studied Spanish in college, she understood nothing from their exchange. But whatever it was, they both relaxed measurably. Mr. Roussard spoke quietly to him as he offered the platter of filets on his right, while Mrs. Roussard refilled his glass from a third bottle of Rothschild.

This weekend is going to be interesting. "May I ask what business you're in, M'sieu Auxier?" Cora asked, drawing his attention when Mr. Roussard moved on.

He promptly took the forgotten bowl from her hands and spooned a portion onto his plate. She couldn't help but notice his helping of *tournedos of boeff* was smaller than hers. She instantly regretted taking so much food. "You've got to stop eating like a field hand if you want to catch a man." One of her sister's favorite admonishments rang in her head, triggering a grin.

"I am in the import/export business, Ms. Dearing, but I would love to know what brought that lovely smile to your face."

Cora thought about it for a moment before answering. She opted for the truth. "I remembered my sister telling me that I eat like a field hand. I had been comparing my plate to yours."

Ethan's blue eyes twinkled with warmth and kindness as they bore two round holes through her heart. "Your sister's fears are unfounded. It's a joy to meet a woman who knows her own mind and takes what she wants in this world and doesn't value other opinions over her own."

"Here, here." Brian Guierre lifted his almost empty glass. "I agree. Plus, men like a woman with a little meat on their bones." He playfully pinched his wife's bare shoulder. Susan giggled in response.

The Guierres were getting a little tipsy. Susan's eyes glinted like sapphires in the candlelight.

"Somebody hand me a shovel," Mrs. Rothman said to her daughter.

"He is correct," Ethan said, ignoring the other comment. "And my own appetite is usually much heartier than this. Something has taken it away." He shot a glance across the table where Mrs. Rothman picked at something on her plate with the tine of her fork.

"Well, the food is very good. You have my compliments, Mrs. Roussard," said April.

Mrs. Rothman, finally satisfied that the offending ingredient had been removed, took a forkful of the pecan wild rice. "Yes, but I must ask you to look at our room air conditioner. It makes an awful racket. I'm afraid it's going to keep me up all night." She finished the champagne in her glass. "Our room smells a little musty, too. Can't you get central air put in this old house? It would certainly do a much better job than these window units."

Cora glanced at April. Her jaw was set in a hard line, but she made no attempt to stifle mama as she helped herself to another beef filet.

Mr. Roussard gave her a deprecating smile, and took a breath before replying. "I'm afraid not, Madame Rothman. The walls will not accommodate running the ductwork. And to box the ductwork on the surface of ceilings would destroy the integrity of this two-century beautiful lady." His eyes glanced lovingly around the room as he spoke. "But I will switch your unit with ours immediately after dinner and hope it will prove more satisfactory. My wife and I are at your disposal to assure that Water Lilies is a most memorable experience."

"Well, everything's been great so far," Brian piped up.

"Our room is beautiful, Mrs. Roussard. I would love to own a gracious home like this one day," added Susan.

"And I would like the recipes for tonight's dishes," Cora said in a quiet voice. "Everything was delicious. Thank you both."

Mr. and Mrs. Roussard beamed with pleasure.

Mrs. Rothman was not finished yet, however. "What

is there to do out here in the bayou?" She put a distasteful inflection on the final word that made Cora wonder why in the world they chose this for their vacation destination. April immediately answered her question.

"Mother, I showed you the brochure. And you promised you wouldn't whine while we're here if I did Vegas with you in the fall. There are airboat rides on the lake, the gator-watching expedition, and the Audubon bird watching tour. I'm looking forward to all of it." Her eyes shone like glass, while a slight slur to her words betrayed her fondness for the champagne.

"It all sounds buggy to me," Mrs. Rothman said with a sigh.

"I have arranged for our son to take anyone interested on a swamp tour tomorrow. It will be a full day with a stop for lunch at a local spot we think you'll enjoy," Mr. Roussard said pleasantly.

Everyone, including Cora, voiced approval of the idea, although Mrs. Rothman's could hardly be described as enthusiastic.

That is, everyone but Ethan Auxier. He said nothing. He simply stared at Mrs. Rothman with cold loathing in his eyes, a tic in his left cheek and the muscles in his neck bunching tightly.

"I wanted to thank you, Mr. Auxier." Cora's voice sounded small in the darkness of the back porch. She had waited until the others had drifted up to their rooms before helping herself to a cup of coffee from the sideboard and following him out through the back door. Magically she located a rocker in the complete darkness and lowered herself into it.

"Ethan, please, if I may call you Cora. And what have I done to deserve your gratitude?"

She sensed, rather than saw him stand when she'd

entered the porch. "For the champagne, of course. That was you in Black Orchids the other night. Don't even try to deny it."

"I wouldn't dream of denying it, if the champagne pleased you. And you are welcome."

This time she spotted his grin as her eyes adjusted to the dark. "I'd just like to know why, that's all. That was an expensive bottle, sent without any reason whatsoever. If you have money to burn, there are many charities in New Orleans eager to take some off your hands."

"Don't worry, they've already contacted me. I give till it hurts to a long list of worthy causes."

"And I have no nasty little secret. I couldn't help over-hear that couple's conversation, since they were speaking so animatedly." Cora couldn't stop herself from defend-ing her behavior in the restaurant.

"Well said. I stand corrected. I made an unjust as-sumption."

"Anyway, lots of people eavesdrop. It's a harmless past-time."

"Completely harmless," he agreed. "No one's ever died due to eavesdropping. At least, not to my knowledge."

Cora shifted uneasily in her rocker.

"I had no intention of embarrassing you. That's not why I sent the bottle over." His voice could barely be heard above the tumult of the swamp. Every frog and toad had to be searching for a mate tonight.

"Then why did you?" she asked, holding her breath for his answer. But it was not the answer she anticipated.

"I've never seen anyone so thoroughly enjoy a bowl of gumbo in my life. You wiped the sides of the bowl with your bread crust. I thought you should have something better to accompany such good soup than that swill you were drinking."

Cora was grateful for the darkness on the porch as her cheeks flushed with color. "I order what I can afford, Mr. Auxier. Not everyone's born with a silver spoon in his mouth."

There was a several moment silence. "Forgive me, Cora. My criticism was directed at the overpriced house wine at Orchids, not you personally. I'm afraid I'm a little out of practice making polite small talk." He reached a hand out and brushed her arm lightly. "Please accept my apology. My nasty disposition has already robbed me of many friends and acquaintances."

Cora pulled her arm away from his touch. She didn't like the electric jolt it sent through her body. "Well, considering you are it in terms of weekend companions, except for a honeymooning couple, and the delightful Rothmans, I suppose I'll overlook the insult."

"I'll make you glad you did, I promise," he whispered. "Thank goodness the rooms are all filled. I couldn't stand it if I had to compete for your attention with new arrivals, being so rusty in social graces."

"You don't strike me as the type who's lived a reclusive existence. I'm sure your charm usually compensates for your manners." Cora heard him take a sip of something. Ice clinked in an unseen glass.

"I sent the bottle over because you were the most intriguing woman I'd seen in a long time. For that reason and no other. Now you know the truth."

"I see," she answered and began to rock in the chair. "And that was your first time out in public since a long, protracted recovery?"

He laughed and sipped his drink again. "No, I see and meet people all the time, or rather, I seem to meet the same person over and over."

Again she was glad for darkness since her face flushed

to her hairline and the little hairs on her arm prickled like needles. She'd received more than her share of compliments over the years, delivered with varying degrees of sincerity, but this man's praise unsettled her. "Well, thank you for the gift. I took it home and enjoyed it while watching the world go by on the street."

"Do you like living in the Quarter?"

"Yes, but I just moved to the quiet end, far from the bars and hurricane vendors. I still have the ambience without the shouted obscenities waking me up at four A.M."

"Sounds perfect. What brings you here to Water Lilies?"

She remembered the opportune meeting of Frederick, but thought against bringing that up in the complete darkness. "Research for a story I'm working on," she answered. "It's hard to believe I can enjoy the incredible amenities here, then write the whole thing off on my expense account." She cringed as soon as the words were out. First, he had seen her scraping her bowl with a crust, now she was bragging about traveling on the dole. *Perhaps I should hang a sign around my neck: Will work for food.*

"So you'll be exposing evil corruption out here on the bayou? Who'll be the focus of your exposé? Crooked politicians accepting bribes for looking the other way to swamp polluters? Or perhaps you'll lay open the weak underbelly of a prominent family and bare their secrets to the hungry trash-reading public?"

Cora strained to see his features in the thin starlight. His voice sounded deadly serious. "Nothing like that. I'm just here to do a feature story on romantic retreats. I'd say Water Lilies qualifies for that distinction, wouldn't you?"

"Yeah, I do, but I'm not sure Emil and Marie would

appreciate the advertisement. They do plenty of business by just word of mouth. That way, they can be selective about who they have as guests in their house."

"Well, they'd have to sign a release before I could publish the story if they're mentioned, so they can decide after seeing my copy." Cora thought for a moment about the Roussards' selectivity. "How did the Guierres rate an invitation?"

"Susan's mother went to school with Marie Roussard." There was no hesitation in his answer.

"And you? How do you know the Roussards?"

"Our families are connected back through our grandfathers."

"What about the charming Ada and April Rothman of New York?"

"How they found Water Lilies remains a mystery for now." His voice drifted through the dark-like fog approaching from the swamp.

Something smacked on the water and drew her gaze. Cora watched tendrils of mist reach from the bayou with a shiver. She forced her attention back to him. "But I don't know anyone. I'm not even from Louisiana." A long moment passed while Cora listened to nothing but tree frogs and cicadas, and the roll of thunder far off in the distance. She grew almost reluctant to hear the answer.

Then he finally replied, "You should consider yourself lucky to have found this place. I know I consider running into you fortunate indeed. Tell me about your work, Cora. Being a writer must be fascinating."

She hesitated a moment to be sure he wasn't making sport of her. "Fascinating? Only on rare occasions, since I cover nothing more exciting than gallery openings, human interest stories to tweak heartstrings and open pocketbooks, plus an occasional non-political scandal."

"You enjoy that? Ruining reputations? Causing untold damage to people's lives?"

She burst out laughing. "You've overestimated both my job description and abilities. The last scandal I reported on involved shady accounting during a fund-raiser cookie sale. It turned out to be a case of miscommunication and lousy math skills among the parents. I assure you, no reputations were harmed during my reporting."

"Happy to hear it! The world already has enough despicable corruption. What about the nice stories? The dog-saves-little-old-lady-in-a-fire, the-teenager-returns-the-purse-with-lottery-winnings-intact tales, do you enjoy writing about them?"

She wished to Heaven she could get a good look at him. The disembodied words floating through the humid air disconcerted her. "Actually, I do. I love the people stories. How humans live their lives, how they choose to fill their days fascinates me. People are far more generous, kindhearted and self-sacrificing than I believed possible."

"Surely not the young ones. Only those about to meet with the Grim Reaper bother to behave with such altruism. Like my grandmother, for instance."

"I'm glad you have a grandmother to keep you from sliding into complete cynicism. I'll bet she's a gem."

"That she is. A perfect lady. Very old fashioned, only modern thinking in her desire to right every one of society's wrongs. No hungry children, no students denied college scholarships, no sick person refused treatment due to lack of insurance. You get the picture."

"Wow. She takes on all that? What's left for the non-profits to worry about?"

He laughed with a rich, warm intimacy. "There's still plenty of deprivation left in Louisiana since Katrina."

"Were you in town then, during the hurricane?"

He exhaled air through his teeth. "No, I was in New York on business. I tried to get back in time but there were no flights. I don't know what I could've done anyway—hold back the storm surge? Keep old levees from crumbling? I would've liked being with my family when they evacuated. My grandmother was stronger, more fearless than anyone. She handled the repairs to her home, then pitched in to help many others in her neighborhood. Unfortunately she received little commendation for her efforts. I'd like you to meet my *Grandmère*. Perhaps you'll find how she fills her days…fascinating."

Cora had no idea what to say to this. She leaned forward in her chair to see his face, but he'd retreated into the shadows. Only the creaking of his rocker spoke of his palpable proximity. Again anxiety tumbled in her stomach for no reason.

"Yes, that would be nice," she said to end the silence, then stood abruptly.

"Are you hurrying off again, Cora? At this rate, I'll be old and silver-haired before we get to know each other better."

"I don't like to give away too much during the first evening. You might grow bored with me, leaving only the Rothmans for my weekend companions," she whispered.

He stood and stepped closer until only inches apart. "Oh, I wouldn't worry about boredom ever being an issue between us."

Cora reared back as though stung by a bee. What was with this guy that made her so nervous? But if there was one thing she had no doubt about. It was no accident, no chance happenstance that she was at Water Lilies.

Ethan waited until he heard the heavy door shut behind Cora before he leaned back in his chair and laughed. He had loved the wide-eyed look on her sweet face when she realized she may have been set up. Then she'd set down her coffee cup and fled back to her room like the devil himself was on her heels. *Maybe he is, cher. You're not quite so brave in the dead of night, are you?*

He loved seeing her hair loose instead of the severe knot she'd worn at Black Orchids. It trailed across her shoulders and down her back. Several times he had to stop himself, or his fingers would have entangled themselves in the thick, luxuriant mane. Each place on her neck or shoulders where a silky strand caressed, he yearned to reach out and touch that place, too. He couldn't keep from stealing none-too-subtle glances at the dinner table, where the reflected candlelight changed her green eyes to exotic golden orbs. She looked like a storybook sorceress ready to seduce the unsuspecting into her web, instead of the other way around.

But being charmed by a sorceress was exactly what he didn't need. Right now he had a job to do and couldn't afford to forget why he was here. He pulled his cell phone from his pocket, then punched in a number. Ethan waited impatiently as the other end picked up.

"Yes, they're here… No, I'd say you under-exaggerated them, if anything…they are without any redeeming grace. This will sincerely be a pleasure… I'm using my mother's maiden name. No, they won't recognize it… Don't worry about a thing. I've got it under control."

When the line went dead, he clicked the phone shut and retrieved a sterling silver flask. It had been his great-grandfather's. Galen men had sipped spirits from this priceless piece of French-American antiquity for two hundred years. He hoped his ancestor's whiskey didn't burn a hole through a gut already filled with anger.

The Rothmans of Manhattan. What did that viper say? "The rest of the city can fall into the river? And even better—the War's over and you all lost."

"I'm afraid that's where you are mistaken, Mrs. Ada Rothman," he said to the pervasive darkness. "This war is just beginning."

Ethan Galen took another swig from the flask, settling back into the chair. His thoughts turned from the abrasive harridan back to Cora. She was even lovelier than he'd remembered in Black Orchids with haunting green eyes and a figure to tempt a saint. She was a strong woman who spoke her mind and knew what she wanted in life. Someone very much like—Chloe. He smiled at the striking similarities between Cora and his sister, evident even on such short acquaintance. Chloe, too, possessed a hearty appetite and a taste for expensive things, although affording them wasn't a problem for his strong-willed younger sister.

This was the first woman he'd seen in years that intrigued him. He just hoped that the headstrong Cora Dearing wouldn't get in the way of what he came here to do.

THREE

CORA HADN'T SLEPT so soundly in years. The noisy air conditioner that so irritated Mrs. Rothman had lulled her to sleep within minutes of her head hitting the pillow. She stretched like a cat, then looked around the expansive room. Cool mint walls, a high white ceiling, and polished wood floors. Oriental area rugs lay scattered about, while tall hurricane shutters flanked the windows. The furniture was heavy, old and provincial. A fireplace graced one wall between floor-to-ceiling bookcases, which held everything from antique leather-bound classics to the latest paperback thrillers.

Cora showered in the porcelain clawfoot tub with its rigged shower enclosure, then padded back into the bedroom with her hair wrapped in a turban. A tray of juice, coffee and croissants had been left on the table along with another vellum note.

Mrs. Dearing: The boat leaves our dock at nine. Please join us for the swamp tour. Max Roussard.

I wouldn't miss it for the world, she thought, as she sipped coffee and dried her hair.

She had changed clothes three times, but finally settled on a cotton sundress that would be cool and comfortable and a broad brimmed straw hat. Too long out in the sun gave her a headache, and she wanted nothing to intrude on her enjoyable getaway.

She arrived at the boat dock behind Water Lilies at 9:03. Luckily, she hadn't missed the proverbial boat.

"Ah, Ms. Dearing, I presume." A young man around twenty-five, ruddy dark from the sun and very blond, held out his hand. She shook it heartily.

"Cora, please."

"Max Roussard." Not letting go of her hand, he drew her into the rocking boat. His accent was stronger than his parents', his sunglasses mirrored, and his clothes baggy, like most men his age. Her first impression was favorable.

Cora spotted the only vacant seat in the boat that happened to be next to a brightly smiling April Rothman. Unfortunately, her mother perched on the small seat in the bow and would therefore face them for the entire excursion.

What did I do to deserve this? Once the boat moved away from the dock, Cora suspected the effusive Mrs. Rothman became mildly seasick, since the woman said little during the trip. She simply fanned herself with a rolled map, keeping her eyes focused on the bank.

Cora glanced behind her during Max Roussard's explanation of the flora and fauna around the pier as he readied the boat to leave. Susan and Brian cuddled next to each other on the bench, oohing and aahing about each plant identified. One would think a couple from Baton Rouge would have been in a swamp before, but Cora loved their enthusiasm.

Ethan sat in the stern in front of Max Roussard wearing the straw hat from their first meeting pulled low on his face. A Styrofoam cooler reposed on the seat beside him. The beginnings of a beard sprouted along his jaw line and chin. At first glance, Cora would have sworn his eyes were closed and the man asleep.

"Trying to disguise your identity, *M'sieu* Auxier?"

He tipped up the brim of his hat and nodded with a

grin. "Good morning, Cora. I trust nothing but pleasant dreams visited your sleep."

"Nothing but, Ethan," she answered.

"Please sit here with me. I saved you a seat just like the good old days of our youth." He moved the cooler to the floor behind him, then stood to extend a steadying hand. "I did hope to get better acquainted with you during the tour."

She grasped his hand and settled herself next to him, keeping as much space between as possible. "I'm afraid you probably know everything there is to know about me already. I live a simple life. No hidden motives, no private agendas." She had hoped to get a rise out of him, maybe even a blurted confession as to what he was up to. What she received instead was another rich, resonate laugh from deep within his gut.

"Everyone has an agenda, whether they're consciously aware of it or not. Everyone desires to further their own plan for the future."

"Well, I'm out here to get a story on the romantic Water Lilies. There, my big secret agenda is out. Now it's your turn to come clean." She spoke in a low voice, turning enough on the seat to face him.

He studied her for a moment from under his hat brim before answering. "Well, all right then. What the heck? I'm out here to get you to do a story on my grandmother and her good works." He stretched his legs out under the aluminum seat in front of him.

She stared speechlessly. "That is the most ridiculous thing I've ever heard." She waited for him to amend or change the explanation as the boat passed water hickory, tupelo, and hundred-year-old cypress trees, dripping with Spanish moss.

"Do you really think so? But it is the truth, *ma cher*."

"Look there, folks," Max called, pointing at a snake coiled around an extended branch over the water. "Duck your heads."

The creature had to be at least a dozen feet long. Mrs. Rothman screamed and clutched her purse to her chest as the boat passed beneath the reptile. Perhaps she'd heard the species were adept purse thieves.

Cora kept her eye on the snake but felt Ethan's gaze on her instead of the overhead danger. "That's the story you're sticking to?" she asked once well past the branch.

"Absolutely." He reached into his pocket, withdrew a paper, and began to unfold it carefully. "I read your article about these two ladies and thought you might do the same—"

She pulled the paper from his hands, not believing her eyes. It was the article she'd written a couple weeks ago about two tireless volunteers in the newly rebuilt Head Start facility. The story had run last week, garnering little feedback from the readers. A minor blip on the journalism radar screen.

Ethan leaned over her shoulder as she stared at the full-color feature. "That's you, isn't it? Cora Dearing?" He stubbed his forefinger on her byline. "I do have the right Cora Dearing, don't I?" His eyes crinkled into deep furrows as he offered an exaggerated wink.

"I read that story, Ms. Dearing," Susan said. "It was very good. Those ladies should get a community award, or something."

"Thanks," Cora mumbled to Susan, reserving a hot scowl at Ethan. Under her breath, she said to him, "You brought me all the way out here to trick me into writing a glowing feature on the humanitarian work of your grandmother? Do I have the story right?"

"Pretty much, but I'm loathe to use the word 'trick.' I'd much prefer 'invite' or 'encourage.'"

"You've got that kind of time on your hands? I thought you said you worked like a normal person."

"I do work. I have other business in the neighborhood and thought I'd kill two birds with one stone."

Cora stared off past Ethan into the shadowy gloom of the waterway, allowing this to sink in. Muskrats and turtles moved through the dark aisles of reeds and palmetto fronds as the insect racket reached din level.

"What kind of business would a man like you have out here? Insect repellant trial tests? Research into the economic effect of invasive plant species? You don't seem the type. You don't even sweat," she added for no particular reason.

"I assure you, Cora. I do sweat." He patted her knee lightly.

She swatted his hand away as though it were a mosquito. "And you consider me a…bird?" Her composure was rapidly deteriorating for no apparent reason other than the heat and his proximity.

He lowered his sunglasses to peer over the top. "I beg your pardon?" he asked.

"You said you're here killing two birds with one stone."

"I just hate that particular expression. I wish people would come up with a better analogy for multi-tasking," Mrs. Rothman interjected. Although Cora and Ethan had been talking quietly, the rest of the party seemed to be taking interest in their conversation despite the stunning scenery all around them.

Cora chose to ignore Mrs. Rothman. "Just another pigeon roosting on Stonewall's statue in Jackson Square?"

Ethan pushed his sunglasses back up the bridge of his

nose and leaned back against the cooler. "Oh, no. Not an ordinary pigeon. I think of you more as an eagle, soaring free on the wind currents, or maybe a swan, gliding through the water with majestic dignity."

"They're still birds. Maybe you shouldn't think of me at all in terms of a creature that eats its body weight daily, defecates anywhere and everywhere, and has a brain the size of a grape."

Susan and Brian laughed loudly, while even Max's chuckle could be heard over the hum of the engine.

"Duly noted," Ethan said, slapping a bug on the side of his neck. "Let me rethink my analogy."

"On the right, folks," Max called with the inflexion of humor still in his voice, "our featured attraction of the afternoon."

Blessedly the attention of the passengers was directed toward a pair of alligators sunning themselves on the riverbank. Everyone but Ada Rothman leaned to get a better look. Neither gator paid them any mind as Max killed the engine and let the boat drift closer. Cora gazed at the leathery hides of the creatures with amazement. She'd never been so close to something so ancient and wild before, yet still watched to be sure they didn't slip into the water in pursuit when the boat passed.

"The male is on the left, female on the right," Ethan said after a moment. "They mate for life, often dying within weeks of each other. They lose all desire to live once their mate is gone."

"Is that so? Much unlike humans with all our machinations."

"I seem to have struck out in the charm department, haven't I?" He whispered his words next to her ear, so that no one could overhear.

"Perhaps you should try a little less intrigue and a

bit more honesty. It's still the best policy, you know," Cora snapped. She scooted as far from him as the boat would allow.

"Ah, honesty." He spat the word out as though he'd caught a nasty bug in his mouth. "I think it's overrated, since it's purely subjective anyway."

"What do you mean?" This raised the dander of the journalist in her.

"What strikes you as the truth may be mere embellishment to others. Truth is an abstraction, existing only in principle. The spoken or written words are always subjective interpretations."

"And yet you want my subjective opinion in a story about your family."

"I thought words could be used to build up instead of tear down for a change. To honor an old woman for the good she's done while she's still alive. A woman who still places high value on other's opinions. Forget I mentioned it. It was presumptive of me, at the very minimum. You have my sincere apology." Ethan settled back against the side of the boat, tipping the brim of his hat a bit lower.

His tone, his bearing, his body language changed so suddenly, Cora thought she felt a cold breeze come from the moss laden trees, despite the intense swelter.

So much for finding a non-manipulative man, Cora thought. Probably just a statistical impossibility after the pre-pubescent stage. Even on a casual level, every man wanted something, and Ethan was no different.

She shook her head as though waking from a bad dream. Concerning herself with this rich, indolent man wasn't why she'd come to the bayou. She trained her gaze on the river's edge and watery lanes branching off both directions. Despite the oppressive heat, she enjoyed the tour. She loved the unspoiled, overgrown lushness of the swamp, and despite the constant hum of insects and birds, it was remarkably quiet as the boat sliced through black water.

"I'd imagine it would be easy to get lost out here, Max," Cora said. "All of the canals leading to this channel look exactly the same to me."

"Very easy. It can turn into a maze with one wrong turn, especially at night. I do have maps tucked away even though I've lived here my whole life." He patted the lift top of the seat beside him. "So don't fear you'll never see civilization again."

As he spoke, the crowded feel from the low hanging vegetation gave way to open grassy fields dotted with an occasional cypress. From a distance it almost looked like a western prairie if you didn't look too close at the water between the hummocks of higher ground.

"These were called 'the quaking' or 'trembling lands' by the Indians," explained Max, taking on his tour guide voice. "They look like solid land, but they're deceptive. In most places the ground floats on the bayou and will support only the weight of small animals. Most people would break through, so venture from the boat at your own peril," he warned, leaning against the stern, utterly comfortable in the stifling humidity. "The swamp has fooled a countless number of adventurers. If a person falls through, it'll close the gaping hole, swallowing the unsuspecting without a trace."

"All of them Yankees, young man?" Mrs. Rothman asked.

"The vast majority, ma'am." Max answered with a wink.

No use angling for a big tip from that one, Cora thought. *She's saving her tourist dollar for more jewelry.*

Just about the time she was growing stiff from sitting

and thirsty from the unrelenting Louisiana sun, the boat turned into a manmade canal and pulled up to a rickety dock, the pilings green with moss. Two barefoot little girls waved and greeted the boat as they tied up. The dock Max selected leaned so far over, Cora was leery to step onto it, probably courtesy of the storm surge. She let the younger and more flexible Guierres get out before her.

"Not to worry, Ms. Dearing. That dock is sturdier than it looks." Ethan's musical accent tickled her ear. She pivoted to find his face within inches of hers. She smelled his heady aftershave, looked into his pale eyes and stumbled in the slant-bottomed boat. He grabbed her before she tumbled over the side, then placed both hands on her waist to steady her. She had no idea why the man made her so fidgety, but she was barely able to step onto the dock with both him and Max Roussard supporting her arms.

"You've been here before, Mr. Auxier?" Cora asked, glad to have solid ground beneath her feet. He looked cool and relaxed in his cotton shirt and silky black pants. The shirt, open several buttons at the neck, displayed surprisingly well-developed chest muscles for a man she suspected didn't work. She felt hot and sticky, despite the thinness of her dress.

He didn't answer right away, but led her up the worn wooden steps. The place looked more like a botanical camp for fisherman and shrimpers than a restaurant. She caught the fragrance of jasmine before spying it climbing the fence that camouflaged the filleting tables. Their sweet scent masked the odious smell of fish entrails. White oleander trees drooped with glorious blossoms while creeper covered posts and lattice, wherever it had gained a solid foothold. Morning glories flanked the doorway. All this went far in softening the ramshackle appearance of *Le P'tit* Fisherman. The sign proclaiming the name hung askew by a single remaining bolt.

"Yes," he finally answered. "I believe I was here once on a fishing expedition."

The thought that this suave, distinguished man would fish struck her as humorous, but she let it pass. Mrs. Rothman could already be heard complaining about the choice of lunch destinations.

"I can assure you, Mrs. Rothman, the kitchen is quite clean. You may have a look if you like. And I am sure you will find the seafood the freshest to be had anywhere." Max's voice wafted out through the screen door as Ethan and Cora entered the low-slung building. It reminded Cora of a cabin with large, screened-in windows on two sides and a corrugated tin roof. She loved the sound of rain on a metal roof and judging by the lowering clouds in the distance, they might just get a downpour during lunch.

"Mother, let's not make an issue of this, please. I'm starving," April Rothman pleaded irritably with her mother.

"I think the place is darling," enthused Susan Guierre as she slipped into a chair next to Brian at the only large table in the place.

"I do, too. And if it has indoor plumbing, I'll give it five stars," Cora joked, glancing around for the restroom. "What more can someone even from New York want?"

"That's right. You can eat at a mall food court anytime."

Cora smiled at Susan, so spirited and full of life. So much like her when she was a newlywed. No, don't think about that. Happily-ever-after does happen for some people. She just hadn't been one of the lucky ones.

"I'll go with you to the ladies room," April said, rising to her feet. "I definitely drank too much coffee at breakfast."

No cutesy sign hung indicating the location of the facilities, so Cora headed toward the back swinging door.

"No, not that way. The restroom is down this hall." April grabbed her elbow and steered her into a narrow hallway where they found the single unisex bathroom. April pushed past Cora to use the facility first without so much as a second thought.

Cora took in the curious scene while she waited for her turn. A cluttered bar ran the length of the back wall. Several men, fisherman she guessed by their clothes, argued between long pulls on bottled beers. They weren't speaking English, so she hadn't a clue regarding their point of contention. Mrs. Rothman pouted at the round table that had been set up for the group, while Brian and Susan kissed and nuzzled as though they were the only inhabitants on the planet.

Cora spotted Max Roussard speaking to a rotund, jowly-faced man by the door who wore tattered shorts, a spattered white apron and flip-flops on his feet. He must be the manager, and probably owner, cook, bartender and cleaning staff, she mused. Ethan leaned against a post with his hands buried deep in his pockets. He listened as the other two talk animatedly in French, glancing up from under the brim of his hat.

I guess I studied the wrong foreign language in high school. How am I to eavesdrop on good story material when I don't speak the native language?

When Cora returned, she took the seat next to Brian to watch the group by the door. Auxier suddenly straightened and spoke in low tones, punctuated by fervent gestures. His hand cut through the air in staccato jabs that left no doubt he possessed a strong opinion on the topic of conversation. The man with the apron nodded his head in agreement to Ethan, said something to Max, then approached the table. A cold shiver raced up Cora's spine. Something told her they hadn't been discussing the fresh catch of the day. She would've loved to know what had irritated Ethan.

"Welcome folks to *Le P'tit* Fisherman," he addressed their table in broken English. "My name is Antoine. Our menu is there," he said, pointing to a chalkboard against the wall. "Plus we have full bar service. Do not hesitate to ask for whatever you want."

Oh, please don't say that to Mrs. Rothman. We'll be here all day, Cora thought. The woman was already complaining because the chalkboard listings were in French.

"Are you hungry, Cora?" The smooth, mellow accent made the inquiry sound lyrical as Ethan slipped into the chair next to hers. He removed his hat, then raked long fingers through his hair. Deep, white squint lines webbed his eyes in contrast to his tan.

"Yes, as usual, I'm hungry," she said, offering her best smile. He intrigued her despite his machinations. She smelled an interesting story in this man's life, spicier than yesterday's leftover special, and she doubted it would have anything to do with his grandmother. "Would you mind translating the menu for me? My years of Spanish classes aren't serving me in the bayou."

He leisurely wrapped an arm across the back of her chair. "Cora," he repeated. "Your name suits you and I like the idea we're back on a first name basis." He enunciated each word slowly and deliberately in a way that had her wondering what else he'd be slow and deliberate with. She blushed at her wandering fantasies and stared at the chalkboard as though it would suddenly make sense.

"May I order for you instead of translating?" His gaze flickered for a moment from her eyes down the front of her sundress.

"Please do." Somehow he made her feel like a shy schoolgirl on her first date and out of her league. Or in over her head.

"Why don't you order for all of us, Mr. Auxier? Request a variety of house specialties that we can share," April said to the dismay of her mother.

"That's a great idea," piped Brian, then resumed cuddling with his wife.

"It would be my pleasure," Ethan answered. He spoke fast and furious French to Antoine who nodded but wrote nothing down. Antoine disappeared through the swinging doors as though on a mission. Pitchers of cold beer and iced tea materialized, followed by a huge bowl of steamed shrimp, another of crayfish, baskets of crusty bread and a tureen of sauce.

"Dig in, folks," said Max. He scraped a pile of shrimp onto his plate, then ladled on the pungent sauce. No one had to be asked twice. The bowl was passed and emptied quickly. Even Mrs. Rothman ate without complaint as she peeled off the shells and pulled out the shrimp. Cora watched her lick hot sauce from her fingertips, then take huge gulps of beer.

The main course soon arrived on blue spatterware plates. Cold, grilled chicken breasts rested atop beds of wild rice with chickpeas, onions and green peppers. She watched Ethan dress his with a drizzle of Rose's lime juice and did the same. Everything tasted delicious. Antoine hovered around their table solicitously. He spoke only French and only to Ethan who relayed any requests from the others.

Cora was finishing her second mug of beer when it hit

her: an odd, disjointed, spacey feeling. She put her fork down carefully on the side of her plate, then took a long drink of water. The water hit her stomach with a somersault. She stared at the glass suspiciously as her lunch churned in her gut.

Damn. I should have asked for bottled water. Who knows what their water source is out here in the boondocks, she thought miserably.

"Are you all right, Cora?" A strong hand gripped her forearm, drawing her attention back to her luncheon partner. Ethan pushed away his half-eaten plate and stared at her with concern on his aristocratic features.

"I don't know actually." As she looked at him, his face blurred out of focus. Her throat tightened and parched. She took another sip of beer. The chatter of the other diners vacillated between loud and soft in her ears. Cora, for the first time, felt scared. "I don't feel very well. Must not have been a good idea to try crawdads for the first time," she quipped. Her voice sounded foreign to her ears. The room swayed as she struggled to her feet.

Ethan immediately wrapped an arm around her waist and headed her toward the ladies room. Cora feared her spongy, rubbery legs would buckle. She concentrated on putting one foot in front of the other and transferring her weight with each step.

If this is food poisoning, I can think of a hundred better ways to die.

"Mrs. Guierre, Ms. Dearing is not feeling well. Can you help us, please?" Ethan called over his shoulder.

Immediately, Cora felt another arm slip around her waist.

"It's just the heat, Cora," Susan said in her ear. "You're probably just dehydrated. I know the beer started to go right to my head until Brian moved it out of reach."

Cora was only vaguely aware that she and Susan had entered the stuffy bathroom. She locked herself in a stall.

"I'm going to wait right out here, Cora. You let it all come up if you've a mind to. Sometimes that's best in the long run. I'll fetch you some water. I won't be gone a minute."

Cora listened to the door shut behind Susan and relaxed a bit. No one wanted to vomit with a listening audience. She sat on the toilet for several minutes but felt no inclination to purge, only overwhelming, staggering fatigue. When Susan returned sometime later with a glass of water, she had left the stall and washed her hands and face. But she still couldn't stand up without leaning against a stationary object.

"If I can lie down for just a few minutes, it'll pass. I don't think I'm going to be sick after all." Cora spoke with extreme deliberation. She concentrated on forming each word with her tongue and lips like a stroke victim relearning to talk.

"I'll go find the owner and tell him." Susan looked both scared and relieved that she could turn the responsibility over to someone else. Even the dim light of the restroom hurt Cora's eyes. She couldn't gauge how long Susan was gone this time and was only dimly aware when the glass of water slipped from her hands and shattered on the tile floor.

She heard voices: Susan's, Ethan's and Antoine's, but all were an indecipherable jumble. She couldn't open her lips without great difficulty, and it hardly seemed worth the effort. Everything swam before her eyes, unfocused and distorted. She felt a cool breeze on her sweated skin. Ethan loomed briefly before her constricted eyes as strong hands lowered her down to something soft, something pleasantly unmoving.

"You can rest here for awhile, Cora. You'll feel better soon." The familiar voice drifted down from somewhere above, but she couldn't open her eyelids. They were glued shut. She would never see again. All sounds receded as she tottered on the edge of a precipice.

Then finally, blissfully, utter nothingness.

CORA OPENED HER eyes with great effort as a sharp pain spiked somewhere behind them. The room swam around her. She swallowed hard, trying to moisten her lips with a tongue that felt twice its size. She struggled to form words with thickened lips. "Where is everyone?" There was no reply.

She was incredibly thirsty, while her throat felt scraped raw. Every movement brought shattering pain in her head. Her perceptions of the room waxed and waned like a swinging light bulb. She closed her eyes again to see flashes shoot like a meteor shower. She forced herself to focus on her surroundings. She was on a metal bed in a small room that held mostly stacked cases of beer and had no idea where she was. Struggling to her feet, she walked to the sole window to look out between the scraggly branches of a cypress tree. Nothing—only endless bayou. Memories of a boat ride, of an alligator sunning on the bank, and of lunch at a fishing camp flooded back.

At least I don't have amnesia, she thought gratefully. She spied her purse at the foot of the bed. Wonder if they took out for my share of the tab?

Cora rubbed her hands across her face to banish the last of the cobwebs, then headed for the door. She'd had enough of the swamp for one day and longed to be back in her room at Water Lilies, or better yet, in her new cottage in the Quarter. So much for the story on romantic retreats in the bayou. *Le P'tit* Fisherman was officially off her list of getaway destinations.

"Hello?" she called, venturing down the hallway from her room. All heads pivoted as the rustic bar opened before her. Faces turned to gawk, but not one of them looked familiar. None of these customers had even seen civilization in a while, let alone the quiet elegance of the Roussard B&B. A small lump of panic rose in her throat, then Antoine appeared from the back carrying a huge platter of steaming crayfish which he delivered to a burly man at the bar.

"Ah, Mad'm Dearing. You are awake. I am pleased."

Cora was rather pleased to see him, too, especially since he spoke English after all. "Antoine, where is everybody? Are they outside in the boat already? I hope I haven't kept everyone waiting too long." She dug in her purse for her wallet. She didn't want to pay for food that nearly killed her, but she didn't want to offend anybody either. When she glanced up, Antoine was staring at her.

"The others returned to your lodgings yesterday, ma'am."

Cora stopped rummaging. "What? What are you talking about?" She looked around the room at the shrimpers who quaffed beer and watched her curiously. "What day is this?"

"It's Sunday, of course. You slept through the remainder of Saturday." The man spoke like this was an everyday occurrence while he washed glasses in the bar sink.

"What the hell happened to me?" she demanded, approaching the sink.

He shrugged, barely glancing up from his domestic duty. "It must have been something you ate. Something did not agree with you, I imagine. None of the other guests became ill, and you all ate the same thing." He looked past her to the men at the tables to assess their needs, before returning his attention. "Only you."

This was too much. "I ate something in your establishment that made me so sick I was unconscious, for what…twenty-four hours? And you act like this is just business as usual?"

"Please keep your voice down, Mad'm Dearing. Business is not what it should be after the Big Nasty. The shrimping industry is in a slump."

Cora stared at him. "I could have died, Antoine."

"Oh, no. Not at all. You were in no danger. I assure you. *M'sieu* Auxier called the local doctor to look at you and check your—what do they call them—vitals—and he assured me you were in no danger. A non-threatening allergic reaction, I believe was the diagnosis." His dish-washing finished, Antoine wiped his hands on his apron before pulling it over his head. "Your friend, *M'sieu* Auxier was very concerned about you. He paid the physician to stay most of the night here."

"He is not my friend. I barely know the man." The whole thing was too much. Cora strode out of the dimly lit bar onto the porch. The intensity of the afternoon sun sent shards of pain ricocheting through her head. She had no choice but to stand still for several minutes, allowing her eyes to adjust to the bright light. Antoine appeared at her side and opened his hand to reveal two white tablets in his palm.

"What the heck are those?" she snapped and knocked them to the ground.

Antoine merely shrugged. "They were just aspirin. You looked like you might have a headache." He shook his head in dismissal, then walked halfway down the pier. "Are you ready, Mad'm Dearing? I'll take you back to Water Lilies in my airboat. My son will tend to the customers."

"No, I don't think so." She backed up from the bartender so fast she almost stepped off the dock. Cora looked frantically for alternatives as she circuited around the fishing camp and restaurant. The man who might have poisoned her, then held her prisoner overnight, was now inviting her for a ride in the swamp.

But in the end, she accepted Antoine's offer of a lift, since no road connected to *Le P'tit* Fisherman to the rest of the world. Hard to imagine beer deliveries by boat, but only waterways led to the ramshackle outpost. The fishing boats she saw tied to the dock while their owners ate lunch barely looked like they'd stay afloat.

Cora kept close to the edge of the seat during the airboat ride from the camp. She decided to take her chances with the alligators if he tried anything, but the Cajun merely pointed out more swamp highlights he thought Max might've overlooked. Cora felt so weak from whatever sickened her, she couldn't offer much resistance even if Antoine did have evil ideas.

They cut down one waterway and headed up another until Cora thought she'd never see civilization again. Finally, the sight of Water Lilies, sitting like a jewel above the expansive lawn, made her giddy with relief. She hadn't noticed the second smaller dock, nearly hidden by vines and Spanish moss, during her initial inspection of the property. Antoine pulled through the hanging foliage with expert assurance. Cora once again extracted her wallet. "What do I owe you, Antoine?" He looked momentarily confused. "For the ride and everything else." Like your lovely backroom accommodations. She couldn't wait to get out of the boat and away from him.

"Oh, nothing. Your friend, *M'sieu* Auxier, arranged the ride back and paid me in advance."

"He is not..." Cora thought better of arguing with him

and struggled onto the dock. The sun beating down during the ride did nothing but intensify her headache. Her legs still felt like lead as she labored up the steep incline toward the house.

She didn't notice the commotion until she reached the flat expanse of lawn and stopped watching her feet. Blue lights, spinning incongruously in the parking lot, caught her attention. They flashed from two police cruisers while a small crowd milled on the porch. As though her stare held magical powers, the lights stopped rotating while she watched, and a portly officer stepped out of one vehicle.

Cora turned back to Antoine, but he and the airboat had already pushed off and disappeared down the waterway. Only a ripple in the black water marked their passage. A second skinny cop leaving an SUV spotted her and stopped in his tracks. Cora returned the man's stare with little else to do. *Was this all for me? Where were you all yesterday when I needed rescuing?* She glanced down automatically at her appearance as the man approached. Her sundress was stained and wrinkled, looking every bit like she'd slept in it as she had.

"Who are you?" the young deputy asked without preamble.

"I'm Cora Dearing," she answered, trying to comb her fingers through her tangled hair.

"That so. You were with the group of them yesterday?" He finally pulled his gaze from where it had landed on her chest long enough to light an unfiltered cigarette. His mother obviously had never taught him the good manners of maintaining eye contact.

"Yes, I was with the other guests from Water Lilies on the swamp tour."

If you two good-old-boys were out hunting for me,

why are you asking me that? And why did no one mention my name to the authorities? All this thinking made her head hurt worse. She staggered for a minute, then lowered herself slowly to the ground. "You'll have to forgive me. I'm not feeling well," she drawled in a voice reserved for pantomimes of her upbringing in Columbia, South Carolina.

"Where the hell is Mrs. Rothman?"

Cora's head snapped up. "Who?" she asked stupidly.

The deputy took a long pull on the cigarette before flipping back the cover of his notebook to read something scribbled. "Mrs. Ada Rothman. I thought you said you were staying here. So why don't you know who I'm talking about?" He glared down at her.

"I know who Mrs. Rothman is but don't have the slightest idea where she is. I thought you'd been looking for me." She rose slowly to her feet, not enjoying him glaring down his nose at her.

He glanced at his notes again. "Says here you were too drunk to take the boat back from Antoine's, and that you slept it off in his backroom." He flicked the cigarette down in the oyster shell gravel. "Now, what do you know about Mrs. Rothman turning up missing?"

Cora put two fingers on each temple to stem the pain, then stepped past the man. "I don't know anything about it. I didn't know she was missing." She had to get out of this sun and lie down or she was going to be sick. "And just for the record," she pointed at his pad, "I wasn't drunk at Antoine's. I had food poisoning. I strongly urge you to avoid the raw shrimp when you're there."

"The sheriff hasn't released none of you yet. He'll have some more questions," he called after her.

She stopped and looked back. "I can't leave?"

"That's right." He dragged out the last word as though

it contained two syllables. "Y'all staying right here until the sheriff says it's okay to go." He rested his hand on the butt of his gun as though he'd shoot if she headed toward her rental car.

Despite the fact her mouth felt like she'd eaten dirt, her stomach churned like a blender crushing ice, and her head felt like it would explode, Cora broke out laughing.

Well, you wanted a big, fat, juicy story to investigate— your ticket into the Reporter Big Leagues. Now if she could just keep from throwing up the nothingness in her stomach, this might just be her chance of a lifetime.

"Don't shoot, Deputy," she said. "I'm only heading to my room."

She crossed the side lawn and climbed the steps. She didn't want to talk to anybody, just get to her room, crank up the AC and collapse. As she pulled open the screen door, movement caught her eye from the left. There under the shade of the live oak stood Ethan Auxier, cool as an ice cube in a T-shirt and pale linen pants. He stood talking to a man who had to be the sheriff. Ethan removed his sunglasses when their gazes met and nodded his head in greeting. The sheriff stopped whatever he was saying and looked, too.

Even at this distance, Ethan's eyes sent a wintry shiver up her spine and stopped the beads of sweat in their tracks. So much for the romantic fantasy concocted for her sister, then fanned into possibility by a lonely imagination. As attractive as this man was, he could be far more dangerous than James Dearing ever was.

Something wasn't right here, but she was in no shape to figure out what.

DOZENS OF MOSQUITOES buzzed and hummed, yet none lit on his skin. Ethan Galen stood on the small dock staring down into the water. The dense matting of lilies that gave the B&B its name lay just beneath the surface. Beautiful flowers, water lilies, but they proved to be the scourge of Louisiana fresh waterways. Since their introduction in the bayou, they'd spread everywhere, choking out the indigenous plants and threatening the vital fishing industry. Men had actually died falling from boats into the swamp and becoming trapped by the entanglement of lilies.

Beautiful, but deadly—lilies had to be female, he thought.

The sound of his cell phone jarred his attention. "Yes?"

"I got your message. Don't tell me it's over."

"I'm afraid so. Now, who'd ever think it would happen in the bayou? There's just so many better places with easier logistics."

"Someone might have recognized you. Someone might have thought time was getting short."

"I don't think so. Neither woman paid me much attention. Other than the usual contempt for someone Southern by someone thought to be more…cosmopolitan."

There was a snort of disgust from the other end. "They sure had airs about them."

"Mommy dearest was the biggest pain-in-the-ass I've ever met, even including my former mother-in-law."

"That bad, huh? Perhaps, it was a blessing in disguise that that part is over, no?"

"Time will tell."

"When are you coming back to New Orleans?"

"Soon, I hope. Dear, sweet April is kicking up a mighty fuss to the local authorities. That woman must be a clone of her mother, without the benefits of daddy's genetics, whatsoever. The Sheriff has ordered us to partake of Marie and Emil's hospitality a bit longer."

"What do they know?"

"Nothing."

"And the other little distraction that you mentioned—the magazine writer on assignment?"

"It was handled. I don't think she'll present any trouble once I get back to the city."

Ethan let his mind wander for a pleasant moment to the way Cora's cotton dress floated over her hips and breasts when she returned from Antoine's today. Even drugged and bedraggled, she looked beautiful, with her mane of wild hair running down her back and her posture erect despite everything she'd been through.

"She won't present any trouble," he repeated into the phone.

He had to make sure that remained true. He couldn't let her get in the way. It had been a mistake orchestrating her to be here this weekend, but she was here now.

There was something appealing, some odd innocence worth protecting in the woman from Columbia with shrimp sauce on her chin and sheer abandon in her eyes. And Ethan knew she could easily become more than a little trouble in his life.

FOUR

"Ms. Dearing?"

Cora had just latched the gate behind her and stood contemplating the route to take to the restaurant. She hadn't taken a single step yet, and already perspiration beaded on her forehead. This was the drawback of living in the quiet end of the Quarter—a long hike to get anywhere you wanted to go.

She turned toward the voice and allowed her face to register the shock of finding a limousine standing by the curb with a liveried driver leaning against it.

"Ms. Dearing?" he repeated. "Mr. Auxier sent his car for you." The man straightened up and peered at her.

"I made it quite clear to Mr. Auxier on the phone that I would meet him in a public place to talk. I am not crawling into the backseat of that thing with a stranger." She tried to peer through the tinted glass.

"I understand completely, Miss, but Mr. Auxier's not in there." He pulled open the door with a flourish. "He's waiting for you on the outdoor terrace of Three Sisters. You'll be perfectly safe. They get quite a crowd." Cora caught the smirk that he quickly banished in the blink of an eye.

She looked into the empty limo then studied the chauffeur. He obliged her by removing his mirrored sunglasses and offered a charming smile.

The drop of sweat that dripped off her nose helped

make up her mind. "All right, but don't lock me in and don't go over twenty."

"As you wish, Miss."

At least he didn't call her madam, as many did. She couldn't get past feeling like she was a proprietress of a brothel with that title. The ride across Decatur in heavy traffic proved long enough to work up her courage. She wasn't sure why she'd accepted a dinner invitation from Ethan two days after returning from the bayou, but something told her he knew a lot more than she about what happened. There was a story here, and she was going to get it. This was exactly the break she needed. So far her paper reported that a wealthy New York socialite had disappeared during an alligator watching expedition, and that the N.O.P.D. and the Lafourche Parish Sheriff's Dept. were investigating foul play. No kidding. You go into a bar in the bayou for lunch and nobody sees you again?

Jim Matthews insisted she furnish the reporter assigned to the story with everything she knew. He got the byline, and all she got was "Thanks, Cora. I owe you one." Andy Bowen was not going to crack this case; she was. She just didn't have the slightest idea how yet, but this mysterious rich man knew something. She could feel it in her bones.

The day at the B&B following Ada Rothman's disappearance had been interminable. She had crawled into bed as soon as she returned with Antoine and slept until the late afternoon. Then the sheriff had questioned her while she sipped tea and nibbled toast, courtesy of her hostess. Mrs. Roussard was distraught that something bad had happened to one of her guests. *Adds a bit of color to the old brochure*, Cora thought, finally returning from her mind fog. The sheriff had made her repeat the story as though she'd break down and confess at any minute.

He couldn't grasp the notion she'd passed out and slept through all the excitement. She couldn't grasp that notion either. Try as she might, she didn't remember anything after Susan Guierre helped her to the bathroom. She had no idea how she ended up in the backroom or anything else until she awoke at noon the next day.

The Guierres insisted they had checked on her before leaving in Max's boat to return to Water Lilies. Apparently Mrs. Rothman disappeared soon after Cora nearly upchucked her lunch. According to Susan, everyone had been concerned about Cora, and no one paid much attention when April Rothman started whining about not being able to locate her mother.

"I thought it was a blessing," Brian had said. "I didn't know she really was missing. Where could she go? There're no roads to that place, only waterways. She didn't swim back to Manhattan."

Apparently, some time had passed before people took April seriously, then everyone, including the other bar patrons, searched the grounds for Ada. Several fishermen even took their boats into the surrounding area to look. The consensus was that the out-of-towner had gone off exploring and gotten lost.

Sounds awfully buggy to me. Mrs. Rothman's words drifted across Cora's mind as she tried to make heads-or-tails of the story. There was no way that lady would have wandered into a swamp and jeopardized her Ferragamos, but Cora kept her opinions to herself. She would get a whole lot more info if everyone thought she was a feature writer, not a would-be reporter. Too much was at stake to tip her hand.

The limo pulled up in front of the restaurant and a doorman opened her door. "Safe and sound, Ms. Dearing. Enjoy your dinner," the chauffeur said with a grin.

Cheeky little devil, she thought, but quickly forgot him in lieu of the ambience of Three Sisters. It was an enchanting fairyland of dichotomies. Elegant and formal, but comfortable wrought-iron tables and chairs lent casualness; hot and sultry, but air-conditioned breezes wafted from the interior; dark and mysterious, but at least a thousand little white lights twinkled from every branch and potted plant. She had heard rave reviews on the food, but her salary never allowed the experience. When she mentioned the Auxier name to the maitre d', she was whisked to a table next to a waterfall, ahead of a long line of wilted tourists.

"Cora," Ethan murmured and stood when she approached the table. She immediately felt underdressed. He wore an impeccably tailored dark suit, white shirt and conservative tie, yet managed to look cool. She wore a gauze sundress and high-heeled sandals with bare legs, but still felt sticky. "I'm so glad you agreed to join me for dinner." His smile was warm and engaging, and that French accent tipped the scale in his direction.

"Hello, Ethan. Nice of you to invite me. I always wanted to try this place, but I've been so busy." She straightened her back against the chair, willing herself to relax.

"I hope the evening lives up to your expectations." He made a small hand gesture, then the wine steward materialized to open the champagne.

"You drink it like water?" Cora teased, motioning toward the bottle after the steward left.

"Oh, no. Just on special occasions."

Again butterflies raged a battle in her stomach. She didn't dare ask what the occasion was.

"How are you feeling since your ordeal?" he asked, pouring champagne into her glass.

She took a sip before answering. "Fine, now. Just not anxious to recommend *Le P'tit* Fisherman to my few friends in town. Have you heard anything more about Mrs. Rothman? I still can't believe she disappeared like that."

Ethan shrugged his shoulders, drawing her attention to their breadth. Amazing what good tailoring can do. "Strange things happen in the bayou. They always have." He opened one menu and handed it to her. "I'll let you do your own ordering tonight, since my recommendations turned disastrous the last time." His lips formed a smile that didn't quite reach his eyes. "I am truly sorry that had to happen to you."

Cora looked over the extensive menu as she considered his choice of words. "Had to happen to me?" She locked eyes with his icy blues.

"In terms of fate." His returning stare didn't waver.

"I'll have the crab-stuffed flounder." She set her menu down and took another sip of the tiny, smooth bubbles. "You're a firm believer in fate, Ethan? You strike me more as the scientific type."

"Hardly. I believe we set our own course and operate with a certain amount of free will. Yet there are things beyond our control that could change life on a dime."

Cora finished the champagne in her glass. She couldn't help but believe his innuendoes and insinuations were directed at her. Maybe the fact his eyes kept roaming over her while he talked had something to do with it. At any rate, she felt skittish and wary. "Let's get back to the weekend-from-hell. Shall we? Just where were you when I passed out in Antoine's charming back room?"

He leaned across the table so that she could feel his warm breath on her cheek and smell his citrus aftershave. For a wild moment she thought he might kiss her, then felt a pang of disappointment when he didn't. "Keeping a vigil at your side. Making sure no nasty mosquito landed on your fair skin."

Cora felt her color heighten. She reached for a roll. "You didn't look for Mrs. Rothman?"

"No." He helped himself to a piece of bread and slathered it with butter.

"Why not?" She waved her butter knife in a small circle.

He tore the bread in half and ate a piece with relish. "There were enough people running around the swamp looking for that obnoxious woman. I chose to stand as sentinel by your bedside." He popped another piece of bread into his mouth, studying her from under his thick eyelashes.

The thought that this man, no matter how attractive, had been watching her sleep while everyone else scurried on a wild goose chase made Cora uncomfortable. Yet, she didn't possess half the guts to say so. She dabbed at the breadcrumbs on her lips. "Ethan, let me ask you something." Now it was her turn to lean over the small table conspiratorially. "And rest assured, it won't go any farther than right here. Do you know where Mrs. Rothman is?"

His reply was not the penitent confession and crack-of-the-story she hoped for. He threw his head back and laughed. "No, Cora, I don't. But I also don't care where she is." Two waiters materialized from the palm fronds to set steaming plates before them simultaneously. "Thank you. It looks wonderful, as always." The waiters bowed graciously and left. Ethan slipped off his suit coat and rolled up his sleeves. His arms were strong and tanned, not what she had expected.

Cora narrowed her eyes at him. "A woman vanishes into thin air, and you aren't concerned?"

"There were a dozen people combing the swamp for sweet Ada Rothman. I was concerned about you." His voice softened to just above a whisper. "You were very sick—food poisoning, allergic reaction, who knows? I felt you needed my help more than the search party." His gentle words were spoken matter-of-factly while he dug into his crab legs with gusto.

Cora popped a small spear of asparagus into her mouth. "Do you think she's dead?"

"Maybe." He cracked another claw.

"That doesn't bother you?"

"Not too much."

"Just because she wasn't the world's nicest person, she deserves to die?"

Ethan set down his fork and crab cracker and gazed patiently at her. He poured them both more champagne. "I don't know if she deserved to die, or not. Probably not. But since she wasn't the world's nicest person, I'm not too bothered." The small dimple in his cheek ticked slightly. "How's your fish? If it's not to your liking, *cher*, they'll fix you something else in the blink of an eye."

His slow, melodic accent entranced her. This was a man who could charm an old lady out of her false teeth. She took her first bite of the flounder.

"It's fine. Very good, in fact." Cora had been starving when she'd arrived; now she could barely eat the delicious fish. "I just can't believe a woman like her would wander off into the swamp on her own. She didn't strike me as the nature-lover type."

"I agree. So does Detective Rhodes, for that matter." Ethan finished his last claw.

"Who's Detective Rhodes?" Cora asked, taking another sip. She could already feel the effects of the wine.

She forced herself to eat more of her dinner not wanting to get drunk.

"He hasn't questioned you yet?"

Cora nodded to the negative.

"He's a New Orleans detective that's helping out the Lafourche boys because charming Ada was rich and her daughter is kicking up a fuss in the papers. She's screaming that a proper investigation is not being run. You know how they are."

"No, I really don't. How are they?"

"I mean the newspapers; they'll print anything. They'll distort any story, cast around nasty aspersions, just to sell copies. The paper heard she disappeared from a place where they had a sheriff instead of a police department and had a field day with April's ranting. As though hailing from the country made one incompetent." He swiped his mouth with the napkin then threw it down on the table. The linen and his plate were quickly whisked away.

Cora kept any comments regarding newspapers to herself. No use alienating her only source of information, but the fact that she was trying to scoop the story unsettled her. "What is April saying?" Cora asked quietly. "You can't blame her for being upset. Her mom is missing. Even nasty women are usually loved by their daughters."

"Dear, gentle Cora. You are a tribute to loving daughters everywhere." He covered her hand with his much larger one. The effect was electric, almost paralyzing. His touch felt strong and tender at the same time. Crazily she wondered what that hand would feel like running down the rest of her body. "I'll bet you love your mother, *ma petite*."

"I do. She still lives in Columbia and teaches third grade. I don't get to see her much and I miss her." She pushed her plate away. "How about you and your mom?"

Cora gratefully allowed the subject to be changed away from *The Times*.

He studied her for a moment before answering. "I adore her. She is the quintessential Southern lady, right down to her lace gloved hands, but she never was afraid to show emotion to her children." Another hand gesture and the empty ice bucket and flutes disappeared. Two snifters and a crystal bottle of cognac appeared from the wings.

"How does that happen?" Cora asked, nodding at the new libation. "I've never had servers wait on me so efficiently, let alone read my mind."

"I'm just a regular, Cora, and a creature of habit. They've learned my tastes, that's all." His eyes darkened to a rich sapphire.

Again the flutter in her gut told her they may not be talking about the same thing. His flirting was subtle, almost ambivalent, yet hit the mark every time.

"You said 'children.' You have brothers and sisters?" she asked, anxious to get back on comfortable ground.

"Yes, I have a brother, Hunter, and a younger sister named Chloe. You remind me of Chloe in many ways." This time his smile reached his eyes.

"Should I take that as a compliment, Ethan?" Cora sipped the tiniest amount of cognac and prayed this wouldn't be a repeat performance of the day at Antoine's.

"You may indeed. She is beautiful, charming, bright, and I thought the most engaging woman in Louisiana, until recently. She wrapped me around her finger a long time ago."

Cora relaxed somewhat. A man who adored his younger sister couldn't possibly be a mad killer, could he? "And your brother? What about him?"

"He, I'm afraid, is a younger version of myself. He

has too much money and too little ambition for his own good. We get along perfectly, of course." He shook back a lock of black hair that had fallen into his eyes.

"I guess we all have crosses to bear." This was all very interesting and made her a lonesome for her own sister, but it wasn't helping to get the story. And that's why she agreed to have dinner with him, wasn't it? "What did this Detective Rhodes think about what happened? I haven't read the papers," she lied.

"Typical of a detective, he didn't give up his thoughts, merely pried mine out of me." He lit a cigarette, took two drags, and snubbed it out. "April Rothman insists her father is behind some plot to kill dear Mommy."

"For what motive?"

"For the alimony he has to pay out every month. April says Daddy has a new girlfriend that prefers the cash to be squandered on her." The shiny lock of hair fell back in his face. This time when he raked it back, he stared at Cora intensely. "Some men would do anything for a woman they're infatuated with."

"I wouldn't know about that." Cora struggled to her feet. She certainly should have eaten more of the expensive entree. "Thank you for dinner. It was great." She pushed back her chair with a clatter, drawing a waiter from the shadows to assist.

Ethan grasped her arm lightly; his touch burned into her flesh where their skin met. It'd been a long time since a man touched her, let alone made her feel so vulnerable.

"It's early, Cora. You haven't finished your cognac. What about dessert? I thought we could walk the river-front later." He rose to his feet in a fluster, his napkin falling to the floor.

"Not tonight, I'm afraid," she said, reaching for her bag. She swallowed hard and steeled her resolve. If he pressed her, she may just agree to walk with him any-where.

Ethan bent down to scrawl his signature across the bill that appeared from nowhere. No credit card. He just signed his name. *Why didn't that work for me?* she won-dered.

"At least, let me drive you home. I'll run alongside the car if you still don't trust me," he added with a laugh.

Cora walked toward the entranceway with Ethan prac-tically on her heels. She felt like Cinderella—and had to get out of there before she changed into a pumpkin. "No, please." She pivoted and placed both palms on his chest, stopping him abruptly on the sidewalk. "Not tonight. I need to go home. Goodnight." He opened his mouth to protest, but she quickly retreated into the crowd on Bour-bon Street and was lost in the tide of people moving in one direction or the other.

She didn't look back. If she had, she would have seen the consummate expression of frustration skewer his fea-tures.

ETHAN WATCHED HER GO, helpless to stop her. Helpless in stemming his disappointment, too. Nate Price stepped from the shadows. "How ya' doin', boss?" he drawled. The livery jacket and jaunty cap were nowhere to be seen. His shirt was open, wrinkled, and spotted with what Ethan suspected was spilled hurricane.

"I'm fine. I see you're a mess and already drinking on the job," Ethan said without rancor and lit another cigarette.

"Hey, I thought you quit," he said.

"I did. This means nothing." He took a second drag before crushing it out.

"Anyway, I shared a hurricane with a lovely belle from

Mobile. We got a little frisky in the backseat of the Town Car, if you know what I mean."

Ethan looked at his friend with a wry grin. "You're using my car for your love nest? I will never give you a job recommendation if this keeps up."

"You only get what you pay for, man. And I'm off-duty. I knew Ms. Dearing wouldn't be riding home with you." Nate threw his arm around Ethan's shoulder. "Let's go in O'Malley's and have a nightcap. Maybe Miss Mobile has a friend."

"What made you so sure?" Ethan shrugged off Nate's arm.

"Oh, maybe the fact she's afraid of you had something to do with it. Or maybe the fact you're not her type." Ethan's murderous glare obviously made Nate rethink his words. "I mean, she's not your type, man."

"What exactly is my type?" Ethan's lips stretched into a thin line.

"You know what I mean. Hell, she probably teaches Sunday school back home and doesn't take the free shampoo from a hotel room."

"And I am, what? The Grim Reaper?"

"You're taking this too seriously. I'm just ramblin'. Let's go get that drink. You gettin' hung up on the chick, or somethin'?"

Ethan didn't answer. He gave Nate a final glower, then stuffed the cigarette into an empty soda can next to the trash barrel. Since Katrina, it was impossible to find a trash receptacle not overflowing in town.

"Suppose you won't be needin' the car anymore tonight?" Nate called as Ethan filtered into the crushing crowd.

Ethan shook his head but didn't turn around. He needed to walk and think. He didn't like the comparison made by his friend, even though he suspected most of it was true. If Cora could see how he had spent his time and money, up until three years ago, she'd be aghast. He'd spent more on drinks for people, most of them strangers, than her schoolteacher mother earned in five years. Such a waste—he knew that now. The job of living down the reputation of New Orleans' most notorious playboy was not easy.

He shouldn't be thinking about Cora Dearing. Despite his money, all he had to offer her was a share in the shame that his family endured. Not exactly an attractive proposition. Plus he'd gotten involved with something and had to see it through. At best, Cora would only be in the way, and at worst, she'd be in danger. He had no right to pursue anybody until this business was finished and the money restored to the Galens. He had to do something right for the family. His idea to seduce Cora at Water Lilies had been borne of loneliness and the need to connect with someone pure. It had been a selfish mistake. He'd put her in jeopardy there. He wouldn't allow anything to happen to her, but Ethan knew some things, many things, were beyond his control, no matter how much money he had, or however noble his intentions. He was smack in the middle of a mess that was no place for her.

"Damn it," he muttered. "Damn you, Cora. Why did you have to waltz into my life now?"

"Ms. Dearing? You in there, Ms. Dearing?" A middle-aged, balding man in a linen suit peered through her screen door from the back patio.

Her heart stopped for a moment at the intrusion, but her uncanny intuition told her immediately who he was. "Detective Rhodes, I presume?" she said, unhooking the screen and stepping into the garden.

"Yes, ma'am. You were expecting me?" His brown eyes crinkled into a smile as he dug in a pocket and extracted a pair of glasses.

"A little bird told me you might pay a call. Most people knock at the front door, Detective." She placed her hands on her hips and waited.

"Yes, excuse me. I did knock, but when no one immediately answered…well, I've always been curious about peoples' gardens. You see, I'm a gardener myself. I just love to see what folks got planted." He went through the motion of perusing the flora of the small backyard.

"A-ha," she said, sitting down on one chaise and gesturing at the other. "Well, considering I'm a renter and just moved in, I take no credit for anything that impresses you. What can I do for you, Detective?"

"Just a few questions, ma'am, and I'll be on my way." He pulled the ubiquitous notebook from his pocket.

"Did you know Mrs. Rothman or her daughter before last weekend?"

"No."

"Did you know Mr. Ethan Auxier before the weekend?" This time he looked up from his notebook to meet her eye.

"No." It felt like a tiny lie, but it really wasn't. She hadn't known him. He'd only bought her a bottle of Dom Pérignon and, she suspected, followed her through a cemetery. That's all.

"So you met Mr. Auxier at Water Lilies for the first time. Is that right?"

"Yes, Detective." She shifted in her chair.

"Did you…get to know him pretty well at that B and B, ma'am?" The question made them both blush slightly.

"No, sir. Mr. Auxier is pretty much a stranger to me." She was growing perturbed with his line of questions.

"Why would a stranger pay your bill at Maison Provance on Chartres?"

"He did not pay my bill at Maison Pro—" She broke off abruptly feeling foolish. Obviously the detective wouldn't say so if it wasn't true. Small details of her move flooded back, like the manager insisting they'd send the final bill instead of allowing her to put it on a credit card. Since when did hostels allow you to do that? "Suffice it to say, I did not know he'd paid my bill until now," Cora lowered her voice, "and I have no idea why he'd do such a thing, but I intend to ask him if I see him again."

"He didn't mention it when you two had dinner last night, ma'am?"

She felt a jolt of fear? Guilt? Shame? She couldn't name it, but didn't like it one bit. It reminded her of the time her mother asked how a dance had been, and she guiltily confessed to kissing a boy in the hallway.

"No, he didn't." She kept her voice low and controlled. "Have you been following me, Detective Rhodes?"

"No, ma'am. Getting back to Mrs. Rothman, how did Mr. Auxier act toward her and her daughter at Water Lilies?"

Cora blinked her eyes and thought for a moment. "I don't think he cared for the mother and didn't notice the daughter much at all."

"Why would you say that?" He jotted something down in his notebook.

"I don't know." Her voice rose in agitation. "You asked for my opinion and I gave it. Mrs. Rothman has a natural capacity to alienate people and I think she rubbed Ethan the wrong way."

"Ethan?"

"Yes, that's his first name. I'm sure it's in your notes."

Cora stood abruptly. A metal ashtray from the arm of the chaise clattered to the flagstones.

The detective fastened his eyes on the ashtray before replying. "Yes, ma'am. It is." He flipped a couple pages back in the pad. "And you had a reaction of some sort at the fish restaurant? Are you allergic to certain seafood, Ms. Dearing?"

"Not to my knowledge. I think it was food poisoning." A breeze finally wound its way into the back garden, cooling her overheated skin. When would she get used to the steamy humidity of New Orleans?

"Food poisoning, ma'am? Didn't all the members of Max's tour eat pretty much the same thing? Why would it…cause such a ruckus, shall we say for you, and not for the others?" He smiled almost paternally at her, and for one absurd moment, he reminded her of her dad.

"I have no idea, Mr. Rhodes." Anger crept into her voice. "Why don't you ask the doctor that supposedly examined me while I was unconscious."

"Yes, ma'am." He flipped maddeningly back another page in the pad. "Dr. Borrell of Lafourche. I intend to." He stood and straightened his suit jacket. Cora rose to her feet, too. "Oh, one more thing. April Rothman said she saw Mr. Auxier talking to Mrs. Rothman down by the dock the night before the swamp tour." He waited for some reaction, but Cora remained motionless. "April said they appeared to be arguing about something. April saw her mother slap Mr. Auxier, then he grabbed her by the arm. Do you know anything about what they may have been arguing about?"

Cora stared at the detective. There was no way Ethan Auxier would manhandle a woman, especially an older woman, no matter how offensive she happened to be.

April must be mistaken. "I know nothing about that. I went to bed shortly after dinner."

He gave her an odd look.

Cora couldn't help herself. She didn't like how this whole thing was starting to sound. "All I know is I cannot believe Mr. Auxier would grab Mrs. Rothman's arm under any circumstances." She crossed her arms indignantly over her chest.

The wide smile returned to Rhode's deeply lined face. "I thought you said the gentleman was a stranger?"

CORA BREATHED A sigh of relief when the detective left. She felt she'd done enough damage for one night but couldn't put her finger on exactly how. Why was the man so interested in Ethan? Of what did he suspect him? Kidnapping? Money would hardly be a motive. You could practically smell the stuff on him from across the room. Murder? With what motive? Because Ada was a haughty rude person that hated old houses and was contemptuous of anything Southern? People didn't kill because of rudeness, or overcrowding would no longer be a problem in the world.

Ethan, with his soft voice and charming manners, wouldn't swat a fly. April Rothman was either mistaken or lying. Cora rubbed her temples. She was getting a headache. Getting to the bottom of this story will be like finding the bottom of the swamp.

Something else nagged at the back of her brain.

Why would the food cause such a ruckus for you…and not the others? Ruckus? As in diversion? Did he think she had gotten sick to distract attention from whatever was happening with Mrs. Rothman? Is that why he kept drawing a connection between her and Ethan before the weekend? *Yeah, Columbo, I plotted this entire crime so*

I'd get the scoop on the story and retrieve my pathetic career from the doldrums. A shiver ran down her spine. How did he manage to find out Ethan had paid her bill at the hostel even before she did? And why did he pay the bill?

Cora heard something move in the bushes and jumped a foot. She peered into the darkness and met the stare of a large, yellow-eyed cat. Then something else caught her attention. The largest vase of bougainvillea she'd ever seen sat on the patio table under the tree. She wouldn't have noticed it until morning if not for the overgrown feline. There must be three dozen cut stems in an antique-looking Chinese vase. She started toward the flowers, then halted midstride. How did they get here? Certainly the detective from N.O.P.D. didn't bring them, no matter how much of a garden fanatic he was. The gorgeous blooms began to take on a sinister appearance.

Cora turned on her heel and ran to her back door with the speed of an athlete. It was time she got behind a locked door before her imagination had her seeing the ghost of Ada Rothman, covered with seaweed and water hyacinths, bringing her another plate of tainted Cajun shrimp.

FIVE

"CORA. CORA, GET IN HERE. And bring that story you've been working on!" Jim Matthews's thundering voice turned most of the heads in the office, except for Cora's. Frantically typing away at the keyboard of her computer and glancing back and forth between the screen and her notes she answered, not looking up, "Be right there, sir."

"Now, Ms. Dearing. I told you I wanted that story today." He slammed his office door.

That was not a good sign. He almost never closed his door, preferring to keep an ear on what was happening in the office. Cora hit the save button, grabbed her notes, and prepared for some employer verbal abuse. "Good morning, Mr. Matthews," she said cheerily, walking into his office. "That is a great tie. Was it a gift?" She clutched her notes to her chest and rocked on her heels.

"Cut the crap, Cora, and sit down." She obediently complied; her smile faded.

"Tell me how the feature story is coming and don't hand me any bull. I need to know if I should run the piece on the possible redevelopment of the levee into a fitness trail." He leaned back in his chair. Coffee dribbles and sugar from his morning beignets dotted his starched white shirt. *He must drive his wife crazy*, she thought.

"Well, I've got three truly romantic restaurants, two haunted inns in the Quarter, and a super walking tour through the Garden District and Lafayette Cemetery pretty well tied down. I can have the whole story finished by five o'clock." She lied through her teeth. If she worked like a fiend right through lunch and wasn't interrupted, she might have a rough copy done by six.

"Lafayette Cemetery?" he wailed. "The story is supposed to be about the ten most romantic spots in the Big Easy. You do understand the concept of romance, don't you, Cora?" He laughed hard enough to jiggle his plentiful belly above his lizard skin belt. "I'm afraid to ask what Bob O'Brien's little girl finds romantic in a bone yard." Then he narrowed his eyes and glared. "You're not one of those gothic types, who go around and…you know, do the nasty business during the dead of night in graveyards, are you?" He looked truly mortified.

Her editor got like this every now and then—treated her like she was a niece to be looked out for, instead of one of his employees. All because her dad had been his best friend for a number of years. Cora cleared her throat. "If the nasty business you refer to is sex, then no, I don't have it in cemeteries. Not that it's any of your business, Mr. Matthews. And regarding the tour, why don't you wait to read the copy, then pass judgment. The stories that came from that tour were steeped in enough intrigue and passionate vignettes to get the juices flowing, so to speak."

"Yeah, well, I still have the final word on what gets published around here, so let me take a look before you think you're done." He swiveled around in his chair and poured two cups of coffee from the carafe, then handed her one. It was the first time for that particular gesture. "What about the trip to the spooky B&B in the bayou? That's what I want to hear about in your story. Bowen tells me you were right there when that lady from New York disappeared into the swamp. That's the kind of stuff

I'm looking for." He leaned back in the chair gulping his coffee.

Cora brightened. "I'd love to work with Andy on the piece. I've got a couple leads I'm following, and working together, we can crack this story before anyone else does." She sipped the coffee to wet her dry mouth.

Jim looked confused for a moment, then perturbed. "No, Cora. Bowen's got the story covered from the disappearance angle. Looks like a paid hit by the old lady's ex-husband to get him off the alimony hook." He laughed like this was somehow amusing.

Cora's scowl stopped his tittering. "Perhaps I should warn your lovely wife of this dark side of your personality, boss."

"Not unless you want to join the soup line at St. Louis Church, you won't. Anyway, I happen to love my wife. Not all women are so lucky as my Peggy."

Cora rolled her eyes.

He glowered in return. "What I need from you, and by five today, is a rundown on that place. Everybody and his sister wants to go there since the disappearance hit the paper. I want to feature this B&B as the central focus of your article since the timing couldn't be better, eh? What would you say if I told you I'm thinking of moving it to the magazine insert, with a shot of Swamp Lilies on the cover?" He waited for the effusive gratitude to start rolling in.

It was quite an honor, she knew. Too bad her conversation with Emil and Marie Roussard before leaving had changed everything. Cora's enthusiasm faded. "I don't think so, boss. And it's called Water Lilies, by the way." She drank her coffee before he retracted the generous gift and pulled the mug from her hand.

"Whatever. What do you mean, you don't think so?" He squinted his eyes under lowered eyebrows.

"I talked to the Roussards, the proprietors, before I left. They wouldn't sign a release for the story or the photos I took. Apparently, they don't need the business and don't want the publicity. They guard their privacy zealously, believe it or not. They've called me since I've been back in the city and reiterated that position, since the news story has caused quite a commotion for them."

"Hogwash," he growled. "What tourist trap doesn't want free advertising? They're just playing hard-to-get, that's all. Have accounting cut them a check for five hundred. That should take care of their tight rein on the photos. They know a body disappearing into the bayou is good for business in this part of the world." He started shuffling the mountain of papers littering his desk.

Cora knew this interview was drawing to a close. "I don't think so. The delightful Roussards are the exception to the greed rule."

Jim looked up, surprised to see Cora still there. "Well, get them to change their mind, Cora. I didn't send you out into the backwater to work on your tan on company time and expenses." His voice rose several decibels.

"I'll try." Cora offered her best smile. The effort was wasted.

"Just do it. Today." Cora started to leave.

"Oh, I almost forgot. Bowen told me one of your fellow guests at Swamp Lilies was one of the Galens, but for some reason, he registered under the name of Auxier." He dug around on his desk. "Ethan Galen. His old man and granddaddy were the movers-and-shakers of the Quarter in their day. Sonny-boy doesn't have a logical reason why he'd be out at some old tourist plantation that weekend. That's definitely not the crowd he runs with." Jim scratched at his chin. "Dig up some dirt on this Galen fellow, since you two are old swamp tour buddies, and give it to Bowen. We want to play the angle of Galen being out there. The Old Guard just laps up any story with that name in it and begs for more. Their lineage is supposed to trace back to Marie Antoinette or something. Nothing like peeling off a layer of that family's patina." He stood and shrugged into his suit coat.

Cora took a moment to regain her composure. "Dig up dirt on his family? What makes you think he had anything to do with the disappearance, anymore than I did?"

"That's funny, Cora. You don't like it when they throw lobsters into the crab-boil at Antonio's. You want to rescue them and let 'em go in the river. You aren't exactly known for your killer instincts." He headed for the door.

"And Ethan… Galen is?" She followed him into the main office. Some illogical compulsion forced her to defend the man while her mind tried to dig up a logical reason for someone to use a fictitious name.

"Look, Cora. I don't know one way or the other. He could be altar boy material, for all I know. But I do know crap on his family sells newspapers, so go get some. And finish that story with a focus on the B&B." He practically roared the final command, turning heads in the office in their direction. The editor took off down the aisle. This discussion was over as far as he was concerned.

Cora walked back to her desk and slumped into her chair. Not one, but two, major problems, and it wasn't even ten o'clock. There's no way she could put the story and photos of Water Lilies in the feature without the Roussards' release. She would have to use another antebellum inn in the area from a local tourist magazine. She could send a release over and have it back by five.

If only the second solution would be so simple.

"Newspapers print anything; they'll distort any story, cast around nasty aspersions, just to sell copies." Ethan's cryptic words floated through her head like a chant. How prophetic of him, or perhaps, he'd lived through it before. More likely the latter. She couldn't imagine a life in which your family attracts fish-bowl attention because of its wealth, position, or ancestry. She remembered a few of her own antics during her college days and was very glad that Cora O'Brien was no one the news-reading public was interested in. Her brief life with James K. Dearing, distinguished corporate lawyer and Columbia elected official, gave her a taste of life under the public microscope.

Cora, for god's sake, that dress is slit up the back all the way to tomorrow. Don't you ever look in a mirror at anything other than your face? And lose the hooker stiletto heels. Put on some pumps and your gray suit. I didn't think I'd have to tell a grown woman how to dress.

Her ex-husband's words didn't singe her insides anymore. They were more like mild heartburn instead of a raging bellyache. But she wasn't about to make that mistake again—to marry a man you thought you knew, who you thought liked you, besides loved you, then discover he wanted to change everything about you from top to bottom. There were some things better than having a large balance in the checking account, she mused as she booted her computer.

The article flew from her fingers—it flowed together from her notes and memory—and turned into a great piece, if she said so herself. After printing a copy and placing it on the ever-growing stack on Matthew's desk, she headed for the door.

The long way home—along the levee, with a stop for coffee at the French Market and time to think—that's what she needed. Ethan's disparagement of her profession haunted her thoughts, almost as much as his cool, collected face, since he seemed to smile at her from every shop window. She hadn't been aware of how lonely she was until recently. And she hadn't minded her solitary status until Ethan showed an alternative.

The dust and sweat clung to her face and arms as she opened the gate and walked to her cottage. The garden welcomed her like a cool, tall gin-and-tonic, usually partaken without the gin. She couldn't wait to strip off her damp clothes and get into shorts.

"Ms. Cora Dearing?"

She nearly jumped out of her skin.

"Sorry, ma'am. Didn't mean to startle you." A rangy teenager dressed in a jacket with the FTD logo advanced, holding out a large white box. He had come in from the side service entrance, whose opening in the fence wasn't even discernible if you didn't know where to look.

"Thank you," she said to the boy's retreating back. Inside were at least two dozen white Calla lilies. They were breathtakingly lovely but somewhat morbid at the same time. They reminded her too much of funeral gladiolas. She put them in her largest vase and set it in the middle of the table. After all, they had to cost someone a small fortune. Maybe they were from Andy Bowen to bribe her for more help, but she knew, at least she hoped, they came from someone else. She found the card at the bottom of the box.

We need to talk. I want to see you. Meet me at Lowry's at 8:00. Please come. Ethan.

He had invited her to another place she couldn't afford on her salary. This wasn't fair. He knew she was weak-kneed when it came to resisting culinary delights and used it to his advantage.

But it wasn't just because she was dying to try Lowry's crawfish étouffée—reputedly the best in town—that she knew she'd go. Cora was dying to see him. She knew it from the moment she dropped the card and flew up the stairs to the shower. She knew it when she changed outfits three times, finally deciding on a slinky black dress with a lace wrap. She was positive it was more than the promise of good food when she spent thirty minutes on her hair and painted her toenails—something she hadn't done since her high school days.

At seven-fifty she walked through her gate, expecting and finding the limo with the same cocky blond driver. The only difference was this time she couldn't wait to get through the traffic to Lowry's. She couldn't wait to see Ethan.

Knowing what her editor wanted, demanded from her if she wanted to keep her job, she knew this wasn't a good idea. However, she was helpless to stop herself. This dinner would give Ethan the chance to explain a few things and satisfy her curiosity. For instance, why did he tell her his name was Auxier instead of Galen? And why was he at Water Lilies in the first place?

CORA WAS LED to a quiet alcove where he waited. He rose when she approached, offered a fabulous smile and extended his hand. She clasped it, allowing herself to be pulled to the same side of the banquette. Sitting so close would make it difficult to maintain her professional distance. After all, wasn't that why she was here? To dig up dirt on the Galen family?

"I'm glad you could join me at short notice." His voice, low and husky, charmed her like a snake. He brought her hand to his mouth and brushed his lips across the back. Her heart pounded in her chest so hard she feared it would be overheard.

"I've been anxious to try this place," she said, sitting as far away as the banquette would allow, "and anxious to ask you a couple questions. I thought I'd give you the opportunity to explain your sudden change of names, Mr. Galen." She watched the color rise in his cheeks while his eyes darkened to turquoise.

"Any reason to bring you into my company is reason for me." He whispered something into the sommelier's ear and the man beat a hasty departure. Ethan settled back to study her, then drew a deep breath. "It's silly, actually. When I travel, as long as no passport is involved, I like to use my grandfather's name." He cocked his chin higher. "I like the anonymity, and I liked my grandfather very much." He flashed straight, white teeth that glowed against his dark tan.

Cora pursed her lips, waiting for more explanation, but his expression turned to flinty steel.

"You look lovely, Cora. Black becomes you."

"Doesn't it look good on just about everybody? And nobody says 'becomes you' anymore." She tugged at the hem of her short dress. She hadn't planned to bare quite so much leg and had forgotten how short the dress rode when seated. He looked rather appealing himself, dressed in chinos with a dark sport coat, but she decided not to mention it.

"Why don't people say it anymore? It's a perfectly fine phrase. And black doesn't look good on everyone. Some should wear it only after there's been a death."

"Ah, well, there's been one. Hasn't there?"

"Surely you don't mourn the passing of Ada Rothman? The woman had few redeeming qualities." He shrugged, then nodded to the waiter who hovered nearby. The man poured a dark, rich red wine into the glasses. "I hope you like a dry Cabernet. I won't let you think I only drink champagne."

"How do you know that, Ethan? How can you pass judgment on a woman's life based on behavior at a dinner party and a sweltering cruise in the swamp? She was out of her element and perhaps, under other circumstances, would have acted differently."

He smiled over the rim of his wineglass. "Cora. You are the consummate humanitarian. Will you judge me so compassionately when the time comes?" He had leaned back against the seat so that his face was shadowed, unreadable.

"We'll have to see about that. Now there is something else I must know." She waited but received no encouragement. "Did you leave a vase of flowers on my garden table?" She hated her tentative, childlike voice.

"No, I must confess I did not." He leaned forward into the glow of the table lamp to meet her gaze. "It looks like you have another secret admirer, *cher*. And I hate the very idea of it. When I discover his identity, there will be the devil to pay." He laughed at his own jest, but Cora didn't. She squirmed in her chair, studying the menu with intense concentration. Then she remembered the delivered flowers and blushed profusely. "Oh, I almost forgot. Thank you for the lilies. They were lovely."

"Ah, but more easily forgotten than the vase left in your yard."

"Only because the gift was an invasion of my privacy and I'd like to know the donor," she snapped.

"It was not me," he said. He stretched out his hand but only touched her wrist with an index finer. The sensation delivered a jolt to her funny bone. "What appeals to you tonight? I am starving," he said. He hadn't picked up his menu, however, but simply allowed his gaze to rove the neckline of her dress.

When she didn't withdraw her hand, he began to trace an imaginary map on her skin. "I heard the crawfish étouffée is wonderful here. That's what I'd like."

"My Columbia belle has developed a fondness for Cajun cuisine, true?" She nodded an affirmative response, then sipped the wine. It was so dry it nearly puckered her mouth.

"Well, all right then." He spoke to the waiter who lurked behind his chair. "We'll have *andouillie* gumbo to start, crawfish étouffée, shrimp Creole, jambalaya, crab cakes, lots of bread and—" glancing at his watch, "two bottles of Pinot Grigio."

Cora's hand flew to her mouth to stifle a giggle. "How hungry are you, Ethan? That is enough food for a party."

"It's a party I had in mind. I invited a friend to join us. I hope you don't mind."

"Not at all," she said. You could learn a lot about a man from his friends. And she had much to learn about Ethan Galen, although with someone else present it might be difficult to pump for information to smear him with, she thought wryly.

"Here he is, right on time. A free meal must be involved. Hey, Freddie."

Cora looked up from her wineglass. It was Frederick from the cemetery tour. She stared from one to the other with growing vexation.

"Good evening, Ms. Dearing. I was looking forward to renewing our acquaintance." He slumped into the banquette across from them, not bothering to brush his long hair out of his face. But he had shaved and his clothes were pressed. He didn't appear quite as gothic as her initial impression.

"I thought you didn't like to be called Freddie," she said.

"I don't. I hate it. As soon as Ethan found out I hated it, he's called me that ever since." The two men exchanged familiar comrade looks, while a waiter materialized with a glass for Frederick.

Cora drew a deep breath, collected her thoughts into one location, then turned on the seat to face Ethan. "So you two are old friends."

"*Oui, ma petite*. From Tulane."

"And you are not really a tour guide," she asked Frederick.

"*Oui*, madam, but I have a friend who is and loves an afternoon off. I am a thespian, should you have need of my services." He bowed slightly.

"An out-of-work actor will do almost anything legal for money," Ethan added. "Illegal will cost you extra."

"And that's how I managed to arrive at Water Lilies, even though the place is practically by invitation only." She had swiveled back to Ethan.

"I cannot tell a lie, *m'amie*. It was a set-up." He pulled her hand to his mouth and kissed the palm. "I invited Freddie here tonight so I can come clean with my chicanery. Honesty is the best policy between man and woman, *n'est pas?*"

"You were helplessly caught in the seductive snare of a Galen, madam. There was nothing else you could have done," Frederick said, downed half his wine, then refilled the glass.

"Is that so?" she asked. The waiter set steaming bowls of gumbo before them.

"Pay no attention to him," Ethan said, picking up his

spoon. "You had, and always will have free will, in what I hope will be a long-term relationship." He took a spoonful of the soup. "I was pleased and honored that you accepted my suggestion to weekend in Lafourche. I thought it might help the article you were writing."

"And did it, Cora? Did you discover anything romantic to write about at Water Lilies?" Frederick baited.

"A lady never kisses and tells, Freddie. You'll just have to wait and buy Sunday's newspaper to find out." She returned the banter, fortified by the wine and spicy soup filling her empty stomach. "Sunday's paper? You're a reporter? I thought you were a women's magazine writer or something like that," Ethan asked.

Cora remembered his less-than-fond feelings for *The Times*. "Oh, I just write women's stories for the Sunday insert, that's all. Nothing dangerous." This was not the time to mention her long-coveted career goals. She reached over and locked her hand over his. His face brightened measurably at the gesture, while he stared at their entwined fingers. "Nothing damaging," she added. Her voice trailed into nothingness when he leaned forward and placed his lips on hers.

It was a simple kiss. No open mouths, no twisting tongues, yet the effect was overwhelming. When his lips touched hers, her skin sizzled with a vibrancy she'd effectively buried for a very long time. His hand snaked through the hair, pulling her close as he kissed her again. She touched his cheek, returning the kiss hungrily. His male scent blended with the patio flowers, almost intoxicating her. She felt his fingers spread at the nape of her neck, flooding her with good old-fashioned lust. Each spot his fingers reached tingled with energy, while his tongue continued to trace the curve of her lips. No one had ever kissed her like that. She melted into his embrace like ice cream on hot apple pie.

"Cora, Cora. I expected rude behavior from Galen, but not from you. Take pity on me. Don't you have any girlfriends you could call to join us for this banquet, and perhaps pay me a little attention?"

Freddie's tone, plaintive and sincere, pulled Cora's attention from Ethan's delicious mouth. Her eyes rounded with amazement at the impressive array of food that had been set before them and overflowed onto a cart. At least seven platters of Cajun delicacies steamed their spicy aromas.

"Good grief," she murmured. "We'll never eat all this."

Ethan handed her his cell phone. "Call someone. Anyone, *cher*. Otherwise Freddie won't leave us alone. He's very jealous, you know. He's always wanted everything I have. You will be no exception." He leaned close and kissed her hair. His warm breath by her ear sent shivers of excitement to her toes, jolting long-dormant sensual zones into full alert.

Cora took the phone, dialing Lara's number from memory. Lara from accounting was her only girlfriend in New Orleans. She was young, spontaneous and free-spirited. If anyone would show up on short notice, it was Lara.

"If you're in Lowry's with two men, a ton of food, and plenty of wine, and you think it's a good idea, I will be right there," was Lara's reply. And she arrived in less than twenty minutes. By that time, Freddie was slightly drunk, while Cora was practically levitating above the seat. Wine was not the cause of her excitement. It was the way Ethan looked at her and murmured her name.

Lara, who had been watching a nature special on sharks, joined in the revelry as though old friends with everyone, even though she didn't even know Cora all that well. She and Freddie hit it off immediately. By Lara's second glass of wine, she was running her fingers through his tangled mane and laughing at his silly stories.

"So, you were behind the idea of my weekending at Water Lilies?" Cora asked, laying her fork on the side of her plate. She slanted her gaze at Ethan.

"It was no devious plot, sweet Cora. Merely a suggestion, since I was already going there. I thought," he said, popping a shrimp into his mouth and chewing before finishing his thought, "that we could get to know one another better."

"And what about your paying my bill at Maison Provance?" she asked in a quiet voice. "What was that all about? I found out yesterday."

He hesitated for a moment from industriously extracting a crawfish from its shell, surprised by her revelation. "That was...nothing, *cher*. Only money. I have a lot. I like to be generous with people I'm fond of." He didn't look at her, only at the seafood on his plate.

"One would consider such a gesture a bit presumptuous on your part."

His steely blue eyes fixed on hers. "I presume nothing, Ms. Dearing. I only have my hopes and aspirations, same as any man, rich or poor. If my gesture offended you, I apologize." Indignation colored his words, immediately making her sorry she brought the matter up.

She realized then that she was no match for him. She had been born yesterday, and he sometime in the last millennium in matters of the heart. "Thank you for your generosity, but I prefer to pay my own way in this world. Please don't try to buy me." She rose from the table. *My, am I going to rush out in a hurry again? I seem to be doing a lot of this lately.*

"Please, Cora, don't go." He clutched her forearm with a tight grip. "I'd never try to buy you. I'm used to spending my money, that's all. No offense was intended."

Cora tried to pull away and found she couldn't. She glared at him until his grasp lightened to a gentle rub across her skin. "All I know is," she spoke slowly and calmly near his face, "since we've been acquainted, a woman has disappeared, flowers have mysteriously appeared in my private garden, your name is changed, my bills get paid without my knowledge, and a detective keeps asking how well we know each other, *cher*." Cora mimicked his endearment, but without the pleasing French accent. The effect was deadly. Lara and Frederick turned their attention from feeding each other peeled shrimp to stare at Cora.

Ethan removed his hand altogether and leaned back from the table. "And you think I had something to do with that woman's disappearance?" His voice was close to a growl.

"Yes, I do. I don't know why, but I do."

"I did not, Cora." Pain etched his words, replaced by anger. "What reason would I have? What would be my motive?" He sipped his wine with cool detachment.

"I don't know, Ethan, but I'm going to find out." She turned to rush out of the restaurant—her recently adopted MO since meeting him.

Truth was she actually didn't believe him responsible for the disappearance. At least she didn't want to believe. A man that charming could *not* be a cold-blooded killer. In an instant, her mission became clear. She needed to get to the bottom of the disappearance, not for story background for *The Times*, but for Ethan's sake, and her own.

She didn't get far from the table, however, because a large man in a wrinkled sport coat and a blindingly bright tie blocked her path. "Detective Rhodes," she said, noticing an odd glimmer in his eye.

"Hello, Miss Dearing. I didn't think I'd find you together, but I guess I've just saved myself time and energy tracking you both down." He fanned himself with a straw hat seldom worn by anyone but tourists on a beach. "Good evening, Mr. Galen. Mind if I sit? Whew, it's humid tonight. I think I've sweated a quart." He lowered himself clumsily into the chair vacated by Cora. Ethan, Lara and Frederick stared at him dumbfoundedly.

"Were you on your way out, Ms. Dearing?" the detective asked. "My, you folks really had yourselves a feast here." He stared at the almost empty platters.

"I'm in no particular hurry." Cora sat back down on the banquette next to Lara, glancing at Ethan. He stared at Detective Rhodes. "What did you want to talk to us about?"

"Oh, yes." He pulled his attention from the platters, sobering visibly. "I'm afraid I have some bad news. Antoine from *Le P'tit* Fisherman was found dead. Floating in the bayou next to his restaurant." He looked from Cora to Ethan.

"Dear me," she breathed. "Was it an accident?"

"I surely doubt it, ma'am. Considering he had put the muzzle of a shotgun in his mouth and pulled the trigger."

SIX

"IT ALL MAKES perfect sense to me." Cora paced Andy Bowen's small office in front of the window.

"What makes sense?" Andy asked, finally looking up from his word processor.

"That Antoine kidnapped Mrs. Rothman in the bayou."

"I thought you said he was busy in the kitchen whipping up his famous recipe for food poisoning?"

"He could have slipped out the back door any time that afternoon. He has other employees, you know. Or he could've hired one of those seedy fisherman to bag Mrs. Rothman while he kept a visible profile in front of us."

"And his reason for bagging an old lady he'd never laid eyes on would be…what?"

"Money, of course. The prime motivator for most crime. He told me business was bad out in the bayou," she added, lending additional strength to her theory. "Money paid by Mr. Rothman," she said with conviction. "I know Mr. Galen didn't have anything more to do with the disappearance than I did." She stopped pacing long enough to pierce Andy with a glare.

"Yeah, Mr. Galen. I was hoping we'd get to him," he said cheerily and shut down his computer. "How was dinner last night, Cora? A little bird told me you and Mr. Galen are getting to be rather good friends." He walked over to the window, slipped his hands into his pockets, and leaned against the sill expectantly.

Cora reeled around, ready to deny the allegation, then

remembered. She was the one who had invited Lara to dinner at Lowry's. Lara, the office blabbermouth. "We are friends, Andy. That's all."

"Well, you and I are friends. How come you never kiss me?" His expression reminded her of the taunting boys from eighth grade.

"Maybe because you're a total jerk." Cora headed for the door.

"Don't you want to hear my theories?" His voice lost its teasing inflection.

She turned around slowly. "All right."

"Someone snuffed out Antoine. Somebody who was in on the plan and didn't want to share the bounty." He waited for a reaction from Cora. She yielded nothing. "April said that that someone would be your new boy-friend. She said Antoine and Galen had a heated argu-ment right before lunch. In French so she couldn't get the gist of it."

Cora remembered the fervent words between the two men that had struck her odd at the time but forced them from her mind. "Perhaps Ethan didn't like the daily spe-cials," she said.

"And Ethan," he mimicked her tone, "was arguing with Mrs. Rothman down by the boat dock the night before. That's what the police report says anyway." He softened his words against Cora's expression.

"If you've been so busy investigating, Andy, then you'd know Ethan hardly needs Mr. Rothman's money. He's got plenty of his own."

"The rich always need extra, more so than you or I." He crossed his arms. "I'm just telling you this for your own good. He might be in this up to his silver spoon."

"Thanks for worrying, Andy, but I'm a big girl." Cora pulled open his office door. "And I'm only seeing him to dig out the story. I'm not staying in the feature department forever."

"You're no match for him. The next time you meet him, take me along. Tell him I'm your big brother, or something."

"Yeah, right. Okay."

"Look, I'm willing to share the byline with you, Cora. It's Matthews that's against bringing you in on this story. He says you're greener than a kiwi."

"A kiwi?" A red cloak had just been waved before the bull. Cora gritted her teeth and marched to the editor's office.

Lucky for him that he was out to lunch with the business staff.

She glanced into her own cubicle at her notes on the next feature story—the genealogical roots from the past three centuries of a Garden District matriarch—and frowned. She should work on the story. Jim hadn't been pleased with her final copy of the romantic retreats article, since she'd placed the other B&B on the cover. But time was so short, he'd no choice but run the feature as it was. "Time for you to start following orders around this place" had been his final words on the matter.

So it was also lucky for Cora that he was out to lunch with the business staff.

Now she could slip out of the office and pay Detective Rhodes an afternoon call.

JEANETTE CARRIED THE luncheon tray out to the dining terrace completely secluded by the spreading branches of a magnolia tree. The limbs drooped with heavy, fragrant blooms. Her lip furled imperceptibly when she spotted whom Ethan dined with today.

"Good afternoon, Jeanette. You are looking in perfect health, as always." Nate Price's drawl pierced the somnolent afternoon drowsiness. Gone was his chauffeur's livery. Instead he wore jeans with a Tulane University T-shirt.

"Good afternoon, *M'sieu* Price." She didn't look at Price, merely cast her employer an odd appraisal. "I've brought iced tea, *M'sieu* Ethan. Will that be sufficient for your guest?"

"That will be fine. Thank you, Jeanette," Ethan said, folding the newspaper and setting it aside. He wore a faded shirt that at one time had been identical to Nate's. Now his was ripped off at the bottom and sleeveless, showing toned stomach muscles and biceps that attested to his determination to make more than money in his spare time. His hours at the gym each week did as much for his psyche as for his body. Every frustration, every setback could be allayed with a grueling workout.

Nate waited until Jeanette had reentered the house. "I have no idea why that woman hates me so much while she absolutely adores Freddie. I'd love to get on her good side."

"Not in this lifetime. She's known Freddie since we wore short pants to St. Cecilia's. Plus, she has to have someone to blame for my bad character. Since you're usually around when I've gotten falling-down-drunk in the past, it must be your fault." He shot Price a crafty look. "Just don't accept anything to eat or drink from her when I'm not around." Ethan divided the food on the platter between two plates and poured the tea.

Nate leaned near, as not to be overheard. "She's not, you know, into voodoo or something. Is she?" His grin held little humor.

"Nah. She gave up the gris-gris for Lent one year and

never went back. Far as I know anyway." Ethan bit into his crab salad sandwich.

Nate cast one last look at the louvered back door. The window curtains fell back into place. "Well, we've got something bigger to worry about right now. April Rothman has vanished." He didn't look at Ethan.

"What?" Ethan said, controlling his temper with great effort. "I pay you an extreme amount of money to keep tabs on that viper." Ethan tossed the sandwich back on the plate, his appetite evaporating.

"I tried to, man. But she gave the slip to the tail I put on her. Somehow she spotted him. There's no other explanation."

Ethan leaned back, his teeth locked in the set of his jaw.

"She's been back to the police three times, cooking up a new-and-improved twist to the story each time," Nate said. "The latest has Antoine being paid by daddy to bump off mother. After all, times are hard in the shrimping business these days. Might as well raise a little spending cash offing tourists." Nate took a bite of his sandwich.

"And now that Antoine is dead, too? Does darling April have a theory on how that came about?" Ethan asked, but he already knew the answer.

"Oh, yeah. And that culprit would be...you."

Rage crept up Ethan's neck, into his face, all the way to the hairline. His grip on the iced tea glass threatened to crush the fragile stem. Nate pulled the glass from Ethan's grasp. "Easy, old buddy. We're not done yet. Not by a long-shot."

"Find her, Nate," Ethan said, pushing back from the table.

Nate rose from his chair. "You can count on that and not because you're the best employer in town. I'll take great pleasure finding this one. I'll be in touch." He picked up the other half sandwich, munching it while he let himself out the back gate.

Ethan was left alone except for his thoughts. Ten million dollars is at stake here. Ten million dollars his family could not afford to lose. Everything he had worked for to restore the family's standing will be wiped out in an instant. Hadn't he already paid enough for mistakes he made in the past? He remembered the grim scene when his feckless wife of eight months had left him. She'd grown bored with married domestic life and feared his father was cutting off his trust fund. If he didn't stop April, she would cost him his future. He couldn't afford to let the woman get away with that.

"Is *M'sieu* Price gone?" She received no response from him. "Ethan?" Jeanette's voice finally pierced his reverie, and he glanced in her direction. "Is Nathan Price gone?"

"Yes, Jeanette. He's gone." He didn't meet his housekeeper's eye. He had no desire to debate whether Nate was a bad influence or not.

"That is good. I wanted to ask you about dinner."

"Please don't trouble yourself. I'll just grab something out if I get hungry." He just finished lunch and received news that had soured everything he'd eaten. The last thing he wanted to think about was food. He walked past her toward the house, but the small wren-like woman was quicker. She blocked his exit.

"I thought about a dinner party, *M'sieu*. Something elegant. A nice Chateaubriand with spring vegetables and a dessert soufflé out here on the terrace."

Ethan looked at her as if she'd lost her mind. He took another step toward the house.

"For you and the young lady." She back-stepped quickly to stay in his path.

"What young lady?" This riddle was getting on his nerves.

"Miss Cora Dearing," she replied as though he were an idiot.

He stopped trying to get around her. "How do you know about Cora Dearing?"

Jeanette exhaled a rasp of air that dismissed the question. "I know much, *mon ami*. I know you should spend more time with the likes of her and less with your old college chums." She spat the last two words as though they were especially distasteful. Ethan managed to get around the determined woman. "You are not getting any younger," she called to his retreating back.

"That is *la vérité*, Jeanette. Thank you for your concern. Perhaps another night would be better suited for your scheme." He turned on the back steps and flashed her a smile before disappearing into the house.

She's who I should've put on the trail of April Rothman, he thought. All would be taken care of by now.

THE AFTERNOON HAD grown stickier with the threat of rain hanging in the air like moss from the trees. It was a long walk to the police station, through a rebuilt historical neighborhood of dogtrots, shotguns, and camelbacks—architectural housing styles unique to New Orleans. Cora had contemplated a taxi, but the walk would do her good, despite the humidity. She could plan her attack on Detective Rhodes. She would have the upper hand this time, instead of him turning up in her back garden like a phantom. She had to find out all she could about April Rothman. Something had convinced this crazy woman that Ethan was involved with her mother's disappearance.

That just wasn't true. A hit man paid by her father certainly wouldn't make himself so obvious by checking in as a guest. He could stake the place out in a boat from anywhere in the swamp. He could've been watching them their entire time at Water Lilies and chosen the afternoon at Antoine's to make his move, especially since she had conveniently created a diversion by getting sick. Antoine didn't necessarily have anything to do with it either.

A blasting car horn made her jump back onto the curb. She ignored the impolite hand gesture from the driver and crossed the street behind the car. Or Antoine could've been in on it and slipped something into her salad plate to put her out of commission. Great. *If I can't figure it out, how will I convince Detective Rhodes that Ethan had nothing to do with it?* The key somehow rested with April, now that Antoine was dead. *I guess that cagey Cajun won't be serving up any more tainted shrimp,* she thought and immediately crossed herself, her religious upbringing ever apparent. *Don't think ill of the dead.*

"A penny for your thoughts, *cher.*"

The voice was a welcome, cherished sound in her ears. She hadn't noticed the Town Car pull along the curb and slow to her walking pace. Ruined office equipment still waited on the sidewalk to be hauled to the recycling facility. Only so many trucks to tackle the monstrous task.

"Ethan. I'm glad to see you." She smiled and brushed her bangs off her forehead. Could the man ever see her when she wasn't wilting from the heat? At least she had pinned her hair off her neck this morning and wore a cool, cotton sundress.

"You are a summer oasis for a thirsty man, dear heart. Get in. I'll give you a lift to wherever you're going. I'm at your service." The door swung open and Cora contemplated the offer for less than two seconds. She stepped into the cool confines of the limo's backseat. The chilly air immediately raised goose bumps on her flesh, or perhaps it was the close proximity to Ethan. He smelled woodsy and fresh, and she yearned to bury her face in his shirt and inhale deeply.

"Let me give you something to drink." He opened the small refrigerator door.

"Please, no champagne. I still have plenty of work to do this afternoon."

He withdrew two bottles of water. "Just spring water. No champagne for my industrious writer of women's stories." He twisted off the cap and handed her one. His fingers brushed hers, sending shivers down her back and raising the little hairs on her neck. "What are you working on?"

"I'm on my way to see Detective Rhodes. Antoine had to be responsible for Mrs. Rothman's disappearance, and now Mr. Rothman has done away with Antoine. It all makes sense." She took a long drink of the cold water and watched the smile melt from Ethan's face.

"I thought you wrote feature stories, touting the romantic, gastronomical and artistic attributes of our recovering city. Why do you concern yourself with that nasty business out in the bayou?" He made a dismissive hand gesture as though the nasty business was nothing more than a bad case of poison ivy. "Let the good detective do his job, Cora, and don't trouble yourself." He wiped away a drop of condensation that had fallen from the bottle to her arm, then put his finger to his mouth.

The gesture mesmerized her. She took another sip of the water. "I don't think I'm preventing anyone from doing his job. The whole thing…interests me, that's all. Nobody I've known has ever disappeared before."

"You did not know her, *cher*." This time his finger

retrieved a drop that clung to her lower lip. She stared as he sucked the moisture from his fingertip in an exaggerated fashion. She moved on the seat, imperceptibly closer. He moved closer, too, not bothering with subtlety.

"No, but I'm already involved. Remember Detective Rhodes came to my house asking a lot of questions... mainly about you." She kept her voice light and teasing.

"It could get dangerous. One person is dead already, maybe two. Stay far away from the treachery until the culprit is captured," he drawled with exaggerated drama.

Cora raised the bottle to her mouth to drink again as his hand held her arm. She turned her gaze on him like an old-fashioned movie in slow motion. His pale blue eyes darkened with desire. He chewed his lower lip in a manner she often engaged in. Helplessly she reached out to touch the mouth that captured her attention, holding her breath as she did so. He needed no further encouragement. He pulled her head close with a firm hand and covered her mouth with his. "Cora," he said with that devilish accent.

Cora melted like butter on a hot griddle. She wrapped her arms around his neck and kissed him back with all the passion she'd hidden away for years. His scent, his touch, his taste—all conspired to reduce her to a besotted, quivering mass. He pressed his tongue past her lips deep into her mouth. The intimacy intoxicated her. Shivers danced down her spine. At that moment she was incapable of letting him go as a feeling of helplessness washed over her. It was as though she'd lost her free will and must succumb to his whims or dictates. Even more unnerving was the vague notion of danger that cloaked him, making any hanky-panky all the more thrilling.

She wrenched free of his mouth, scooting back along the seat. "Ethan, please stop. Haven't you ever been told no before?" Her tone sounded unintentionally snippy. Most of her exasperation stemmed from the impossible logistics of the situation.

His gaze raked her with desire. "I have, but never when it's mattered so much."

"We're in the backseat of a limo. Your driver is right there." She drew a halting breath and pushed his unnerving kiss and her own lack of control to the back of her mind where she kept things she refused to deal with.

Ethan leaned forward and knocked on the glass privacy screen. It lowered a few inches. "Pull over and park the car, Nate, and take a coffee break."

The car swerved out of traffic, coming to an abrupt stop under the shade of several trees. The chauffeur pulled a thermos from somewhere on the seat and began to pour liquid into the thermos top.

"Take your break outside the vehicle, you idiot," Ethan snarled.

Cora stifled a giggle. "My, that's not a good way to talk to your employees, Mr. Galen. You'll soon be driving yourself wherever you want to go if that keeps up."

"Excuse me, Mr. Galen," Price said into a speaker. "My little wife fixed this thermos and I thought I'd just partake a little of it." Nate tipped his brimmed hat up and smiled at Ethan in the rearview mirror.

Ethan scowled. "He and I...go way back. He's well compensated for the verbal abuse he receives. He enjoys it actually, and by the way, he doesn't have a wife." He glowered back at Price.

"That's right, ma'am. Don't you worry 'bout me. Mr. Galen, he's a generous employer."

"Well, whatever, you stay put, Nate. I need to get out anyway. I'm close to where I'm going." Then she fixed her gaze on Ethan. "The Police Station," she said in a tone of challenge. "I'm going to talk to Detective Rhodes. And you're not going to stop me."

"Rhodes, the estimable investigator trying to capture the kidnapper. From here in downtown New Orleans? What do you think he'll tell you, *cher*?"

She ignored his question and asked one of her own. "What makes you think Mrs. Rothman was kidnapped and not just missing? Or murdered, for that matter?" she asked, watching his reaction.

"Just a guess. If she's rich, perhaps someone is holding the woman for a hefty ransom. They will soon be ready to give her back, even if the money hasn't been raised. She has that effect on people." His grin lit up his entire face. He reached out and stroked the side of her face. "You just let the good man do his job. Do not distress yourself. I'm sure he will soon get to the bottom of this."

Cora blanched at the patronizing tone. "I am not distressed, Ethan. I think I can help him. I may have information for him, or at least ideas he might find useful." She didn't miss the squaring of his jaw or the downturn of his mouth.

"You poke your nose around, Cora, and it will look like you had a part in this when you didn't."

"Have a part in what, exactly?"

"In whatever it turns out to be, my love." He leaned to brush her lips with his, but she turned her head and caught the kiss on her cheek. "Why don't I drive you home and pick you up later for dinner? Someplace out of the city, perhaps in Mandeville on the lake. My family has a summer home there. I think you would like it." His fingers drifted from her face down the bodice of her dress. The movement was deliberate, intentional, yet casual, as though he fondled her on a regular basis. Her breasts tingled with the touch.

She grabbed his wandering hand and resolutely lowered it to the car seat, not releasing her hold. "I'm sure your summer home is lovely, Ethan. Maybe I'll see it one day, but I'm staying in the city today, and right now, talking to Detective Rhodes."

"As you wish. My desire is only to make you happy."

Cora scooted across the seat and grabbed the door handle before she changed her mind. Nate set down his coffee and jumped out, drawing open the backdoor with a flourish. "Are you certain there isn't someplace I could drive you, Miss? It would be my pleasure."

"No, thank you. I prefer to walk."

Ethan caught her hand as she was getting out. "I'll pick you up in front of the station, Cora. You won't be in long. Detective Rhodes isn't there. He went to Lafourche for the afternoon."

Cora yanked her hand back and stomped away from the car. *Just how did he know that?* She walked hard and fast from the limo, not noticing it trail her progress half a block behind.

That was a good thing because when she talked to the desk sergeant and discovered that Detective Rhodes was indeed in Lafourche for the afternoon, she was fit to be tied.

HOME NEVER LOOKED so good. Cora quickly regretted her hasty decision to slip out the back of the police station after learning Rhodes wasn't there after all. She wanted some time to think, and not just about the disappearance story. Things were rapidly careening out of control with Ethan, and she hadn't exhibited much self-control in the man's presence lately. But the seven-block walk in ninety-eight degree heat had been more conducive to frying eggs on the pavement than plotting a course of action. She turned the key in the door and stepped into the coolness of the cottage, provided by overhanging shade and eighteen-inch stone walls.

She smelled the rich, heady fragrance the moment she entered the house. She knew it wasn't the fading blooms she'd gathered the other day and set on the windowsill that overpowered the room. A huge mass of beautiful gardenias tumbled over the sides of a Chinese vase in the center of her dining table. The same vase she had found in her back garden.

It had been outside on the patio when she'd left.

Her heart lurched; her breath caught in her throat. Whoever had made the latest floral gift had been in her house.

Flying on her feet, she found the back door closed but not locked. Without signs of forced entry, Cora wracked her memory for this morning's activities, then remembered a trip to the trashcan next to the gate before rushing off to work. Did she neglect to lock the backdoor? Maybe, but who would dare to enter her domain whether the door was locked or not?

Cora retraced her steps to the garbage can and pulled off the battered lid. There lay the bouquet of bougainvillea that formerly resided in the Chinese vase. *Well, at least this stalker cleans up after himself*, she thought, but couldn't bring herself to laugh. The idea that someone had been in her house, whether the door had been left open or not, gave her the creeps. She spent the next hour going over every inch of the house to determine if the intruder had stolen anything. Nothing was missing, and nothing seemed out of place. *I apparently have a stalker obsessed with flowers. One mustn't have wilted blooms gracing one's table.* That was something her grandmother would say, and Cora smiled at the pleasant memory of a type of woman long gone from the world.

She slammed her vanity drawer and straightened her back. Nothing had been taken, as far as she could tell. Out of the corner of her eye, she saw through the streaky window something move in the garden below. Cora jumped back a foot, then fled down the stairs, grabbing both her cordless phone and a butcher knife from the block. A shadowy silhouette moved on the other side of the drawn shade, triggering Cora to action. Sticking the phone into her waistband, she raised the knife high with her right hand, and flung the door wide with her left.

Detective Rhodes stood on her stoop, his pleasant smile fading as he spotted the eight-inch knife blade she brandished above his head. He jumped back two feet.

"Ms. Dearing, please don't stab me. I apologize for not coming to the front door, but I wanted to bring you these." He held out a tray of six plastic pots, each holding a scrawny plant. "These are rare African primroses that I started from seeds. They tolerate the shade well," he said, flourishing a hand toward the overhanging branches, "and love our Orleans humidity." He never took his eyes off the knife in her hand.

Cora gawked at him, then at the plants, utterly speechless. Slowly she lowered her hand holding the weapon. "Sorry, Detective."

"I'll just set them here, ma'am. Be sure to get them into the ground within the day and give them lots of water." He walked to the patio table with his wilted plants looking a bit crestfallen. "And I'm sorry I startled you."

Cora set the knife and phone inside the door and stepped down into the stifling heat. She heard the shuffling of feet and a woman's laughter from over the fence. The disembodied noise of car horns, barking dogs, and music from a radio floated on the thick air. "That's okay, Detective. I'm glad I didn't stab first and ask questions later. I thought you were in Lafourche." She sat on the edge of a chaise, rubbing her temples with the tips of her fingers. A ferocious headache gripped her mercilessly.

His lips thinned with the question. "Yes, I was. I just got back to town. Lovely parish, Lafourche, or at least it will be again. Still needs more recovery time."

"Did you stay in town during the hurricane?" Everybody had a story to tell if they were here during the Big One.

He didn't seem anxious to tell his. "Yes, I was here." His gaze looked skyward for a moment. "Those were dark days, Ms. Dearing. I went house-to-house marking front doors with red or orange X's signifying it'd been checked for bodies. Dark days, indeed. Hopefully, never to be seen again in my lifetime." His florid complexion had paled considerably.

Cora decided to change the subject. "Detective Rhodes, did you bring me flowers the other night and leave them on that table?" She motioned to where he'd set the primroses, then looked at him expectantly.

"Oh, no, ma'am. I surely did not." He blushed profusely. "My wife doesn't mind me sharing some of my plant progeny, but she draws the line with bringing another woman flowers." He raked a hand through his gray hair. "She'd be next to take a butcher knife to me." He forced an unnatural laugh, his gaze darting between Cora and the house. "Why do you ask?" he asked, watching her.

Cora rose. "I was trying to figure out which of my beaus left them, and I wanted to rule out non-romantic sources first." She flashed a magnificent grin and hoped he believed her capable of multiple beaus. "Was there a reason for the visit, other than sharing your plants? Thank you for them, by the way. I'll get them into the ground tonight."

"Yes, ma'am. I almost forgot. I was curious about the other night. You know, when I ran into you and Mr. Galen having dinner in Lowry's? They're supposed to have good food—my wife is always nagging me to take her there."

Cora sat back down and waited, offering no opinion on the cuisine. He smiled and extracted a photo from his pocket. "I was curious about the other gentleman you were dining with. I didn't get a good look at him, but I think it was this man." He turned the photo over and held it under Cora's nose. It was a picture of Frederick in all his punk-Goth glory. He wore at least a dozen earrings and his pale complexion hadn't seen sunshine since his playground days.

"Yes, that's the man we were dining with. His name is Frederick."

"Yes, Frederick Bearnard. Old family, the Bearnards, not from the Quarter though. His granddaddy had a big place that got torn down, and well before Katrina. We call that area the warehouse district now. It was a ramshackle, falling down mansion that his granny rented rooms out to anybody with fifty bucks for the week. The Bearnards fell on hard times after the war."

"And what war would that be, Detective?"

"Why, World War II, ma'am. His granddaddy didn't change with the new economy. Terrible shame, to have wealth and watch it dwindle to nothing."

"All this is fascinating about Freddie, but I'm curious why you're so interested in a tour guide."

"Oh, he's not a tour guide, ma'am. He calls himself an actor, but that isn't how the man pays his bills. And he's got lots of bills." He paused and dug in his pocket. "I was just wondering about his connection to Mr. Galen, and yourself."

"Why?" Cora stood, planted her feet, and crossed her arms.

"Well, Miss April Rothman says this man," he tapped the photo with his finger, "has been stalking her. She said he was sweet on her in college. Followed her around like a puppy dog, he did. Never got over the fact that she... spurned him. You know anything about that, Ms. Dearing?"

Cora couldn't picture Frederick following any woman who wasn't interested in him. Especially not April Rothman. Even in dim light, she was only marginally attractive. "Now how would I know anything about that? I only know that Frederick is an acquaintance of Mr. Galen's. I don't know the man, but I'm having a hard time believing any of that."

"Well, seeing that you hardly know him, anything's possible. Right, Ms. Dearing? And the other lady, she is your friend?"

Cora had to think for a minute. Lara. "Yes, she is. She knows nothing about Freddie." She could have kicked herself for saying that. It sounded like she was trying to cover up something but hadn't a clue what it was.

The detective walked toward the gate. Cora followed. She was rapidly losing her chance to get information for her story.

"What have you learned about Mr. Rothman? Has anybody questioned him about his whereabouts that weekend?" She maneuvered herself directly into his path.

"Oh, yes, ma'am. We certainly have. Mr. Rothman is remarried and living in Cincinnati, Ohio. Hasn't been in this area ever, for all we could tell." He found what he'd been looking for in his pocket and pulled a small plug of tobacco from a tin. "Funny thing. He says he hasn't seen his first wife in sixteen years, and he never had to pay any alimony. Only child support while April was young."

He gave her a peculiar look and nodded his head like a well-bred Southern gentleman. "Good afternoon, Ms. Dearing. You be careful with those butcher knives."

SEVEN

As it turned out, there wasn't any time. No time to worry about Frederick's possible connection to Mrs. Rothman's disappearance, although Cora did have difficulty believing the detective's story that Freddie was sweet on April in college. She was hardly his type. There wasn't a body piercing or tattoo anywhere visible on her body, and she seemed far too conservative for flamboyant Frederick's tastes based on Cora's short assessment. The amusing memory of him and Lara alternating shots of raw oysters with shots of tequila, on top of all the wine they had consumed, flitted through her memory. How Lara managed to function at work the next day and not appear green around the gills astounded her. Cora knew she would have kept her head buried under a pillow close to the bathroom for at least a twenty-four hour period following similar excesses.

There wasn't any time to fret about the vase of gardenias gracing her dining room table either. She simply left them where they sat when she locked the door behind her. Their fragrance imbued the air with such sweet recollection she couldn't bring herself to throw them out. Gardenias were her mother's favorite flower. Seldom did the house not have a bouquet adorning the mantel while in season. Perhaps they were from the caretaker's wife—the elusive Mrs. Vacherie—as a belated house-warming gift, she mused. Surely some demented stalker wouldn't bother to clean up after his last offering. At any rate, the call from Andy Bowen precluded any serious anxiety over the flowers' origin.

She had exactly twenty minutes—to wash her face, put on a little makeup and throw some clothes in an overnight bag—before he picked her up in his battered Audi. A bag of sandwiches and bottles of water sat on the seat between them. They were on their way to Lafourche Parish, he had announced, the destination of choice for the day.

Andy had received a call from April Rothman herself. The grieving daughter of the missing woman was willing to talk to a small group of reporters tomorrow morning. They would drive out to the bayou tonight since the conference was scheduled for eight A.M. It would be the first official press conference April had called, with no one admitted except those she selected. Andy Bowen's name resided at the top of the short list.

"She says she trusts *The Times* to print the truth," Andy explained, waiting in a long queue of traffic at a light. It was still suffocatingly hot, even though the sun had slipped behind a bank of ominous clouds in the west. Cora hoped the country would be cooler as she held a water bottle to her forehead.

"She said that?" Cora asked, fanning herself with a map. "And why don't you fix the AC in this thing?"

"She did. And I ain't got a thousand bucks, that's why." He was obviously tickled he'd been invited to the press conference. Cora realized then that his career wasn't exactly shooting skyrockets either. He usually received the less-than-exciting stories to cover, while the plums were divided among Matthew's veteran staff.

April Rothman had been leaking information, different information, to any news service listening, but the gist of it all came back to a paid hit on her mother.

"I told Miss Rothman I'd be honored to represent *The*

Times at the conference and said I'd be bringing along my partner on the story." He glanced at her as he floored the car, finally breaking away from the slow moving traffic. He leered at Cora and waggled his eyebrows.

"Your partner?" Cora asked.

"At first, April said no, nobody not on the list. But when I told her my partner was you, whom she'd met that weekend, she changed her mind."

Cora stared at him. "You checked this out with Matthews? He approved my coming along? I'll be on the time clock tomorrow and not AWOL at work?"

"Yep, but he didn't like it. He didn't like it one bit. Said you stiffed him on the genealogy story, and you'd better fax him something or you're fired." He grinned and opened his water bottle. Andy knew the editor seldom followed through with threats, except every now and then.

"Yeah, I'll fax him what I got when we arrive." She patted her laptop in its leather case by her feet. This was her first real news assignment and press conference. She leaned back against the headrest and tried to recall Water Lilies. She had fond memories of the beautiful mansion, its elegant garden and the genial Roussards. It was where she had become acquainted with Ethan. Just thinking about his sensuous mouth on hers in the limo, while his hands tenderly caressed filled her with desire and brought a stinging flush to her cheeks. She glanced at Andy surreptitiously, as though he could read her carnal thoughts. Water Lilies would always remain steeped in romance, even if Ethan turned out to be a paid killer and took his soft French accent and gracious manners to the state penitentiary.

No. That way lay madness.

She forced the image of Ethan as a murderer from her mind. She knew that could not be possible. He was too gentle, too kind, too generous. Yet she remembered the strength of his grip when he'd kept her from falling on the dock. That, and the anger he'd showed when Ada Rothman behaved rudely to Mr. and Mrs. Roussard.

"Cora. Are you still with me?" Andy shook her kneecap.

"Sorry. I was plotting strategy." She brushed his hand from her leg.

"For what? Your job is to make sure we get every word down on tape and take notes of any theories that come to mind. I'll ask the questions, missy." He grabbed her knee again, just for a moment.

"Are we staying at Water Lilies?" she asked.

"Unfortunately, no. They were filled up. Apparently April booked all the rooms and assigned them at her discretion. She must have paid Emil Roussard a small fortune. Nobody else has been able to book a room there since this happened. They've been keeping a low profile. Now, a news conference. Wonder what gives with that? We're staying at that place you featured on the cover of your article. Boy, Matthews was mad you went against his advice. They were full-up, too, until I told them who was coming along, and they found a room after all."

That snapped Cora's attention from her musings out the window. "What? We're staying in the same room?" She arched her neck, jutting out her chin. "I don't think so, Andy. I'm not prepared to see you in your Spiderman pajamas with the drop-down flap in the back."

"The flap is in the front, baby." He winked and took the turn-off from the freeway way too fast.

"That's even scarier, Bowen. Better let me off here and I'll take my chances hitching a ride back to town." She put her hand on the door handle.

"Relax. They only had one room, Cora. This isn't a

plot to despoil you. And the room's got two double beds. I'll give you the one closer to the door in case I sleep-walk, okay?"

Cora studied him over her sunglasses. He was a nice man. About her age, not bad looking, but too sneaky, too driven, too wiry to have caught her attention before. This was her first, maybe her only opportunity, to do some investigative reporting. So she really shouldn't whine about the sleeping arrangements. "Okay. But we both sleep in sweats or something. I don't want you making jokes about me around the lunchroom when we get back."

"Relax, Cora. I won't spill the beans that you've got Little Mermaid jammies in your overnight bag."

THE BED AND breakfast was almost as pretty as the photo she'd downloaded from the travel site. Almost, but not quite. And it couldn't hold a candle to Water Lilies. The telltale high water line still was visible on the founda-tion despite any and all scrubbing attempts. Only a heavy coat of paint to the stucco would hide this memento of a hurricane's fury. Something nagged at her when they'd crossed the threshold of the house. Something was miss-ing. Something that lent charm and grace that defied even a generous restoration bank account. Cora sent Andy up to the room with their bags and scowled after him when he answered "yes, dear." The young woman at the desk waited patiently as Cora assessed the reception area's appointments.

Cora paused while signing the inn's register with her and Bowen's names. She spotted a small stack of bro-chures on the counter. "Could you do me a favor, Miss?" The young woman smiled and nodded. "The newspaper I work for, *The Times*, well, everybody wants a brochure from this place, and this won't be enough. Could you find some additional, please?"

The girl glanced at the pile Cora shifted in front of her. "Yes, of course. I'll get them from the office. I'll be just a minute."

Cora smiled sweetly until the clerk left the room and spun the register around. Flipping back pages, she quickly located the weekend she'd stayed at Water Lilies. Scanning the names with dreadful expectation, she found what she'd been looking for. Artistically scrawled under Friday, the day before the disappearance was Frederick, with a totally illegible last name. Cora swallowed hard and stared at the slanted handwriting. She could barely turn the book back before the girl reappeared with a hefty stack of brochures. Cora accepted them with a profusion of thanks and headed up the steps. Frederick had been in the area that weekend after all.

Why would a hit man stay at the same place as the victim? It would be so easy to simply stake the place out by boat and wait for the perfect opportunity. The endless maze of watery aisles would provide easy escape for someone who knew the area or hired a local guide. But Freddie the hit man? No, that wasn't possible. He was too irreverent, too spontaneous to live the life of a paid assassin. The only crime she could picture Freddie capable of was filching mangoes from a market stand, or skipping out on a bar tab to stick his drinking buddies. Yet he'd been here. She was sure of it.

Cora found Andy lazily leaning on the doorjamb, waiting for her to come up. He had two glasses in hand; something amber sloshed over the ice cubes as she took one from him. He had set her bag on the bed closest to the door. She spotted an almost full bottle of bourbon on the dresser and he'd opened the French doors to the balcony. A gentle breeze fluttered the sheer lace curtains.

"You brought a full bottle for a one-night getaway?" she asked.

"Never know when something might call for a celebration."

She took a sip, smiled her appreciation, then announced, "I'm going down to the study to finish that story and download it to Jim's computer tonight. I'm not getting fired over a story that's three-fourths done." She saw the look of disappointment on his boyish face. Apparently, he thought they'd tie one on sitting out in the night air, listening to swamp frogs serenade their mates. Not a bad idea, but she didn't want to give Andy any notions. A woman can usually tell when a man was getting a notion, and it was written all over Andy. But he seemed like a schoolboy next to Ethan. A child, an amateur.

I should talk about amateurs, she thought, grabbing her laptop and carrying her drink downstairs. She could count her dates on one hand before meeting James Dearing. She'd been swept off her feet in courtship and married right after college graduation. Her experience with men had been limited to college boys with sex and sports on their minds, then one smooth-talking lawyer who wanted to control her and every other female who ventured into his sphere. She had trusted her ex-husband, and he'd proven not worthy of her exclusive devotion. Was she about to make the same mistake twice?

Andy Bowen was as misguided pursuing her as she was thinking about a future with Ethan. A guy with a chauffeur was definitely out of her league. What would that kind of wealth be like? To open your bills and simply pay them, not bothering to stack in order of dire repercussions as they waited their turn to be paid. Or better yet, to have someone else pay them—an accountant or a business manager. What would it be like to go shopping and not head for the final clearance rack? Yet, she'd never minded the clearance rack, or clipping coupons for the grocery store, or seeing movies during bargain matinees. Pleasure lies in the enjoyment of something new to wear, or the movie, or buying what you need regardless of the measures you took. It wasn't Ethan's wealth that appealed to Cora. It was something far less tangible. Call it *élan*, his aura of cool reserve that said he could handle anything in his path without raising his voice above a bedroom drawl. And that accent—she'd willingly listen to that man recite the phone book some evening, just to hear him talk.

Cora booted her computer, finished her drink, and dug out her notes. Fantasizing about Ethan wasn't getting the feature story done to keep her marvelously low-paid job. She'd polish off this assignment and go to bed early, to be fresh for the morning conference. The key to their story lay with April Rothman. Cora didn't like the aspersions cast on Ethan. She was certain when she got to the bottom of this, his name would be cleared. And the former grew less and less important than the latter. She could live without a promotion to reporter, but Cora didn't wish to consider the day Ethan no longer lurked around the next corner.

No matter how feverishly she typed and edited, the story dragged on past midnight. Her mind kept straying to a tall, narrow-hipped man with large hands and silky hair. She could smell his citrus aftershave and taste his tender kiss even though alone in the room, except for antebellum ghosts from another age.

Hopeless, that's what she was. She just prayed she was hopelessly lazy and not hopelessly in love.

EARLY MORNING IN the Louisiana bayou—there was really nothing like it. Even the light was different—slanted, diffused, soft. The smells of salt marsh and the tangy sea air from afar combined with the scent of dying plant life in the ever-renewing cycle of rebirth. A hush hung over the swamp as if a parochial schoolmarm had finally quieted down the class. The tumult from the night before would start up any moment. But for now, Cora sipped her strong coffee on the wrought-iron balcony and enjoyed the serenity. The coffee had been delivered to her door by the proprietor who again expressed gratitude for her article in his singsong mixture of French and English.

Cora headed into the bathroom with her bag the moment she heard Andy rouse from sleep. The next he saw her, she was dressed in a linen shift and headed downstairs for breakfast. His second look of disappointment ebbed her enthusiasm a tad, but she promised to save his place at the table. The two of them ate hearty breakfasts of mushroom omelets and croissants quickly and headed to Water Lilies. Andy peppered her with questions about her previous stay the entire drive over.

Mr. and Mrs. Roussard greeted Cora with warm hugs and a peck on the cheek. All rather unexpected considering the unwanted publicity that weekend had garnered. Andy and she were shown to an airy conference room, already filled with reporters. Everyone else had gotten up earlier to catch the worm, or at least a good seat. Andy nodded to several other journalists. Cora recognized no one, except for April.

"Good morning, Mrs. Dearing," April said in a smooth cultured voice, not the one used on their previous acquaintance.

"Good morning, Miss Rothman." Cora smiled and offered her hand. "I'm so sorry your mother is still missing. This must be horrible for you," she said in a soft voice.

"Thank you... Cora. No one seems to understand just how dreadful this is." April dropped Cora's hand and picked up a lacy hanky from her lap. Her gaze held Cora's just for a moment, then assessed Andy Bowen, from his tousled hair, down to his scuffed loafers. Cora thought she saw a tiny smile in reaction to his appearance. "We'll begin in a moment, as soon as Marie brings the coffee service."

Marie? Cora thought. Now April was on a first name basis with a woman she'd considered a backwoods anachronism two weeks ago. Cora studied April furtively while she set up her tape recorder and retrieved her pad and pen. The baggy dinner suit had been replaced by a chic outfit with a low-cut jacket and slim skirt. In black, of course. She looked like she'd lost ten pounds in the past two weeks, too. Worrying herself down to a wraith—the diet of the new millennium. Her shoes were expensive wisps that cost a month's salary for Cora, and even the mousy brown non-hairdo had been cut and spiked into a fun style. *This kitten has blossomed, out from under the daunting, critical eye of mama cat.*

April sipped her coffee and cleared her throat, drawing everyone's attention. She crossed her legs at the knee, exposing a fair amount of thigh. A somber pose overtook her features. "I called this press conference today, despite my pain in talking frankly...about my worst suspicions, because I think only the press," she made a small gesture at the journalists hanging onto her words, "will make a difference in this case." She paused again, as though expecting questions.

A middle-aged newsman from the local TV station

did not disappoint her. "What difference can we make, Miss Rothman?"

"I have told many of you my suspicions…that my mother is dead." She drew a halting breath. "Killed by my father, or more likely, by someone hired by my father." Cora narrowed her eyes at April and glanced around the room. None of the other reporters seemed to question that theory. Could it be that Detective Rhodes dropped the tidbit about Mr. Rothman having little motive into her lap and no one else's? Why in the world would he do that?

"He has remarried and perhaps doesn't like the alimony he must pay." She tossed her head. "For whatever reason, I believe my mother is dead." She held a steady posture, meeting the eyes of several reporters in succession before continuing. "The police have more information on this matter than they're releasing. A lot more. As you know, Antoine, the proprietor of the seafood restaurant where we all dined—" She nodded at Cora. "—and where my mother was last seen, is dead. He apparently took his own life." Her face scrunched into a grimace as though she got a whiff of something distasteful. "What they are not revealing is that he not only left a suicide note, written in his own hand, but also confessed to the murder of my mother."

You could have heard the clock hand sweep; it grew so silent for a moment, then a bevy of questions broke loose.

"Why would he kill your mother, Miss Rothman?"

"Why, for money, of course. Mrs. Dearing will attest that that hovel he ran was so neglected, it was about to sink into the bayou."

"How do you think he pulled it off, with all of you right there in the restaurant?"

"He created a diversion. He must have drugged Cora or something because she became quite ill moments after we ate. Everyone's attention was on her." She fixed her green eyes challengingly on Cora.

The faces swiveled toward Cora, but none looked as thunderous as Andy's. "I thought, partner, you would've shared that info with me."

"I told you I got very sick. I thought it was food poisoning at the time," Cora whispered hotly in his ear. He scowled at her and turned his attention back to April.

"My mother wandered outside while everyone hovered over Cora. There wasn't anything she could do to help since that pushy Mr. Auxier kept telling everyone to back off."

Like Ada Rothman wanted to hold my head up while I barfed, Cora thought.

"Of course, I've recently found out his real name is Galen. It's anyone's guess why he was out here under a false name." She shot Cora a curious look then continued. "By the time we got Cora resting comfortably in the spare room, my mother was nowhere to be found." April actually dabbed the corner of one eye with the lacy handkerchief. "Antoine saw his opportunity and made his move. A man like him, a swamp dweller, would know what to do with a woman's body so it wouldn't be found."

Cora stared at her. She'll lose a lot of sympathy in Lafourche Parish if Andy printed April's disparagement of swamp dwellers. What an odd thing to say. Rehearsed, that's how the whole tale sounded. Why would she have to rehearse anything? Then the mention of a name pulled her back from her own thoughts.

"—that Mr. Auxier, or Galen, or whoever he is had a hand in this. He argued with my mother the evening before—an older woman he'd never met before—and spoke exclusively in French with Antoine before and during lunch." She smoothed a hand over a crease in her skirt.

"He knew that none of us spoke French from the previous evening." Again, she fastened Cora with a look that implied corroboration of her story.

"Actually, the restaurant was filled with French-speaking people. I'm sure if Mr. Galen and Antoine were plotting your mother's demise, one of those fishermen would've said something," Cora said, before she could stop herself.

The reporters in the room glanced at Cora for a moment and resumed their rapid-fire questions. But April uncrossed her legs and rose to her feet, keeping her gaze trained on Cora. It was a look of cold, singular anger.

Something very wicked was afoot here; of that Cora was certain.

"I thought you'd become smitten with that man's charm, Mrs. Dearing. Perhaps that has prevented you from remembering things as they really were." April spoke in a smooth, quiet voice as though the two women were alone and not in a room filled with reporters. "That's all, gentlemen and ladies. I suggest you direct your inquiries to the detectives assigned to my mother's case. Perhaps they'll offer logical explanation as to why they've withheld the contents of the suicide note. If they have any, other than perhaps some inside loyalty between the NOPD and the Provincial Trust Insurance Agency." She walked toward the conference room doors as though on a New York catwalk.

"What connection to Provincial Trust, Miss Rothman?" At least three journalists shouted the question in unison.

"I might as well tell you." She brought her hand up to her collarbone and rubbed lightly, as though suffering from mild heartburn. "My mother took out a rather large policy with Provincial Trust last year so that I would be provided for in the event of her death. The life insurer can be forced to pay the policy with a documented signed confession by the killer and not allowed to wait the customary seven years when there's no body." This time her eyes filled with tears, and she allowed one to drop to her pale cheek before dabbing with her hanky.

Too bad the Oscar nominations for Best Actress are already out. Cora followed the rest of the reporters into the grand foyer, but April Rothman had already fled up the stairs. The proprietor blocked the path of two newsmen who tried to follow her.

Andy Bowen grabbed her arm, pulling her away from the milling crowd. "Great, Cora. Now the evening news will have you as the smitten woman, part of the plot, implying you staged your illness to assist the murder," he said, next to her ear.

"I had nothing to do with her disappearance. I really was sick." Cora jerked her arm away from his grasp.

"Look, Cora. I believe you, but just because it's the truth doesn't mean that's what will be printed."

"That sucks, Andy! Why not throw in that I'm pregnant with a three-headed baby, fathered by an alien invader, if we're going to sink to tabloid level?"

Andy took her arm again and dragged her out to the porch. "Better shut up about you being pregnant," he warned softly and didn't sound like he was kidding. "I don't make the rules of the game, Cora. You're the one who wants in on the investigative reporting game. What did you think it was about—telling the truth and nothing but the truth?"

Cora needed a little space away from Andy. She turned, but he held her arm tightly. "And stay away from Galen. There was a ten million dollar policy on old lady

Rothman. That's a lot of money. Enough money to motivate a person to do a lot of bad things."

She yanked away and stomped down the steps, across the long sloping lawn to water's edge, but not before she heard his final admonition.

"Grow up," he hissed at her retreating back.

ETHAN GALEN PACED the length of the expansive living room of his Rue Royal apartment. The French doors to the gallery overlooking the street stood open, allowing the breeze from the bedroom windows to flow through. Today the Quarter smelled pleasant, a rich blend of spicy cooking odors, salty air from downriver and magnolia—at their peak in the square. It helped that the streets had been power-washed last night after the normal business-as-usual spilled beers on Bourbon. But even if the Quarter had smelled like a park pit toilet, as it had after Katrina, it wouldn't have soured his mood anymore than it already was. He had spent the morning with his mother and *grandmère*.

He sweated as he paced like a caged animal, soaking the back of his starched shirt, but he couldn't sit down. He was a caged animal without options to affect the events happening around him. He could only watch while his name was run through the gutter by a newspaper that had no clue what damage it wreaked with innuendo. Not that he and his siblings hadn't given them plenty of legitimate fodder to work with in the past. But despite his every attempt to provide this fellow Bowen at *The Times* with other avenues to pursue, the man had dragged his name into the story. And lately, Cora's, too. Out-of-control—that's what Ethan felt. Powerless to protect his mother and grandmother from embarrassment that their offspring was involved in a woman's murder.

Now he was powerless to keep Cora from being implicated in the whole distasteful mess.

He rammed his fist against the two-hundred-year-old
doorjamb, sending the chandelier into a jangling sway. He
didn't feel the pain shoot up his arm. The memory of the
morning breakfast on his grandmother's terrace caused
a pain far more acute. *Grandmère* was eighty years old
and from an era where honor, respect, and dignity were
qualities people valued more than money or possessions.
She dressed in flowing silk dresses even if she didn't
plan to leave her drawing room. She smelled of verbena
and talcum powder and talked in Parisian French that
put his teachers to shame. She was a lady, down to her
last bird-sized bone.

Grandmère, pale and wan, had hugged him warmly
and asked, "What is happening, *mon petit*? Why do they
keep saying you had something to do with that poor woman's disappearance?"

*Because I'm involved up to my eyeballs. And I would
do anything to spare you this shame. Anything, that is,
but give up the ten million dollars at stake. That, I cannot do. That, the family cannot afford to happen. I am
my father's son. I cannot allow the family to sink into financial ruin if there's something I can do to prevent it.*

But he had only hugged the tiny woman and murmured, "Don't trouble yourself. I will get to the bottom
of this and the paper will print a retraction."

"When pigs fly" had been his mother's uncharacteris-
tic retort. She had glowered at Ethan. "What is that over-
paid investigator Price doing? And what about the team
of expensive lawyers we have on retainer? Can't they
threaten a slander lawsuit?" His mother, a larger woman
than *grandmère*, stood tall in her silk suit and high-heeled
pumps. She spoke English usually in a well-modulated

voice, except when directly addressing her mother, and seldom minced words.

"So far, nothing they printed has been a falsehood. Innuendoes and insinuations, yes, but you can't sue a paper for them," Ethan replied through gritted teeth.

The women had just begun to live down Chloe's latest reckless behavior at school. Luckily, charges against her had been dropped with a stern lecture. The sorority had been placed on warning, which meant no alcohol in the house for six months or they'd lose their charter. That should do the girls' grades a world of good, he thought. And Chloe's promise to her mother to straighten up had seemed sincere. His mother didn't have a chance to recover her dignity from that debacle at her Tuesday bridge games before this story broke.

"Oh, Clotilde, did I read correctly in the paper? Do they really believe Ethan is a murderer? And why was he out there in the bayou using his *grandpere's* name?"

Why, indeed. The latest story, courtesy of Andy Bowen, reported that the mysterious Ethan Auxier was really Ethan Galen of New Orleans, of one of the French Quarter's oldest families. His explanation that he preferred to travel anonymously had received the same cool stare from both women at breakfast. One of them he suspected didn't believe the explanation; the other was insulted by it.

What troubled him most was Cora's potential reaction. He'd not talked to her since the story broke and dreaded facing her after his deception. Her trust of mankind in general tottered on shaky ground. He didn't like admitting he had lied. Not to Cora. She was one person who deserved honesty, and that wasn't something he had to offer at the moment.

The whole idea of wooing her while he had a job to do

had been a mistake from the start. He was in no position to offer a "nice" girl anything. All he offered were lies and subterfuge. Like attracts like—perhaps he should return to the seedy bars of the Quarter and seek his ilk—women who appreciated his easy spending and fast life and didn't give a nickel whether he swore the moon was made of green cheese.

"*M'sieu* Galen?" The soft voice of Jeanette interrupted. "You have a phone call." The dignified woman had glided into the room, handed him his cell phone and slipped out.

"Hello?" he asked expectantly, hoping against the odds it would be Cora. It wasn't.

"Ethan. It's me." Freddie's distinctive voice needed no identification. "You're not going to believe this."

"Where are you?" Ethan asked.

"Lafourche. Listen, I just left Water Lilies. April Rothman was here, giving a damn press conference. Can you believe it? Price lost her, and I found her. How do you like that?" The pride in his voice came through the line loud and clear.

"I don't like it at all. April Rothman called a press conference back at Water Lilies?" Nothing made sense about that. She'd practically disappeared from the face of the earth for the past week.

"That's right. And only certain news services were invited to the little soiree. Bowen was here from *The Times*, and guess who was with him?"

"I have no time for guessing games, Freddie. Who the hell was with him?" he snapped.

"Ms. Cora Dearing, also of *The Times*."

"She's a damn feature story writer. Why the hell would she be there?"

"I don't know, boss. I'm just a gardener, filling in while the regular one's out sick. I just happened to be trimming the hedge by the conference room windows," he said with a smug laugh.

"Freddie, listen to me. Get back to town and stay away from April Rothman. Do you hear me? Stop sticking your nose into this. You're not the one to deal with it." Ethan's anger waned. Now he felt something more insidious. The hairs stood up on the back of his neck.

"Hey, Price can't seem to handle the job. Why not put me on retainer? Just until my next acting assignment comes up, of course."

Ethan heard the note of seriousness in Freddie's usual bluster, and it made him very uneasy. "Get back to town, and we'll talk tomorrow."

"Sure, boss. You want me to fix it so this Bowen guy slips on a banana peel before I go? He seems to be trying to get friendly with your girl." Freddie's voice intoned a decent John Wayne imitation.

"She's not my girl." *At least, not yet*, he thought. "Don't let Cora see you out there, you numbskull. She'll think I put you up to this."

With this, Freddie ranted a string of expletives in French, not pleased with the numbskull moniker. Ethan didn't understand all of them but dared not ask anyone for a translation.

"Freddie, *Je suis désolé*, my friend. We'll talk tomorrow. Please, let Nate and me handle this."

Freddie mumbled acknowledgment in French and hung up. Ethan stared out the open door to the street below and sprang from the room.

"Jeanette? Jeanette, where are you?" He searched the six rooms, finding her on the back steps to the garden, wearing a wide-brimmed hat and carrying shears. He nearly fell over her as he opened the door and rushed through.

"You have found me, Ethan. Although I wasn't trying too hard to hide from you," she said in heavily accented English.

"That's good. What about tonight, Jeanette? You know, for your dinner party idea for Cora?" he asked in a rush. "Remember, the Chateaubriand on the patio? Is it too late to pull it together?"

Jeanette looked steadily at him. "I remember. It is not too late. Call her, Ethan. Don't take no for an answer," she added over her shoulder and continued down to the garden. He could be mistaken, but he'd swear he heard her chuckling.

Ethan knew what he had to do. Cora was getting too close and he knew how dangerous that could be. If he had to, he'd fabricate a bag full of lies to protect her. He couldn't walk away now; he could only pray she didn't hate him when this was over.

EIGHT

CORA SIMPLY SAID yes without even considering the idea. A dinner invitation at Ethan's home sounded like a lovely idea after the interview with April, the fight with Andy, and the long, silent ride back to New Orleans. She was hot, tired, and hungry when Bowen dropped her off at her cottage. He had tried to make amends for his pushy ways, but Cora had ignored him. She didn't like his implication that she was involved in the disappearance. Friends should trust and believe their friends.

During dinner she would have a chance to ask Ethan how he knew the detective would be in Lafourche and a few other things as well.

"Here we are, Miss," the limo driver called, stopping in front of an antique gallery. Nate tipped his hat as their eyes met in the rearview mirror. "I'll leave the car on the street and stay nearby, should you have need to rush out and make your escape." His grin suffused his face, and she couldn't decide if he was sympathetic or mocking her.

"Thanks, Nate. That's reassuring, considering you know your employer better and what he's capable of at a dinner party." She swung her legs out, accepting his hand in assistance.

"Yes, Miss, that is the honest truth." He winked at her and punched a security code into a box mounted on the stone wall. The wrought-iron gate swung open. "Mr. Galen wishes you to join him in the garden." He nodded toward the flagstone path next to the building. "I hope everything lives up to your expectations." Another tip of the cap, then Nate disappeared into the people thronging down Royal.

"I should've brought Lara," she mumbled and followed the pathway to the back. Ducking under an arched arbor covered with wisteria, she found a secret garden behind the gallery, unimagined from street side. A stone wall divided the garden from the one behind and from the buildings on either side. Ethan sat at the table reading the paper, his feet propped on the arm of the other chair.

"Cora," he said, scrambling to his feet. "I'm glad you accepted my invitation at such short notice." He met her halfway across the patio and led her to a chair. A single white rose waited on the seat. She picked it up and breathed in its fragrance, even though she hated the smell of roses. Her eyes took in the elegantly set table, the bottle of wine breathing on the side cart and the massive bouquet of gardenias in the center. Gardenias—he'd have much to explain.

She took the chair he held for her and tugged down her short dress. Suddenly she wished she'd worn something long and baggy, instead of a slip-like dress that her mother would describe suitable only for sleeping. It was so bloody hot, she preferred not to perspire all evening.

She unfolded her napkin but didn't take her gaze off him. "I'm curious about something, Ethan. Why did you really use the name Auxier while you were in Lafourche?" Her eyes challenged him with their directness. She wouldn't let him off the hook this time.

A tiny smile turned up the corners of his mouth and he nodded as though reluctantly acquiescing. "The name Ethan Galen ranks right up there with mold in the Quarter. You are new to town, *cher*. The rumor mill won't touch you for twenty years hence." He poured bloodred wine into two stems and handed her one. "I sowed my wild oats while young, and unfortunately continued my errant ways when not-so-young." There was no swagger, no bravado in his voice. "Right up until a couple years ago, eat-drink-and-be-merry was my sole motto to live by. There was one more verb in that list that Freddie liked to chant, but I'll not repeat it in front of a lady."

Cora inexplicably felt herself flush, as if she hadn't gone to college and spoken that very verb herself occasionally in the sorority house. She sipped the wine; it was very dry and hinted of oak. It reminded her of autumn vacations in the Smoky Mountains. "What made you decide to mend your ways?"

"The wisdom that comes with age, *cher*, but I discovered it's not so easy to turn over a new leaf here. Everyone has expectations, positive or negative, and it'll take years for those expectations to change." He stared over her head, then directly into her eyes. "I disgraced my family with my behavior, my father in particular, Cora. I would give anything to be able to do things differently."

Cora felt the heat from his gaze burn through her, scorching down to her toes and up into her scalp. Luckily, a tiny woman wheeled a cart onto the terrace, breaking the intensity. She parked it next to the table and smiled warmly at Cora.

"Cora, this is Jeanette Peteriere, my housekeeper and lifelong friend. Jeanette, Cora Dearing." Cora extended her hand and the woman clasped it briefly, flashing obsidian eyes. "A pleasure to have you as our guest, Miss." The richness of her Creole accent was more musical than the strains of jazz wafting over the garden wall. Then Jeanette added to Ethan, "I carved the roast, *M'sieu*, so you wouldn't hack it as usual. The dessert is on the counter. I will retire now."

"Thank you, Jeanette. I'm sure it will be delicious."

"It will be. Good night, *M'sieu.*" She nodded at him, then Cora, and walked slowly to the kitchen.

Cora giggled, turning her attention back to Ethan.

Ethan swept off the cover of the Chateaubriand. The mingled aromas of herbs, vegetables and meat assailed them. "I may sign her paycheck, but as you can guess, Jeanette is in charge here."

"She wouldn't have stayed here if you were hopelessly dissipated," Cora said, then regretted it. The subject of his lamentable past deserved to be dropped.

"I'm eternally grateful that she has. She's been the bridge between my parents and me, smoothing things over, telling little lies." He spooned a hearty portion onto her plate. "My mother and grandmother know my commitment to undo the damage my behavior caused."

"Well, then. All is well. Everyone has a wild time in his life, although mine was probably briefer than yours," she teased. "Everything is smoothed over now." She took a bite of the beef. It melted in her mouth like nothing she'd ever cooked.

Ethan watched her eat for a few minutes, delighting in her enjoyment of the meal. Then he spoke in a quiet voice. "Not everything can be smoothed over, Cora. Life seldom offers a get-out-of-jail-free card for our actions. My father died during the height of my…dissipation. He was disappointed in all his children, but thoroughly ashamed of me, his eldest son."

Cora's fork halted halfway to her mouth. The garden suddenly quieted, as though the mosquitoes and crickets were shocked into silence by his story. "Parents often say one thing, but feel another," she offered. "They don't want their kids to grow reckless if they show too much approval."

"Sweet, dear Cora. I'll bet you never gave your mother a moment of heartache. Probably her only worry was whether you took your umbrella if it threatened rain." His face had darkened into the shadows when he'd pushed himself back from the table.

Cora didn't appreciate his Pollyanna idea of her life. It sounded pretty boring. "Well, I'll have you know, I painted my face, rode in fast cars, and even went bra-less once." She popped one last carrot in her mouth and pushed away her plate with a glare.

He reached across the table to touch her hand. "I didn't mean to offend you. *Je suis désolé*, Cora. Tell me about your wild life. Soothe my soul that I'm not the only depraved person in New Orleans." He topped off her glass. "I especially want to hear how you came by the title of Mrs. Dearing. If you tell me the scoundrel led you into your life of debauchery, I will find him and challenge him to a duel." He leaned out of the shadows, his eyes flashing. "Tell me you were married in name only, an arranged marriage by your parents, and the man never joined you here in the New World."

"A duel? What century are you from? I should've been that lucky. No, Jim Dearing swept me off my feet when I was an undergraduate and he was in Law School. He thought I came from a good family in Columbia that would help his political aspirations." She hoped her voice didn't sound as bitchy to his ears as to hers. "We were married after a brief courtship, then he ran for District Attorney. My parents and sister thought I had done well for myself." Cora took another sip of wine, hoping he wouldn't push her for more. James Dearing was her least favorite subject to discuss. And did she really use the word courtship?

Unfortunately, Ethan shook her arm with eyes twinkling with mischief. "And did you do well for yourself, *ma petite*?"

"No," she answered flatly. "He was controlling and vindictive, and…a philanderer. Every woman still breathing was viewed as either a voter to be wooed or someone to be seduced, if the spirit moved him. And that spirit moved him a lot." She gazed into his eyes with determination. "I swore off men for life after going through a nasty divorce. Most of my friends actually believed me silly not to look the other way with his indiscretions. I considered becoming a nun, but the fact I'm Protestant stood in my way." Cora relaxed against the chair back. The retelling had become easier with time.

Ethan leaned toward her and caressed her cheek with his fingertips. "Then I'm glad you're not a Catholic." He brought her captive hand up to his mouth and kissed her knuckles. "But if we wed, my *grandmère* will insist that you convert." A smile widened his mouth, crinkling the skin around his eyes into a web of tiny lines.

"You'd have to hog-tie me, *M'sieu* Galen, to get this girl down the aisle. Once bitten, twice shy." She found herself moving toward him, too, without realizing it.

"I'll keep a length of rope in my back pocket at all times. I'm a patient man." His last two words were barely audible as his lips closed over hers in a kiss both tender and tentative. His mouth teased and played like children experimenting behind the schoolyard for the first time. He nipped her lower lip and traced over her front teeth with his tongue. Strange things happened in Cora's belly and lower down that had nothing to do with digestion. She couldn't pull back from his delicious mouth anymore than she could resist ice cream on a July day.

Ethan shoved aside the dinner dishes and grasped both of her forearms. His mouth sought hers with new intensity, a demand that both empowered and frightened Cora at the same time. His tongue probed her mouth deeply, tasting and savoring, drawing her into a sensual tangle of emotions. Slowly, yet irrevocably, her own needs and desires fought their way to the surface and she returned his kiss with passion to match.

"*Laissez le reste de ma vie avoir lieu comme ce moment*," he whispered when they separated. His hand trailed up her arm to her neck and cupped the back of her head. His fingers entwined in the knot of hair coiled at the nape. He released the springy clip, ruffling her hair across her shoulders and down her back. "Lovely," he murmured.

Cora pulled back from his mouth and hands, which seemed to be everywhere at once. "What did you say?" She gave her head a little shake, as though rousing from a dream.

Ethan stood and walked languidly around the table. "I don't know. When?" He stood over her, looking down with eyes filled with earth-old signs of desire.

"Just now. In French. I need to bring an interpreter to our dates to make sure you're not saying I have butter on my nose or my scuffed shoes are untied." Cora did what she always did when nervous, made little jokes to distract the attention from herself.

"Trust me, *cher*. Any discussions regarding butter or shoelaces will always be in English," Ethan drawled in a husky voice. He pulled her to her feet and backed her firmly against the ancient oak sheltering the table with its massive branches. His mouth found her neck this time, plying the length with nips and laves. Her own hands helplessly lifted from her side to settle around his narrow hips.

"Ahh," he groaned. "I thought I would die waiting for you to touch me," he whispered into her hair.

"I told you. I'm out of practice. I thought I'd grow old celibate." Her hands roamed to cup his butt through his trousers and felt the intimate response press against the front of her dress. He drew her even closer. Both arms tightened around her back, locking her against a hard chest and taut thigh muscles. He felt like raw power; power she'd never experienced before despite all James Dearing's blustery machinations. Her breath caught in her throat, bringing a momentary panic reaction. She pushed against his chest with both hands. He immediately released her.

"What's wrong, Cora?"

"I need some air." She stepped around him, crossing her arms protectively over her chest. "We're going too fast. I need things to slow down, Ethan." Petulant and childish, that's how she sounded. "Let's have some coffee and talk." Her voice sounded alien even to her own ears, like the wrong soundtrack for a video.

"Whatever pleases you, Cora." He walked toward the steps up to his suite of rooms, but pleasure had vanished from his voice.

For a fleeting moment, she considered bolting for the walkway back to the street, but Andy Bowen's admonition still haunted her. *Grow up.* The words echoed in her ears because she knew he was right. It was time to stop hiding and spying and watching life. Time to take a chance, but she doubted the wisdom of taking that chance with a rich, indolent libertine, who most of New Orleans thought was a murderer.

Cora followed him up the steps and into the house. The kitchen glowed from polished brass and white enamel, along with Art Deco light fixtures throwing off diffused light. She spotted an eight-burner commercial stove—seven too many for her needs—but loved the narrow, efficient room immediately.

Ethan was already pouring coffee into two mugs. He glanced up when she entered. "Jeanette left this on the warmer. I don't suppose I could talk you into having dessert up in my bedroom." He pointed to a chocolate torte on the counter, dripping with cherry glacé, and flashed a wide grin.

"No, I think I'll just have coffee with milk here in your kitchen." She returned the smile, slipping onto a tall stool.

Ethan carried over the mugs and pulled up the other stool. "Can't blame a guy for trying, can you? I suppose I'll totter into senility celibate along with you, since there's no other woman for me but you."

Why does he say things like that? Is he trying to be funny? He couldn't possibly be serious.

Could he? "We'll discuss the drawbacks of chaste behavior later," she said, sipping her coffee, fully recovered and businesslike. "I have a theory."

That drew Ethan's attention away from the torte he'd been picking at with his finger. "What is it, my favorite nun?"

"To start with, Daddy Rothman didn't do it." She waited for a reaction and was disappointed. Ethan returned to digging at the cherries in the glaze.

"There was no reason to, besides the fact he'd never been in the South, for all the cops could uncover. No alimony is being paid, never has been. Mrs. Rothman didn't gain her wealth from her ex-husband. He's happily living a middle-class life in Cincinnati. No motive there," she announced.

Ethan barely glanced away from the dessert. He reached for the knife and cut himself a slice. "Are you sure you don't want a piece of this? It is delicious." He brought a forkful to his mouth and savored the taste with enthusiasm.

"Are you listening, Ethan?" She grasped the arm holding the fork.

"Of course, I am, *cher*. Daddy is innocent." He ate another bite of torte.

"But," she emphasized for effect, "daughter may not be." Her voice dripped with mock drama. "There is a ten million dollar life insurance policy on Mrs. Rothman. Ten million dollars, that's a lot of motivation."

Ethan cut himself another slice of the gooey cake and slid it onto his plate. Cora tightened her hold on his arm, shaking it zealously. "And guess who the beneficiary is?"

"The Audobon Society?"

Cora exhaled an exasperated breath. "For a man who half of New Orleans thinks did it, you're not very concerned here."

"*Je suis désolé, m'amie.*" He set his fork down and rocked back against the counter. "I take it April is the beneficiary."

"She is. She probably bumped mother off for the money and had Antoine help her."

"This plot is thickening, no?" He tucked a lock of hair behind her ear with a touch that sent ripples down her spine.

"Yes. Then April bumped off Antoine. That was no suicide. She forced him to write the note admitting the crime, then killed him."

"All by herself? I suppose a Cajun former alligator wrestler would be no match for a Manhattan princess." He waved a forkful of cake before her nose.

Cora ignored both the sarcasm and the cake. He was trying to get her goat. She stood and poured herself more coffee. "Maybe she got the drop on him with a gun. I don't know all the particulars," she snapped. "But I do know that Antoine left a suicide note. The cops hadn't released that tidbit to the papers yet."

This finally got his attention. Ethan set down the fork and waited.

"In this note, he admits to killing Mrs. Rothman. That's supposed to be why he took his own life and stated no one will ever find her body. April forced him to write that; then she killed him," Cora said with great pride.

Ethan was watching her now. "Why would she force him to say that?"

"Don't you ever watch TV, Ethan? With a signed confession, April thinks she can force the insurance company, Provincial Trust, to pay out the proceeds of the policy on her mother without waiting seven years to be declared legally dead, since there's no body."

He pulled the coffee cup from her hand and set it down. "Good work, Agatha Christie. Now stay out of this, my sweet, and let the police do their job. They probably have good reason for not releasing certain information. It could corrupt their investigation and taint evidence. Stick with writing about Mardi Gras preparations for next year."

Cora felt a stab to what only could be her pride. "Do not patronize me, Ethan. The press has a right to uncover information that might protect the public."

"The public would be better protected if they'd just keep their pretty noses in their own business."

Cora sucked in a gasp, silently counting to ten. She was a guest in this man's house. Kicking him in the groin wouldn't make an appropriate thank-you token. "I'd love to continue this stimulating debate with you, but I must use your powder room. Kindly point me in the right direction."

"Through the dining room, up the stairs, the first door on the right. Please don't be angry with me. I just don't want you to get hurt," he called after her.

But Cora was no longer listening. Her eyes had landed on something as she walked through his ornate, expensive dining room. A blue and white Chinese vase sat on a carved armoire. It exactly matched the one that had been refilled twice with flowers at her home. She forced her legs to move through the room toward the bathroom where she splashed cold water on her face in addition to the intended activity. She must reign in her emotions. An hour ago, she thought she was falling in love with the man downstairs. But she didn't like the thought of anyone sneaking around, invading her privacy, and entering her house while she wasn't home. That behavior was over the top, and she needed none of it. This infatuation with Ethan was not a good idea, and the sooner she got over him, the better off she'd be.

Even if he didn't kill anybody.

Cora walked back to the kitchen, allowing her eyes to fasten on the vase again for moral support.

"Ethan," she murmured. "No, don't get up. I'll just let myself out. I'm not feeling well." She kept moving toward the back door.

Ethan flew off the stool and blocked her path instantly. "What's wrong? Was it Jeanette's cooking? I'll fire the woman tomorrow if she poisoned you, too." His signature laugh resounded in the room.

"No, I'm just overtired after my day in Lafourche. Thank you for dinner." She backed away from his hands that tried to embrace her. He looked puzzled and hurt.

She paused in the doorway, remembering something

else she'd learned from the detective, something she had to tell Ethan, even though he was a skulking stalker. "Ethan, the cops were asking a lot of questions...about Frederick."

His laughter ceased. His chin tilted up curiously. "What kind of questions?" he drawled.

"About his connection to you and April Rothman. They seem to think he might have had a hand in this. Helped April with the murder."

Ethan snorted. "That's ridiculous. He doesn't even know April."

"Detective Rhodes said he went to college with her and that he was sweet on her."

Ethan laughed uproariously at this. It rather irritated Cora. "Freddie went to Tulane with me and Nate. That's where he developed the idea of being an actor. He's really not bad on stage."

"Your chauffeur went to Tulane?" she asked after a moment.

Ethan looked a bit taken aback. "Yes, but I didn't say he excelled there." His voice had grown sullen, quiet.

"For the record, I don't believe Frederick had anything to do with it," she said, forcing the memory of Freddie's signature on the B&B register from her mind.

"He didn't. Freddie wouldn't harm a fly." There was no room for discussion in his tone.

Cora glanced back at his set, stony face, then made a quick exit out the door and down the stairs before he could stop her.

And you, cher? Would you harm a fly? she thought.

Cora slipped into the crowd, heading for the opposite end of the Quarter. The walk would do her good since she had no desire to climb into the back of the limo driven by Ethan's chauffeur, Tulane educated or not.

IT WAS A good thing Ethan had been busy all day. First, financial concerns for the family occupied most of the morning. He preferred to look over the mountain of bills for the living expenses for him and the other Galens before sending them to his accountant for payment. He especially loved seeing the tab for tuition and board to keep Chloe in Ole Miss. It helped maintain a hard line during their weekly phone conversation when he counseled her to study more and party less. Then there were the complex adjustments to his extensive portfolio with the help of a broker. He finished around noon with a headache.

He'd woken up with a headache, too, and a dull aggravating pain somewhat lower in the anatomy. That Cora Dearing had escaped from his wit and charm once again last night. Either he was losing his touch with the ladies, or he'd finally met his match. Probably the latter, since she drifted into his dreams and waking thoughts with regular frequency. She was unpredictable, strong-willed, and had a penchant for expressing opinions about things she knew nothing about. But she did so while fluttering the longest eyelashes and adding a shake of her mane of hair for good measure. Hopelessly smitten, that's how *grandmère* would describe him, and it was probably true, as good as that would do him. Cora Dearing would no more take up with him than with Ted Bundy. Each of his moves brought a surprised, wary look to her face. That didn't exactly bode well for him getting-the-girl-at-the-end-of-the-trail.

He'd spent the entire afternoon with Nate in the Jag trying to track down Freddie. He drove the car, while Nate made jokes about him not wearing the livery cap, or not appropriately cutting in and out of traffic like a madman. They had no luck finding Freddie. The search of his haunts in the Quarter—the coffeehouses near Tulane where the streetcar turned around, and the bars in the Garden District where several of his actor friends still lived—proved fruitless. No one had seen him since he'd gone to Lafourche two days ago.

Nate had jimmied the lock to Freddie's tiny apartment with a credit card. Ethan had never been inside his digs before, although he'd dropped him off inebriated at curbside too many times to count. His quarters consisted of three small rooms behind a bar on St. Charles. The stale odor of beer, cigarette smoke, and cooking grease permeated the walls, yet the rooms were not unpleasant. They possessed Freddie's flamboyant, bohemian sense of style with a patched overstuffed wing chair; a tile-topped farmhouse table with three mismatched chairs; and a huge, ornately embellished brass bed. Ethan smiled. The bed was neatly made with a stack of condoms on the nightstand for future needs.

Nothing gave any clue to the whereabouts of the man whose shopping list on the refrigerator consisted of beer, bourbon, and toilet paper.

Ah, Freddie. Reduce life to its simplest terms.

Ethan's attention snagged on a photograph adorning the mantel of the bricked-in fireplace. It was of the three of them in college with their arms around each other's shoulders. The glassy look in their eyes betrayed the fact the requisite beers they showed the photographer hadn't been their first, nor probably even their fifth. The photo, framed and dust-free, brought back fond memories—of youth, friendship, and innocence.

Ethan replaced the snapshot on the mantel. "Let's get the hell out of here. This isn't doing us any good," he said, heading toward the door.

"Hey, let's check if he's got any beer in the fridge," Nate said, walking back into the kitchen. "That mooch drinks all mine every time he stops over." Ethan laughed and waited, anticipating the outcome. Freddie didn't have anything in the fridge but hot sauce, catsup, bottled water, and a jar of peppers with three X's on the label. Nate circled the word beer twice on the shopping list and the two men left, locking the door behind them.

Ethan returned home in a foul mood. A wasted afternoon, and he had no time to waste. Something had to be done about April Rothman, but first, he had to find her. He had made that perfectly clear to Nate when he dropped him off. The last thing he needed to do was read *The Times*, but he couldn't help himself. He was a moth drawn to that particularly blistering flame. It was after six when he opened a beer and settled down on the gallery to read the paper. It didn't take long for him to spot the article.

Police seek man accused of stalking by vacationing heiress. Frederick Bearnard of New Orleans is wanted in questioning for allegedly stalking April Rothman, a former college acquaintance. Miss Rothman is the New Yorker whose mother disappeared mysteriously while alligator watching in the bayou of Lafourche Parish. Bearnard is also wanted for questioning in the said disappearance of Ada Rothman. Bearnard was seen in the vicinity of the Water Lilies Inn the evening before the possible abduction of Mrs. Rothman. Detective Charles Rhodes says foul play is suspected in the disappearance.

Ethan balled up the paper in fury and threw it over the railing, upsetting his bottle of beer at the same time. It crashed to the tile floor with shattering finality. He uncharacteristically left the shards where they fell when he stormed from his apartment a few minutes later. He didn't notice the tiny form of his housekeeper who'd just returned and had stepped into the pantry to stow her umbrella. She noticed him, however, and his agitation. A deeply furrowed brow and pinched lips indicated she shared the same emotion at the moment.

The Jag's tires squealed against the wet pavement as Ethan pulled up in front of the mansion on Ursulines. He knew from Nate that Cora lived in a small house at the back property line. He hadn't bothered to call first or pick up a bottle of wine like he'd envisioned for his first visit to her home. This was not a social call. He could think of only one source where *The Times* could have gotten that information about Freddie. He knocked on her front door, then pounded when no one answered.

"What the devil?" An angry voice could be heard before the door swept open. Cora stood frowning at him, dressed in faded shorts and a cropped T-shirt. Her hair hung in a tangle down her back, with her bangs plastered to her forehead. She looked at though she'd been napping. She rubbed her eyes, not pleased about being jarred awake.

Ethan pushed past her into the cool confines of the room. "You need a doorbell," he muttered.

"You need some manners, Mr. Galen, and an invitation before you push your way into my home." She stood with hands on hips, jutting her chin angrily. "How dare you?"

"How dare I?" he snapped. "How dare you feed that crap to Bowen about Freddie? Knowing full well that they'd print it, not bothering to check if there was even an ounce of truth to it." His tone had lowered to a snarl.

Cora's hands slipped down her sides while the venomous look faded. "Oh, that's what you're mad about," she said, walking toward the sofa and sitting down. She met his gaze, then looked away. "Believe me. I regretted giving the information to Bowen right after the press conference. I wanted to tell you last night, but I didn't."

Her voice faded to a whisper. "I didn't think he'd phrase the article like that."

"How do you think a reporter is going to phrase things, Cora? His job is not to report the truth, but to sell papers. Period."

"I didn't tell him anything that wasn't true." She held up her hand before he could speak. "The detective was looking for Freddie to question him about April's stalking assertion. Rhodes told me so. And he said Freddie was a college chum of April's."

Ethan walked toward her, his anger ebbing in her confusion. He lowered himself to his haunches in front of her. "Cora, I told you. Freddie did not go to school with April. She probably never even went to college." He spoke the words patiently, like to a child.

Cora looked him in the eye. "You didn't tell me that until last night. I'd already told Andy in the morning, and the story had gone to print."

Ethan snaked his fingers through his hair. "All lies, all manufactured lies by that bitch." He put a tentative hand on her knee.

Cora placed her hand of top of his. "Frederick was in Lafourche the night before the abduction. I saw his name on the register of the B and B down the road."

Ethan stared at her, not believing, then blinked like an owl. "Now April knows he had been there, too."

"And why was he there, Ethan?" Cora tightened her hold, but he pulled away and stood abruptly.

"I don't know, but I do know he's not involved with this. You shouldn't have fed this crap to Bowen. And your name is with his on the byline."

She winced at that. "Ethan, that was an error. A mistake. My name shouldn't have been there. Bowen was just trying to score some points with me."

"Why?" he asked. "Is there something between you two? I think I have a right to know." The reason for the visit suddenly turned into something else. Ethan didn't like the intense jealousy he was feeling over this Bowen jerk trying to impress Cora.

You want me to fix it so this Bowen guy slips on a banana peel before I go? He seems to be trying to get friendly with your girl. Freddie's words rang hollow in his ears. Maybe he should've told his friend yes when he had the chance.

Cora rose to her feet. "Ethan, are you jealous?" Her tone teased and baited. "Of little ole me? Boys haven't fought over me since…well, it's been awhile." She gave a little push to his chest.

Ethan grabbed both her wrists. "Don't change the subject, *cher*. Yes, I'm jealous. I want no other man near you until I know what's in your heart." He loosened his grip and lowered his voice. "But I didn't come here to talk about my heart or yours." He dropped his head to be on eye level with her. "You have to decide who you want to be, Cora. You can't have integrity and be a reporter." He released her wrists.

"That's bull, Ethan. Can't you admit you're a bit jaded on the topic from other reporters. Rightly so, I have no doubt, but that doesn't mean all journalists are soulless cretins." She shifted her weight to one hip and glared.

"You must trust me on this. Stay out of it. It's not safe." He paced the length of the room, avoiding her eyes.

"How do you know that? What aren't you telling me?"

Complete silence filled the room as Ethan tried to think of something to say and came up empty. He opened the window, allowing the evening air to fill the room.

"And what's going on with us?" Her voice was softer,

but no less demanding. "You're playing games with me, and I don't like it. Not with everything else going on."

"I'm playing no games, Cora."

"When I got home from work today I found a bottle of wine on my patio that few other people can afford, and magnolias in a vase that exactly matches the one in your dining room. Plus an assortment of pralines on a plate in my own kitchen. I thought the garden visits were rather sweet, but I really don't like anyone coming into my house when I'm not home."

Ethan turned and stared at her. She stood rubbing her forearms as though a chill had come into the room instead of the humid air of August. "I didn't bring you the flowers or the wine or pralines."

"Come on, Ethan. Fess up and I promise I won't be mad. The first time you left the flowers I was kinda spooked."

"The first time? How many times, Cora?"

She studied him with clear intent. "Today was the third."

"On my father's grave, I left you no flowers nor entered your home before tonight," he said softly, and watched the color drain from her cheeks, "but I think I know who did. However, unlike you, I prefer not to accuse the person until I'm certain."

"I never accused Frederick of anything. He's only wanted by the police for questioning."

"The assumption of guilt will remain in people's minds long after they expose the true criminal. It will dog him for the rest of his life by the majority of people who won't bother to disassociate him with the crime."

"You have little faith in humankind."

"*La vérité.*"

Cora opened her mouth to say something, but whatever her retort, it remained unspoken, since her front door opened and in walked Nate Price. His face was colorless, his hair damp and stringy. Both Ethan and Cora stared at him.

"I went to your place," he said to Ethan, "and Jeanette thought you might have come here." His eyes flickered over Cora for a moment, then settled on a spot on the wall.

"What's up, Nate? What's so urgent?" Ethan took a step toward him.

"I was listening to the police scanner and having a few brews." Gone was the country Cajun accent he emulated for Cora's benefit. "It's about Freddie." His eyes darted to Ethan, then away.

"What about Freddie? Spit it out, Price."

"A Frederick Bearnard was found dead in Algiers an hour ago. Narcotics Division is investigating. First officer on the scene described a possible heroin overdose. That's what they reported."

When Nate finally looked Ethan in the eye, his eyes filled with tears.

And Ethan felt his soul drain from his body like rainwater back into the Mississippi.

NINE

"THAT'S NOT POSSIBLE. Freddie didn't touch drugs. He never would." Cora heard the disbelief in Ethan's voice. "It's not possible," he repeated. He stared out the window blankly and lowered his forehead to rest against the window pane.

"I know." Nate's voice was equally filled with pain. Cora never felt so helpless in all her life. Nate approached Ethan and laid a hand on his shoulder. Ethan turned around and the two men clumsily embraced for a minute. Cora felt a stinging longing for a friend who could share such emotion.

Ethan pulled back, bracing both hands against the sill behind him. "Get over to the morgue. Make sure those idiots haven't made a mistake with identification. Find out everything you can." His voice now was controlled, directed.

"You got it, boss." The two men exchanged another poignant look. Nate gave Cora a small nod and walked out into the night.

"Ethan, I'm so sorry," Cora said as soon as Nate had gone. She wrapped her arms around his waist. He didn't pull back or resist the embrace but allowed himself to be enfolded in her arms. She felt him nuzzling her hair while his heart thudded against the thin cotton of her shirt. "You don't think this was an overdose, do you, Ethan?" Cora asked.

"I'm sure it's not. Freddie's sister OD'd when he was

young. He never got over it. He didn't touch the stuff, not even to toke a joint at a rock concert. He just plain wouldn't do it." He trailed a string of tender kisses across her forehead and down her nose. "Please, do something for me without question or argument."

"Anything," she answered without hesitation.

"I have something to do. I'll drop you at my house. You'll be safe there. Wait there until I get back. Can you do that for me, *cher*? I don't want you to stay here alone."

"All right. I'll go to your house, but I don't think I'm in danger." She picked up her purse from the table and allowed him to lead her out to his car at the curb.

Ethan drove like a madman. How no tourists died in the ensuing minutes between their homes would confound anyone. When he pulled up in front of the expensive gallery on Rue Royal, he jotted something on a slip of paper then jumped out to open her door.

"Ethan, I—"

"Later, Cora. Punch this code into the security system and lock up tight behind you. Tell Jeanette not to go out tonight." He pressed the paper into her hand and sprinted back to the driver's side. She stared after him openmouthed. Words tumbled around in her head but refused to organize into one cohesive sentence.

"I adore you, *cher*. Don't be afraid." He flung back a lock of hair that had fallen across his forehead. "While you're here, you might want to ask Jeanette what she knows about the flowers and wine," he said over his shoulder, then ducked into the low car and roared away. There was nothing for her to do but let herself into his home and wait for she knew not what.

"Jeanette?" she called timidly after punching in the code at his back door. She waited, listening to house sounds and strains of rock music mingled with jazz from the bars on Bourbon. She smelled the scent of gardenia before the small, black woman glided soundlessly into the dark kitchen. For an instant, Cora was frightened by the ninety-pound seventy-year-old.

"Miss Dearing? What's happened?" Jeanette asked, with an all-business French accent. She flicked on the kitchen light. All fear faded as Cora saw the look of concern on the woman's aged face.

"Oh, Jeanette. Ethan asked me to wait here for him," she murmured, glancing around the spotless room and met her gaze. "Someone's killed Frederick. The police think it was a drug overdose, but Ethan knows Freddie didn't do drugs."

Jeanette's thin hand grasped her throat. "Frederick?" she gasped. "Who would want to kill little Freddie Bearnard?" Her voice held anguish and pain that only years of friendship could kindle.

Cora smiled inwardly at referring to six-foot-two-inch Freddie as little, considering Jeanette would barely reach five feet tall with heels. "Someone…horrible. I am so sorry," Cora said inadequately and held out her arms to Jeanette. The woman hesitated for a moment and stepped into Cora's embrace. She returned the hug with reserved constraint. Cora inhaled the sweet smell of gardenia on Jeanette's hair and skin.

When the housekeeper stepped back, she dabbed at her eyes and muttered a string of French that Cora thought better than ask for translation. Jeanette walked to the refrigerator and pulled out a pitcher of tea, Ziplock bags of cold cuts, and several jars of olives and peppers.

"Oh, no. Jeanette, nothing for me," Cora said, then realized how presumptuous that might have sounded. "But I'll be happy to keep you company if you'd like a snack."

Jeanette glanced at her over the top of the refrigerator door. "We will both have a sandwich and some tea. No arguments. Ethan tells me you don't know how to cook." She walked to the cupboard and withdrew a two-foot baguette. "So, you probably had nothing to eat today other than Diet Pepsi and Ho-Ho's." The cultured French accent pronouncing the store-bought little cakes made Cora smile. She realized how pointless arguing with this woman would be and sat down at the counter.

Jeanette didn't ask the countless questions most people would when making a sandwich for a stranger. Mustard or mayo? Lettuce and tomato? Peppers, pickles, olives? She made two sandwiches to her own specifications, placing one in front of Cora. Cora took a small bite and smiled. The sandwich was delicious. The two women ate for a few minutes with only street sounds and garden crickets from the back window breaking the silence.

"Ethan thought I should ask you if you knew who might've left flowers, wine, and pralines at my home," Cora asked without preamble.

A rose flush tinged Jeanette's cheeks. Her sandwich paused in the air, midway to her mouth. She lowered it back to her plate and studied Cora. "He did, did he?" She sounded peevish.

"Yes, I don't know why." Cora set her own sandwich down and gestured with her hands. "I was very upset, frightened, really. Somebody's been in my house while I wasn't home. He thought you might be able to shed some light on the matter."

Jeanette thumped her empty tea glass on the counter and released another string of quaint French expressions.

"In English, please."

"If Ethan wouldn't drag his feet, waiting for the right moment, while opportunities slip through his fingers, I wouldn't have had to act in his stead." She flashed an angry look and stomped over to the pie safe. There she withdrew a bottle of bourbon and two glasses. Cora thought better about declining as the woman walked back to the table. "He thinks he has all the time in the world, while it slips through his fingers like sand. He has too much daring in everything else, except women, nice women that is." She appeared to be musing, not addressing Cora at all. "He and that Nathan Price can charm the floozies of Bourbon Street as though a competition, but now that he's smitten by a nice woman, he's bashful and backward like that silly dwarf." Her inflection on the word dwarf rendered the word almost unrecognizable.

"And that nice woman would be me?" Cora asked, taking a small sip of her drink.

Jeanette stared at Cora as though she were a bit addlebrained. "Yes, *M'selle* Dearing. That would be you."

"And you left me the bougainvillea in my backyard?"

"I had too many blooming for house bouquets. They're only at their peak a short while," she said with a shrug.

"And the gardenias?"

"*Oui.*"

"And today's magnolias, wine, and pralines?"

"My sister made those pralines. She has a shop on Decatur. Did you like them?" Jeanette took a sip of the bourbon.

"I haven't tried them yet, but the gardenias were left inside my house, Jeanette."

"That was a lesson for you, *ma petite*; do not leave your doors unlocked. This is New Orleans. Foolish people end up robbed." Then she added quickly, "I'm sorry, *M'selle* Dearing, but it was for your own good."

"Well, I must admit, I'll be careful to lock the doors in the future." It was very hard to stay mad at this determined woman.

"And it was for Ethan's good. He worries about this Bowen boy, but he says nothing to you about his heart." She carried their two plates to the sink.

Cora spluttered on the liquor and set down the glass. "Ethan worries about Andy Bowen? Why?" This was getting interesting.

"I better be quiet now, or he'll make good his threat to fire me. I will be lost if I can't meddle in his life. My grandchildren live in Baltimore. Can you imagine that? Baltimore?" Her tone betrayed sheer incredulity.

"Shocking," Cora answered, since she suspected that was the anticipated reply. "Well, Ethan doesn't have anything to worry about Andy Bowen. He's just a co-worker. Funny, Ethan never struck me as the jealous type."

"He never has been before. Even when his hellcat first wife was caught with a lover in her bed, he didn't raise his voice, or shed a tear, for that matter."

"Ethan was married before?" This time Cora poured them both another shot of bourbon.

"Less than a year. To a woman he met skiing in Lucerne. They lived together for a few months one winter. She told him she was pregnant, so Ethan did the noble thing and married her, bringing her home to New Orleans to meet his family. She wasn't pregnant. That was a lie. A manipulation." Jeanette took another sip. "She was not a wife to him. She spent his money on gambling and cocaine, and buying drinks for everyone in Lafitte's. Ethan was so ashamed to his father for having married someone like that. He wrote a fat check and sent her back to France when he caught her cheating. The only reason she went was because Ethan's father threatened to disinherit him. No more money, no more interest on her part."

Jeanette drained her glass, watching Cora intently. "I have said too much. You now have me at your mercy.

Shall I make an appointment at the unemployment office, *M'selle*?"

Cora smiled. "Absolutely not. I will not divulge the facts revealed here tonight." She made an X motion in the air over her heart.

"They will not appear in tomorrow's *Times*?" Her lips pinched tight; her eyes narrowed.

"No, they won't. Ethan was pretty upset about the story, wasn't he? I couldn't stop it in time. I'm sorry that I said anything to Andy. I thought I owed him something for giving me a chance on a story."

"That is important to you? The story?"

"Well, yes. I want to be a reporter, but I don't want to print lies to get the promotion." Cora felt uncomfortable revealing her career aspirations to the housekeeper, as though she'd just admitted wanting to be the madam in the best whorehouse in town.

"Ah, that is a lesson for you then. Ambition must always be tempered with integrity."

Cora opened her mouth to speak—something to indicate she didn't appreciate the lack of integrity inference, but shut it when nothing brilliant came to mind. "Ethan's father was unhappy with his choice of wife?" she asked instead.

Jeanette remained mute for so long, Cora doubted the woman would answer. "Yes, he was disappointed in Ethan's choice of bride, but that followed other disagreements they'd had. The marriage only brought the matter to a nasty head."

"What did they argue about?"

Jeanette leaned wearily against the chair back. "A parent, especially a father, has strong notions how a first-born son should spend his life. Etienne wanted Ethan involved with the family business. After Ethan divorced

Aimee, he took his papa's advice and came to the office every day. But Etienne died several months later, before…he'd been able to teach Ethan everything he'd wanted." The woman rose and walked to the sink to wash their glasses. "No more, *M'selle*. No more history lesson. You are nosy. I hope that's due to your affection for *mon petit* Etienne, and not for any other reason, or the next bouquet you find on your pillow will be oleander." Jeanette leveled a look that shivered Cora into silence. "Follow me, I will show you where you may retire."

Cora followed the woman into the dining room, through the large living room, then up the narrow stairs. She spied a guest room on the left and a bath directly at the top of the landing. "You'll stay in here," Jeanette said, opening the door to what obviously was the master suite.

"But isn't this—"

Jeanette interrupted with a raised hand. "Lots of towels in the bath. Snoop around to find something to sleep in. You should have no trouble doing that," she said gleefully. Her laugh revealed small white teeth that glowed in the dim hallway.

"Don't you think Ethan would appreciate his privacy when he returns tonight? Perhaps I should stay in the guest—"

"No. Do not argue with me, *M'selle* Dearing. I know what is best." With that she turned and marched down the stairs with surprising agility.

"Good golly, I thought my grandmother was domineering," Cora muttered and entered Ethan's bedroom. It was exactly what she'd expected based on her limited knowledge of his tastes. Elegant, refined, understated, quintessentially male. A massive eighteenth century bed dominated the room, one she suspected wasn't a reproduction. The covers had been yanked up to pillows resting lopsidedly against the headboard. It was the way a man made a bed, not a housekeeper. A matching carved armoire occupied eight feet of wall space away from the gallery, where a battered antique desk sat between the French doors. Its surface was cluttered with coffee mugs, papers, books, a laptop, and boxes of computer discs. The walls held an assortment of framed photographs, mostly of wildlife in the bayou and misty shots of the Mississippi at dawn. Then there was the ubiquitous memorabilia from Tulane and old pennants for the Saints. She shoved over a pile of jeans on the blanket chest and plopped down. The room smelled of Ethan; her skin tingled as the scent elicited memories of his hands and mouth on her skin. Cora sat for several minutes and tried desperately to sift through everything Jeanette had told her. Only slits of streetlight intruded between the louvers in the dark bedroom. Ethan had been married. Why did that surprise her? He was no spring chicken. But in the end, she neither made sense of her conflicting emotions, nor rummaged through his possessions like the nosy person she was thought to be. Instead she undressed, left her clothes in a heap next to his jeans, and slipped into one of his shirts proclaiming *French Quarter: Home of the serious drunk.* She pushed down the covers, crawled under the silky top sheet and fell asleep in minutes with visions of pralines and oleander dancing in her head.

HER DREAMS DID not remain of flowers and candy for long. They were quickly replaced by dreams of a tall, well-built man with big hands. His tender fingers plied her flesh with a touch that electrified every nerve ending before she roused to full awareness.

"Who's been sleeping in my bed, little Goldilocks?" a voice intruded. The dream-man pulled back the sheet, allowing the cool breeze to reach her overheated skin, and reached up her thigh. Cora arched her back, bringing her body closer to his roving hand that halted maddeningly at mid-thigh. Her fingers interlocked behind her head as she stretched out shamelessly before him. "A bit more to the right and a little higher," she instructed in a sleepy voice.

"Anything you wish, *cher.*"

The voice jarred her fully awake. She sat up and stared into Ethan's grinning face. "Good grief. I was dreaming. Sorry. Jeanette told me to sleep in here." She locked her thighs tightly together, drew up her knees, and pulled the sheet over them discreetly.

"Then the area higher and to the right is out of the question?" He leaned forward and kissed her temple.

"For the moment, it is." She leaned against the headboard, rubbing her palms on her cheeks. "What happened tonight? Was it really Frederick?" she asked in a quiet voice.

The question stopped his trailing kisses and roving hands. Cora heard his shoes hit the floor before he stretched out beside her, not touching. He braced his head with his hand. "Yes, Cora. It was Freddie. That bitch murdered him. And she will pay." His voice sounded disembodied and deadly in the darkness. The last of the revelry had died down on Bourbon. The Quarter finally quieted for three hours or so before the shopkeepers returned to sweep the sidewalks of the nightly debris.

"Who? April Rothman? She had something to do with Frederick's death?" She reached out and splayed her fingers across his chest. He had half unbuttoned his shirt and wore no undershirt. Her fingers felt the warm skin and sinewy muscle that covered his ribcage. She heard his intake of breath as he shifted his weight on the bed, but she continued to ply his pectorals with inquisitive fingers.

A hand shot up and captured her wrist tightly. "Do not play with me, Cora. I'm too tired and too strung out. Don't start this game unless you're prepared to finish it." The words drifted on the air, more like a promise than a threat.

"I'm not playing a game with you, Ethan. I assure you, I'll be equally disappointed if we don't see this through." She cocked her head to glimpse his profile in the thin light. Male desire and need never held much appeal to her before. She wanted to make love to him more than draw her next breath. She felt empowered by her own sexuality, not embarrassed by it. This time the urgent touch was hers as she entwined her fingers in his hair and drew his mouth down. "I just hope you're not too tired."

He exhaled a pent-up rush of air. "Don't you worry 'bout that or anything else." He bent his head, brushing his lips against her mouth. Cora kissed him back without shyness, feeling her heat rise in sweet anticipation. Her fingers traced the outline of his stubbly jaw and ran playfully down his chest.

"I want you, Ethan," she whispered, tugging his shirt out of his trousers.

"Ah, but will you still respect me in the morning if I give in to your demands tonight?" he teased, spreading his fingers across her hip and tugging at the thin band of her panties.

"Well, I don't know. Are you willing to take the chance?" She struggled to unbutton his shirt.

"I'm willing to walk across burning coals on my hands if need be. I want you so much." He kissed her softly. "Without an agenda." He deepened his kiss, delving into the inner reaches of her mouth with his tongue. "Without hidden motivation. Just you."

Desire shot through parts of her that had hibernated for years. She arched her back, moving closer to his irresistible caresses. She yearned to discover his body while he explored hers, yet was reluctant to hurry the delicious progression along. His thumbs rubbed her jawline and trailed down the sensitive skin of her neck. He kissed her eyelids, her cheeks, her forehead, even the tip of her nose with childlike exuberance, returning to her mouth with renewed intensity. Mumbled words in French sounded sweet to her ears each time he came up for air.

"In English, please. I want to know what you need to talk about as we make love," she said.

"Some things don't translate, my sweet." He captured her mouth with a crushing kiss that contained none of his earlier playfulness. Soft groans of desire were his only reply as she stroked the length of his ribcage, then tugged the shirt off his shoulder. He sat up to strip the garment off, tossing it across the room in a ball.

In the thin light Cora saw the rippled muscles of his chest and shoulders for the first time. She had to remind herself to breathe since it'd been a long time since she'd seen a male body. She suddenly felt sixteen years old again.

"My, what big muscles you have," she said, mimicking a storybook voice. She squeezed his bicep with one hand.

"All the better to carry you across mud puddles after you eat up all the jambalaya."

Cora punched him in the solar plexus, catching him unawares. "I'm going to develop an eating disorder, if you keep talking like that."

When he tipped up her chin, she saw his eyes glowing like dark sapphires. "Cora. You are complete and utter perfection, inside—" His fingertips pressed the soft flesh where her heart thudded in her chest. "—and out." His hand lightly cupped a breast through the cotton of the shirt. "The only disorder you need to develop is an obsession with me. That way you won't grow bored when I follow you around like a dog for the rest of your life."

His hand on her breast burned away the last of her self-control and she reached for him.

When Ethan finally shifted his weight off to the side, he drew up the sheet to protect her from the night breeze. "You're shivering," he said while his hand cradled her head.

"Not because I'm cold, I assure you." Her fingers snaked a path up his spine as she inhaled the spicy clean scent of his hair.

"You just wait. I'm still out of practice," he teased.

Cora said nothing, only closed her eyes and curled closer to him. She let her imagination wander to the future delights that lay in store for them. Then the memory of where she was and why she was here intruded on her pleasant sensual thoughts.

"Ethan, I'm really sorry about Freddie," she said in a small voice.

"I know you are, Cora." He stroked the hair back from her face, like her father had done a long time ago.

"And I'm afraid for you. Someone is framing you for the murder and that someone murdered Antoine, and now Freddie."

"Don't you be afraid of anything. I won't let this touch you. It'll all be over soon." He pulled a thin blanket up to her knees and kissed her forehead. "No more talk, *cher*. Go to sleep."

But his command proved unnecessary because Cora had already fallen asleep in the protected crook of his arm. Ethan held her for a long time, listening to her slow breathing and reveling in the sheer joy of their union. Blessedly she didn't stir when his cell phone rang.

Ethan slipped from the bed to answer it, grabbing up his trousers from the floor. "Hello?" he whispered, struggling into his pants with the phone clamped with his chin. He stepped onto the gallery and closed the French doors behind him. No sense waking Sleeping Beauty with business.

"I know you were sticking your nose in my business tonight, Ethan. I told you to stay out of it. Let me do my job."

"If you were doing your job, maybe Freddie would still be alive," Ethan said, trying to control his temper.

"The reason he's not is because he refused to stay out of it, too," the voice on the other end spat back. "I warned Bearnard he was getting too close, but he wouldn't listen."

"I warned him, too, but Freddie always did what he wanted in this world. He never listened to reason." The anger ebbed from his voice, replaced by sad resignation as he remembered each clash of wills with his friend.

"That's unfortunate. You stay away from April Rothman. Do you hear me? Don't do anything stupid." Then in a low voice he warned, "And keep your friend Miss Dearing away from her, too."

A muscle jumped in Ethan's jaw as his hand tightened on the phone. "Do you really think you need to tell me that?" he whispered into the mouthpiece. He yearned to grab him by the throat and throttle until every insult had been wrung out.

"Probably not, my friend, but she showed up at that press conference and made herself very visible…and very vulnerable." The man spoke in French, but it was a language he had painstakingly learned in school, not grown up with. His vocabulary was adequate, but his inflection was often on the wrong syllable.

"You let me worry about Cora," Ethan said in a clipped voice. "What about this suicide note found on Antoine?"

"It was unfortunate that the information leaked out. It looks bad for you. We can't have that, can we?"

"Antoine no more killed himself than Freddie accidentally overdosed on heroin."

"What we know, and what we can prove are two different things, *n'est pas*? No one saw April with Freddie yesterday. Nobody seems to have seen Freddie at all until he turned up dead in Algiers."

"That woman got to Freddie, and if you don't find her and do something about it, I assure you, I will." Ethan pressed the disconnect button and slipped the phone back into his pants pocket, as though it had been a normal conversation, not a threat on someone's life. Inside his heart pounded like it would burst in his chest, while his grip on the railing slowly bent the aged metal into a new curve in the filigree.

Mournful sounds from ships' horns on the river drifted on the humid night air, while low voices chattered on the street below as tourists returned to their hotels from the casino. But Ethan heard little except for the roar in his head—a roar borne of anger, fatigue, and loss.

He had lost his best friend tonight. You don't get too many of those in a lifetime.

He'd die before he would let anything happen to Cora.

He'd die, or someone else would. Of that, he was certain.

TEN

"DAMNATION."

Jim Matthew's roar jarred Cora and she spilled coffee across her desk—the coffee she desperately needed to clear the cobwebs from her brain. The last thing she had wanted to do this morning was come to the office of *The Times*. The first thing she had wanted was a repeat of the marvelous performance of last night. The taste of Ethan's mouth on hers remained when she had awakened, and she felt a rush each time she remembered his hands roaming freely over her body, but a repeat performance was not in the cards. She woke in his massive bed utterly alone. The doors to the gallery had been shut and the drapes drawn, inducing her to oversleep without the stimulus of sunlight streaming into the room.

Jeanette had been evasive, pleading ignorance to each question regarding the whereabouts of her employer.

"Oh, I don't know, *M'selle* Dearing. Perhaps he went to the gym. How about a warm beignet for breakfast?" The woman's voice had soothed as she practically pushed Cora down in a chair, setting both juice and coffee before her. "Don't you worry about *M'sieu* Galen. He told me to take good care of you, and that I will." She cut a large wedge of cheese from a wheel and placed that in front of her, too.

"Was he dressed to go to the gym?" Cora asked, sipping her coffee. It tasted twice as strong as any at the office.

"I don't know," she said. "How about some fruit? I

have fresh pineapple. I will get you some." She rose from the chair, but Cora stopped her with a grip on her hand.

"Let's forget about the pineapple for a moment. Did you see him before he left, Jeanette?"

"No, I didn't see him. No way of guessing how he was dressed." She easily tugged her hand free.

"Then how exactly did he convey his wish for you to take good care of me?" Cora could usually smell a liar, and she sniffed a not very good one now.

"He left me a note." Jeanette's hands rested on her narrow hips while she glared at Cora. "Do you, or do you not want pineapple, Miss Dearing? It is very sweet today but won't be so tomorrow."

Cora could also usually sense when she'd pushed someone too far and who would yield nothing more. That message came across loud and clear.

She downed her coffee, drank half her juice, and took a beignet along for the cab ride.

"Where are you going, *M'selle*?" Jeannette looked more formidable than ninety pounds usually permitted.

"Home to shower and change, then to work. The newspaper frowns on dressing like this for the office." She gestured at her shorts and cropped top.

"You are supposed to stay here with me. Ethan will be mad if I let you get away."

"Tell him I escaped out a window when your back was turned." She picked up another beignet and headed for the door. "Thanks for breakfast."

Despite Jeanette's protests and her own misgivings, Cora left the safety and comfort of Ethan's apartment. Things seldom seemed as ominous in bright sunshine. She still had a job, at least she did the last time she'd checked her voicemail, and she was late for work.

Now in her office trying to make sense of sixty-two

emails that queued when she booted her computer, she wished she had the piece of cheese and slice of pineapple.

And maybe enjoy a second cup of coffee with crusty Jeanette. That woman was a font of interesting information, especially under the influence of bourbon.

"Cora, get your ass in here!" The booming voice of Matthews put aside thoughts of returning to Rue Royal to finish her breakfast and await the return of her lover. That conclusion she'd arrived at this morning as she walked double-time to the office—Ethan was her lover. First, they'd made exquisite love the evening before. And secondly, she was in love with him. Plain and simple as that.

Cora knew better than waiting to be called twice by Matthews. She carried in her half-empty cup and prayed her editor would offer a refill from his carafe. The offer was not forthcoming. She spotted Andy Bowen leaning against the window ledge with his arms crossed and wearing a rather bleak expression. He nodded to her when their eyes met but said nothing.

"Cora, what the hell is this? I just heard that this Frederick Bearnard who OD's on smack yesterday in Algiers was a good friend of Galen's, and therefore—" He dragged the word out as though it had three syllables instead of two. "—he must've been a good friend of yours." Matthews leaned forward in his chair, letting his tie trail through the powdered sugar from his requisite beignet. "Would you mind telling me why we had to find out from the news service Bearnard was found dead inside a drug house across the river?" He shook his tie, but it did little good. "I thought you were working with Bowen on this story?"

Cora hunched her shoulders. "I didn't think it was newsworthy since I believed it to be untrue."

"Untrue? What's untrue? It is Frederick Bearnard

lying in a cheap room in a slum of Algiers next to a needle with his fingerprints all over it, a needle mark on his
arm, and enough smack in his system to kill three men."
Matthews poured coffee from the carafe but offered none
to Cora or Bowen.

A thought struck her between the eyes. "A needle
mark? The police found one needle mark? If he was a
junky, don't you think he'd have a string of them up his
arm?"

A slight smile curled the corners of Matthews' lips.
"That was only the preliminary report by the narcotic
investigators at the scene. The autopsy might reveal a
quilt of needle holes all over his ass for all we know."

Cora stole a look at Bowen. He looked skeptical, too.

"'Sides, the *méthode de jour* is to snort the stuff. Your
pal Freddie might have just escalated to the next step."

She tilted her chin indignantly. "Unfortunately, I didn't
know Frederick long enough for us to become friends.
He was an acquaintance."

"Is that so, Ms. Dearing?" he snorted. "Your pal,
Ethan Galen, if that's the name he's going by now, knew
him well. Just what the hell is going on with you two?
You keep seeing this guy, and they'll start looking at you
being in on this."

"Being in on what?" Cora asked.

"Being in on Mrs. Rothman's murder. Are you awake,
Cora?" Jim bellowed. "This is serious. Looks like your
pal Galen, Bearnard, and that Cajun who blew his brains
out were all in this together."

Cora shot Bowen an angry look. The only way Matthews would know anything about her and Ethan would
be from him. Andy ducked his gaze and concentrated on
the wall above the boss's head.

"What evidence do you have for that assertion, sir, or doesn't hard evidence enter into our stories anymore?"

"Don't you take that high-and-mighty tone with me, Cora. And we're not the DA's office. We don't have to provide an airtight case for any jury. We only report the information we're given." The vein in Matthew's head bulged, probably indicating a dangerous rise in the man's blood pressure.

"And we have no obligation to determine if the information holds even a shred of truth?" Cora asked.

Again, a string of French expressions was muttered on her behalf. If she did nothing else while living in New Orleans, she would take up that language in night school.

"We know Bearnard and Galen were friends; they were seen together having dinner in Lowry's, with you, I might add. And that gal from accounting." At that moment, he reminded her much of her late father, but not in a good way. "Galen and Antoine were seen having a private conversation right before the woman disappeared. You were there then, too. Are you still with me, Cora?" He glared at her, more like her father's friend than her employer, for the moment.

"So Ethan was there and had talked to Antoine, same as me. So what?"

"He was using a phony name."

Cora didn't answer. Any rationalization why Ethan traveled using another name would betray something personal he'd confided in her.

"We know from Bowen that Bearnard was in the vicinity of that fishing camp the night before the disappearance," he continued.

Cora pursed her lips and shot Bowen an irritated glance, the irritation more with herself than with him.

He must have seen her checking the B&B register and did a little snooping on his own.

"And from the police report that April Rothman filed, we know that Frederick Bearnard had been stalking her. He'd been fixated on her since college."

"That is all a pack of lies," Cora shouted. "They didn't know each other."

"I'm curious as to how you're so sure about that," Matthews said in a controlled voice, watching her with anger and concern. "Why would April Rothman, who just lost her mother, bother to file a fictitious police report about a man you say she didn't even know?" He narrowed his gaze and waited, like a cat expecting the mouse to rear its head from the hole.

Cora helplessly fell into his trap. "Maybe because April wanted to point the attention anywhere but at herself."

"Hmmm. So you think April might have had a hand in this, Ms. Dearing?"

Cora knew the man well enough to know that he hadn't come up with that idea just now. "She might have. We need proof before we go printing any accusations," she added smugly.

Matthews ignored the insinuation. "And if she did know Bearnard, maybe they were involved romantically, and maybe they planned the thing together for the ten mil. Then they got rid of that Cajun. One less cut of the pie." It was his turn to smile smugly. "Then that smackhead Bearnard started spending his cut a little early and scored some pure stuff that did him in. Another person who doesn't need his cut any longer." Jim rocked back in his chair and waited.

"Freddie was not a smackhead. I know that."

"Care to share your source for this insight, Cora?"

"No, I do not." She banged down her empty coffee mug on the edge of his desk. "I'd really appreciate some of your coffee."

He ignored her request. "The last time I looked you were still on my payroll. If that's changed, I wish you'd kindly clue me in." The vein in his forehead bulged again. "You're not exactly cooperating with this story, especially in light of the fact you were all hopped up to move to investigative reporter."

"I'm doing my job. I'm trying to get the facts, not just make things up as I go along," she said, controlling her temper the best she could.

"Let me spell something out for you, Cora. As your boss, and as your father's friend, if they were all in this together, you better…stay…away…from Galen. Two people involved are dead. You keep asking that man a lot of questions—and I'm assuming that is the reason for your continued involvement with him—and you might be next."

"Thanks for your concern, but I know what I'm doing. April isn't as innocent as that dog-and-pony show she staged at the press conference, and I'm going to find proof of that." She picked up her mug and headed for the door.

Jim rose from his chair stiffly. "Work with Bowen to put the story together. And stay away from Galen," Matthews shouted at her retreating back.

But Cora barely heard the man. She was too busy formulating a plan, a plan that would prove Ethan had nothing to do with April's plot to kill her mother for the insurance money.

April's plot to kill her mother. For a fleeting moment the cruel meaning of her conclusion struck her. Her own mother's loving face flittered across her mind, bring-

ing stinging homesickness. Cora couldn't conceive of a
woman killing her own mother, not for ten million dollars, or all the money in the world. But everyone wasn't
like her.

Anyway, the alternative to believing April a murderess was a paid hit by daddy or persons unknown with
their own reasons for wanting Ada Rothman dead. A
paid hit that may or may not have involved Freddie, Antoine, and Ethan.

And she'd didn't even want to imagine that for a minute.

IT WASN'T EASY getting rid of Andy Bowen. He followed
her to the Algiers Police Station, insisting during the entire ferry ride that he was justified releasing any information he uncovered with the story. "After all, if your
boyfriend is innocent, then he's got nothing to hide," was
his retort twice to Cora's remonstrations. She had stopped
denying that Ethan was her boyfriend for two reasons.
One, Andy didn't believe her. Two, he was starting to feel
like a boyfriend, the first she'd had since her divorce. It
felt good to say it. It felt even better to have him in her
life. Last night had been magical. Silly romantic drivel,
she knew, but that was the only word appropriate for the
chemistry between them.

Bowen was acting like an adolescent whose girl ran
off with the captain of the football team. Only Cora had
never been his girl and never would've been, even if she'd
never met Ethan, but there was no tactful way of letting
him know that.

The trip to Algiers proved to be a complete waste of
time. The police were treating Frederick's death like any
other drug overdose, apparently a regular occurrence
on this side of the river. A desk sergeant impatiently informed her that autopsy results wouldn't be available for

two weeks, and they would never be available to her. The report would be released to the New Orleans Homicide Division, per the request of a Detective Rhodes, and "if *The Times* needed more information, they could just get on back to the Quarter and ask him themselves." Not exactly a pleasant sort of guy.

As an afterthought, Cora sent Andy in search of a soda machine, feigning drop-dead thirst from the heat and asked the sergeant one more question. "Has anyone sent for the body yet?"

"I told you, missy, it won't be released until after the autopsy, and we've got a room full of stiffs before him." He barely looked up from the pile of forms he was reading.

"Yes, I know. But when it is released?"

The man stared like she was a bug who refused to die after a healthy spray of Raid. "I was a friend of Mr. Bearnard's," she said in a quiet voice.

He looked skeptical, but checked a roster under his papers. "Yeah, an Ethan Galen requested that Simone's Funeral Home in the Garden District be called." He issued a sly laugh. "Old Simone probably never buried a smackhead before. He'll probably wear two pairs of gloves." Then he noticed Cora still standing before him. "Is there anything else?" His tone warned that there better not be.

"I gather from your insensitivity you've never lost anyone close. Lucky you." Cora walked out into the blinding afternoon sun and waited for Andy to find her with the soda. Ethan had arranged for Frederick's burial. That didn't really surprise her, but it did make her feel wistful. That kind of loyalty was something she wanted in her life. Right up until the very end, you can count on me. She hadn't enjoyed any of that since she'd grown up and left home.

She never had it with Jim Dearing.

She wanted that desperately with Ethan.

Andy gave up after several attempts at conversation with her on the ferry back. He stared down into the dark brown water, both of them lost in their private reveries. Plenty of debris still floated down the Mississippi, washed into the river after every rain from the endless piles of unsalvageables.

"Be careful, Cora. You are known by the company you keep," were his cryptic parting words.

"Guilt by association? And whatever happened to innocent until proven otherwise?" Her voice called after him, but he didn't respond. She felt an odd sense of pity for him as he disappeared into the crowd. Since it was too late to go back to the office, Cora walked home from the river landing, cutting through the French Market for a *café au lait* and a pastry. What she wanted was a cool shower. What she found instead was Detective Rhodes rummaging around in her tiny back garden with her watering can in hand.

"Are you checking up on me, Detective?" Cora asked, over the man's shoulder. He didn't jump or even flinch. He'd been aware of her creeping up on him.

"Yes, ma'am. I wanted to see how the African primroses were doing. Making sure you're watering them every day."

"I have," she lied. "So, now you're on the plant patrol. Not enough to do in Homicide these days?" Cora hadn't meant that to come out quite so nasty.

He straightened from his crouched position over the flowerbed. "Well, I did have another reason for the visit. The department doesn't allow me to check my plant offspring on company time." He brushed soil from the palms of his hands and looked at her short dress, almost disapprovingly. "I was wondering if you discovered who's been leaving flowers in your yard."

"You have a very good memory, Detective."

"Ah, like an elephant for details. It's the big, obvious things I sometimes overlook."

"I find that hard to believe." Cora sat on the edge of the chaise and motioned to the other chair.

"Thank you, ma'am. So—" He hesitated as though debating whether to continue. "—who did leave the flowers, if you don't mind my asking."

Cora paused before answering. "It was Mr. Galen's housekeeper, trying to…fix us up."

"Did it work?" A slow smile spread across his lined face. "Are you two fixed up?"

"Is this pertinent to your disappearance case or to Freddie's murder?" Cora asked, as politely as she could manage.

"No, I was just a little curious, but you never know what'll turn out to be pertinent in a case like this. We're looking at it like a homicide, since we found Antoine's note admitting his role." He watched her face as he extracted a hanky, then scrubbed his palms with the clean linen.

"Yes, I imagine so." Cora waited patiently, like a teacher waiting for a shy student to get to the point of his story.

"I'm a little curious about something else, too." His smile reached his eyes, deepening the creases in his suntanned forehead. "What do you know about Mr. Galen's friend, Nate Price?"

"Do you mean his chauffeur? I know he drives too fast." Cora rolled her eyes. This man managed to make everything and everyone sound part of a master conspiracy. "He is a bare acquaintance that I met when he's picked me up and dropped me off. I don't have a car here in New Orleans."

"Smart of you. They're expensive to park and unnecessary in the Quarter, ma'am. Unless you must evacuate in a hurry, but we won't think about that today. I only use the cruiser from the department." He dabbed at his forehead with a clean section of the hanky.

"I do know he went to Tulane with Ethan and with Frederick Bearnard, for that matter. If you'd do some digging, I'll bet you'll discover that April Rothman did not go there. So there's no way Freddie could have stalked her in college or have any reason to do so recently."

Rhodes pushed his glasses up the bridge of his nose. "Is that right? Well, I'll check into that as soon as I get a free minute, but I don't suppose we'll be arresting Mr. Bearnard for Mrs. Rothman's disappearance, since he had an unfortunate accident with his drug of choice." He put a sarcastic inflection on his last words and seemed waiting for a reaction.

Cora did not offer one. They just sat, considering the other like two dogs squaring off for a fight. Finally, Cora asked, "Why are you interested in Nate Price? Does he have a string of double-parked tickets in front of the hot spots on Canal? Wanted for driving eighty in a twenty-five?"

He forced a laugh. "No, nothing like that. He's been arrested him for breaking-and-entering. They got him locked up in Metairie." He pushed the sodden hanky back in his pocket. "April Rothman took one of those long-term suites in Metairie. You know, the kind you lease by the month."

Cora shrugged, trying to hide her uneasy feeling upon hearing Nate had been arrested.

"Well, the story goes Miss Rothman came home and

surprised him ransacking through her stuff. She pulled a gun on him, she did. Then called the Metairie Police. She got the drop on him, since he happened to be packing a thirty-eight Ruger." Rhodes waited again for a response from her. Cora only felt the urge to use the bathroom, impatient for the man to leave.

"I have to ask myself, why would a chauffeur need to carry a firearm?" he asked.

"I don't know. Maybe if someone cuts in front without using their turn signal." Cora rose to her feet.

"That's funny, Miss Dearing. You should write for TV not for the newspaper."

"I'll keep that in mind." *And I will, too, since I may be looking for a job in the near future.*

"You don't have any idea what Nate Price might have been looking for in Miss Rothman's apartment?" He followed her toward the back door.

"I have no idea, Detective, but I do think you should check the ballistics of April's gun. You know, the one she pulled on Nate. Just in case her mom's body turns up."

"You know, that occurred to me, too, but I'd need a search warrant to take it from her and run the tests. And there's not a shred of evidence against Miss Rothman in her mom's disappearance."

"I'd say she had ten million reasons."

"Plenty of people are their parents' beneficiaries; that doesn't mean they'd do anything to hurry the process along." He smiled patiently as Cora stepped up on the back stoop.

"There's always the exception to the rule."

"I'm on my way over to Metairie to question Mr. Price. Not about the break-in—that's Metairie's business. But about his whereabouts on the day Mrs. Rothman disappeared."

"Well, thank you for keeping me up to date. The newspaper appreciates your cooperation and forthrightness. And thank you for watering my primroses." Cora opened the screen door and stepped halfway in.

Rhodes looked confused. "I'm not here because of your connection to *The Times*, Miss. I'm here because of your personal connection to this case, although I can't quite say I know what that connection is." He took hold of the door, preventing her escape for the moment. "But if you were my daughter, I'd tell you to keep your distance from Mr. Galen." He anticipated her response and added quickly, "Just until we get this whole mess sorted out. He seems to be in this up to his eyebrows."

Cora scowled. "Thank you for your concern, but I'm a grown woman and not your daughter."

"Two people around him are dead, and another one is in jail, looking to do ten years on the B and E, more if he doesn't have a permit for the gun he carried. Galen didn't have a logical explanation as to why he was in the bayou that weekend, so it sure looks like he followed Rothman out there. We know Bearnard had been there, too. And I'm willing to bet my next paycheck Price had spent that weekend getting bit by mosquitoes, too." Rhodes ran a hand through his hair and sighed. "The only reason we haven't arrested Galen yet on suspicion is because of who he is. The Galen name still carries a lot of clout in the Quarter. My lieutenant wants hard evidence before we bring the son of Etienne Galen in."

"A flimsy frame-up is all that's required for Bearnard and Price since they're poor nobodies. Do I have the explanation correct, Detective?"

His lips stretched in a smile without amusement. "I didn't mean to imply that, Miss Dearing, and I'd hate to see myself misquoted that way in tomorrow's *Times*." He stepped back from the stoop. "A complaint had been filed against Bearnard for stalking. We got a witness that he followed Rothman to Lafourche that weekend. Nathan Price was caught red-handed in her apartment rummaging around while carrying a firearm. No flimsy frame-ups needed there."

"Right, they were both connected to April Rothman. She could be at the center of this, not Ethan. He has no motivation to make Mrs. Rothman disappear. His family is rich, too."

"Not as rich as they once were, and everyone we talked to said Miss Rothman was devoted to her mother. It takes an odd sort for matricide, wouldn't you say?" He held Cora's gaze for a long moment. "Well, I'm on my way out to question Mr. Price. He might want to roll over on Mr. Galen to shave some time off his sentence."

Cora's eyes widened angrily. "Don't be so sure Mr. Galen had anything to do with this!" Cora wondered why she spent so much time defending him when apart, while doubting him so much when they were together.

"Lock your doors and don't do anything foolish, Miss Dearing. I'll call you if we learn anything concrete." He bowed slightly and headed out the gate.

Something concrete that would frame Ethan, you mean. Cora slammed the door behind her and ran to the front window. She wanted to make sure he actually left. Rhodes let himself into the alley through the supposedly hidden door in the fence. Why did everybody seem to know the location of the shortcut?

But Cora had bigger fish to fry. This detective was bound and determined to make Ethan the mastermind of the disappearance. If there was one thing she was certain of, Ethan wouldn't hurt a fly. She just hoped his loyalty to Frederick and Nate wouldn't convict him simply with guilt by association. *You are known by the company you keep.*

Nate Price could very well have been paid by April to pull this off along with Antoine. He'd never really struck her as a chauffeur. He was too cocky, too brash to work in the service industry. His getting caught in April's suite didn't look good. The only explanation was that he searched for something that would connect him with April and the crime. Apparently he hadn't found what he'd been looking for.

The other thing Cora made up her mind about during the time it took to lay out clean clothes and turn on the shower was she wouldn't idly sit by and allow the man she loved be framed for murder. Not as long as she had a single breath of air left in her lungs.

ELEVEN

ETHAN ARRIVED BACK at his suite of rooms hot, tired and in a foul mood after a completely fruitless morning and afternoon. His mood grew worse when he discovered Cora had left the apartment this morning despite Jeanette's attempt to keep her there. She had insisted she must go to the office, or be fired. If everything went as planned, he'd buy the damn *Times* and fire her himself. That way she'd have no excuse but to spend all her time with him.

That was probably the only way he'd be able to get any work done. The stop at his office had been long enough to ascertain everything was running as smoothly as one could expect, but he'd left before even glancing at the reports neatly piled on his desk or the stack of papers requiring his signature. It would all have to wait. He had trouble concentrating on anything but Cora since last night.

Last night. It had been the most memorable of his life thus far, yet he knew it had been a major mistake. Deepening their relationship put Cora in jeopardy. He had known that as soon as things started to get out of hand at *Le P'tit* Fisherman. He had pledged then to put the seduction of Cora Dearing on hold, for her safety, and for his ability to concentrate on what had to be done.

That's what he'd decided with his head, but his heart and that other, even less cooperative body part, had seen things differently. Now she was firmly, resolutely immersed in his life to the point any activity away from her was wasted time. After last night, he couldn't stay away from her any longer.

Only his desperate attempt to find out what had happened to Freddie during his last hours had managed to distract him. Yet no matter whom he questioned or how much money he threw around to loosen tongues, he hadn't found anyone with knowledge of Freddie's death. None of the regular drug users in the area remembered seeing him at all, which had been what Ethan expected. Freddie would no more go to Algiers to score heroin than the local parish priest would. Someone had set Freddie up. Someone had arranged to meet him and arranged that meeting to be Bearnard's last on earth. There was no doubt in Ethan's mind that that someone was April Rothman.

"Hey, Price can't seem to handle the job. Why not put me on retainer? Just until my next acting assignment comes along, of course."

Freddie's words from their last phone conversation haunted Ethan. He knew why Freddie would have jumped at the chance to meet April Rothman. He had wanted so much to outdo Nate. The two had been competitive for as long a time as Ethan could remember, whether it was a rugby game, a challenge over picking up a woman, or a belching contest in a bar. Freddie always wanted to one-up Nate, and it just cost him his life.

The Algiers Police Department wasn't much help either. Right now, only narcotics detectives were investigating, and only from the standpoint they didn't want ultra-pure heroin to start a rash of OD's among users. It was bad for the tourist business when bodies started turning up all over town. And tourist business was bad enough since Katrina. Less hotel rooms, fewer bars and restaurants meant less revenue for those who returned and rebuilt. Ethan's insistence that they should investigate this as a homicide fell on polite, but skeptical ears. He'd received only a vague assurance they'd turn it over to Homicide if evidence from the autopsy warranted. Only a call to the coroner's office by his attorney at least garnered the promise that the autopsy would be thorough, not cursory, as in keeping with the usual junkie death.

This was no death of a junkie. This was the murder of Frederick Bearnard, Tulane graduate, promising actor, ladies' man, drinking champion of Lafitte's, and trusted friend. Nobody would sweep this under a rug.

"Jeanette," Ethan called to the kitchen.

The tiny woman stuck her head around the corner and raised an eyebrow. "I've just tried Miss Dearing at *The Times*. She's not there and not answering her phone at home. Do you have any idea where she might be?"

"I do not. It is not my turn to watch her." She disappeared back into the kitchen. Her voice dripped contempt. Subtlety has never been, nor would ever be, her strong suit.

"Do you have something on your mind, Jeanette? Something you want to discuss with me?" He retrieved a beer from the refrigerator and walked over to where she worked at the counter. After the unsuccessful morning, an afternoon making funeral arrangements for Freddie, then arriving home to find Cora gone, and *in-communicato*, he was in no mood to spar with his housekeeper. But past history had taught him it was infinitely better to hash things out and not allow them to smolder.

Jeanette had been chopping celery, onions, and green pepper, no doubt for a pot of gumbo. She tossed down the paring knife with a clatter. "Why did you sneak off this morning and allow *M'selle* Dearing to wake up alone in a strange home?" She fixed her dark eyes on him.

This was the last thing he'd expected. "What?"

"You heard me, Ethan. You walk around like a love-sick steer pining for a cow in the next pasture, and when she finally agrees to spend the night with you, you find some stupid duck-chase to run off on as soon as you're awake."

He stared at her. "I think you mean bull and not steer, Jeanette," he said inanely, still taken aback they were even having this discussion.

Jeanette picked up the paring knife again, brandishing it in the air. "Don't sass me with farmyard technicalities, my ass-pain. And don't even think of firing me. I won't go. Simple as that. Not until you've straightened out this mess of a life you have." She wielded the knife back to a stalk of celery, creating a row of uniform slices in the blink of an eye.

"Jeanette, I had important business to attend to that couldn't wait. I know Freddie didn't die accidentally; I believe he was murdered." Her fingers trembled as she picked up the next stalk, but she didn't look at him. "If there is any chance we can prove my supposition and lead the authorities to his killer, I had to make sure the coroner proceeded with my speculation in mind. I don't want this treated like a routine junkie overdose." It felt cold and alien to be discussing the matter so blithely. The victim had been his friend since they'd shot spitwads at each other in grade school.

Jeanette glanced up before directing her energy at a large bell pepper. "Then, Ethan, you should have awakened her and explained your need to leave, not just abandoned her, without a word of explanation."

Ethan groaned. He was too tired, too distraught to argue with a *modis parenti* about a breach of etiquette. "I didn't abandon Cora. She was sound asleep when I left, so I decided not to disturb her. I'd planned to explain my reasons for leaving when I got back home." Ethan let the cold beer run down his throat almost without tasting it. He needed something to take the edge off before he yelled at an old woman who only had his best interests at heart.

"And before all that—when you arrived home yesterday evening, did you tell Cora what was on your mind then, or perhaps—" She halved a large onion with a single blow. "—what was in your heart? Or did you just expect the woman to read your mind and draw the correct conclusions?"

Ethan's mouth dropped open as he set the empty bottle on the counter. "I don't have a clue what you're talking about. Perhaps it would be better if we continued this enlightening conversation another time. I've got to get a hold of Cora right now." He pulled his cell phone from his pocket, but her tiny hand clamped down on his wrist. For a woman who'd didn't weigh a hundred pounds soaking wet, her grip was amazing.

"No, *M'sieu* Galen. We will finish the conversation now, then you can fire me, and I'll go to Baltimore to torment my son's family. But I will have my say first." She resumed her frenetic chopping. "I listen sometimes when you talk to her on the telephone. You are very polite. You flirt, but you betray nothing of your heart or your soul. It is as though you expect the woman to fall in love with a stranger wearing a mask. You are nothing more than a facade to *M'selle* Dearing."

This was too much. It was bad enough that she eavesdropped on his conversations, but to use what she overheard to lecture him was over the top, even for Jeanette. "You've no right to judge me, Jeanette. And I don't appreciate you meddling in my personal affairs. I'd put you on a plane this afternoon to your son in Baltimore, but I like the man. I don't want to take this out on him."

Jeanette stifled a smile at that, but Ethan continued. He needed to straighten this out and not back down. "You have no idea what things are happening here, so stay out of my business." His voice rose in intensity. "I don't want to involve Cora either. It's not safe."

"So that's the reason why you haven't explained your hatred for the newspaper who employs her, because it's not safe for her?" Jeanette wasn't backing down either.

Ethan glowered at her. "Of course not. But do you think I want to air our family's dirty laundry? Do you think she even cares about our family?" he snapped.

"I do. And so do you."

He exhaled a sigh. "I have no desire to explain to Cora how my behavior reduced the family's status and how my years of neglect to the business has affected our finances." Pain and humiliation filled his voice. He opened the fridge and extracted another beer. "Do you think any woman wants to fall in love with a man who caused his parents nothing but grief and heartache?" He took a long swig. "I thought I'd save that background information for when I felt a little more assured of her affections. For all I know, she may be seeing me solely to scoop the continuing saga of the Galen involvement in the disappearance."

"No. That's not the way it is. It can't be," but her tone had grown less certain. "Anyway, don't say you caused your papa and mama nothing but pain and heartache. That's not true, *mon p'tit*."

"It is true, Jeanette. Don't lie to hide the truth from me. They were ashamed of me."

She pushed the cutting board away and threw down

the knife. "I don't lie! They were never ashamed of you. It's true," she insisted to his skeptical frown.

"Your mama understood that they had given you, your brother, and sister little to do but play, waste time, waste money. She knew she'd done this, and she was glad. Galens had always worked themselves into an early grave to attain what they had. She was happy that her children wouldn't have to." Jeanette's eyes softened into dark pools with the memories of the past. "Clotilde didn't stop to consider the downside of idle lives—the rumors and gossip when children got into mischief."

"I'm afraid you're simplifying everything, reducing it all to childish pranks."

"But that's what they were," she insisted. "Nothing more. And that's what they still are for *ma petite* Chloe. Childish pranks, because no one expects anything else from her, but she'd do anything for your mama and *grandmère*. She is a good girl in her heart."

Ethan softened now that the conversation had strayed to sweet, sassy Chloe. Jeanette would defend that brat, and him, for that matter, with her last dying breath. "You might be right about my mother, I'll grant you that, but you're wrong about my father. I was there, Jeanette. I heard him. He was ashamed of me. My behavior, my refusal to accept responsibilities in Galen interests, in my selection of a wife." The last word burned a distasteful hole through his tongue. Aimee had never been a wife to him, merely a passing diversion who'd happily gone home once her hands clutched the tidy settlement check.

"What is the matter with you, Ethan? I expect that behavior from Chloe or from Hunter. They still see themselves as children. But not you, Ethan. You know you are a man and still you act like you have no dignity." Ethan

shut his eyes, trying to squeeze his father's words from his memory.

"Yes, he was very angry with you. That is what you remember. He'd lost his temper and regretted his words later."

Ethan looked at her questioningly. "How do you know he regretted anything?"

"You are not the first person I have eavesdropped on." She emitted a strangled laugh. "I know he regretted his words; I heard him say so," she repeated. "He had been angry and disappointed because he allowed Clotilde to let the children run amuck for too long. It wasn't easy to rein any of you in." She lowered her voice to a whisper. "And he knew he had to rein you in quickly, Ethan, because he was sick. He knew he didn't have much time left."

Ethan opened his mouth to speak, but Jeanette held up her hand to silence him. "But he never was ashamed of you. He loved you. And he knew you loved him and respected him, and your mother and *grandmère*. That's all a parent really wants from a child in return—love and respect. Everything else you get is icing on the cake." Jeanette set her jaw, tilting her head upward, finally silent.

So was Ethan. He was speechless. "I didn't—"

"I know you didn't, but don't even think of arguing with me about this because you don't know."

"I wish I could've shown him a little more respect while he was alive." Ethan slumped in a chair and stretched out his legs.

"We all have things we'd like to do over in our lives, every one of us. Don't dwell on it. If he's looking down on the Quarter, he knows you've tried hard since his death. And if he's not watching, you can tell him when you get there, *mon ami*."

Ethan stared out the kitchen window at the steady rain

that thrummed against the pane as Jeanette returned to her chopping with renewed zeal. *If he is looking down, he knows I've got everything at stake here for Galen Enterprises. If the family reputation was tarnished before due to indiscreet behavior, it would pale into nothingness if I sent them into bankruptcy.* Ten million dollars was a lot of money to gamble with. He had to win this sick little battle. He had too much at stake, besides the family fortune. Antoine, a hapless fisherman looking to make an easy buck, and Freddie, his friend, were dead. He had to see this through to the end no matter what—to restore his self-respect, something he'd lost a long time ago.

Then he could be honest with Cora. Then he could admit he loved her more than life itself. Then he'd have something to offer—something more important than wealth and family reputation. He could offer her a man not afraid to look himself in the mirror.

Ethan jumped when the phone on the counter rang. He looked around as though waking from a dream. Jeanette was bent over in the pantry, rummaging for ingredients for her soup. The phone rang again. This time Ethan picked up, walking out of the room into the stillness of the dining room. He pulled the door closed behind him, in light of Jeanette's eavesdropping admission.

"Hello?"

"Hey, old buddy. How you fixed for cash? Or maybe you've got a cashier's check laying around?" The voice of Nate Price sounded far away on the scratchy phone line.

"Where are you?" he demanded. "I've been calling all day, and you don't answer. What the hell am I paying you for when I'm investigating Freddie's murder myself?"

"That's part of the reason why I need the money, boss. They took my cell phone away and will only allow me one call. I hope you'll call your attorney and send him down." The upbeat swagger was still there, but Ethan heard fear in Nate's voice.

"Where are you?" Ethan pronounced each word succinctly.

"I'm in jail, boss. In Metairie. Had a little trouble getting my hands on something to connect Rothman with Freddie's murder."

"What? You're in jail?" Ethan had a hard time putting this together. "You're supposed to point the finger at her, not end up arrested yourself." He tried to keep his voice down, despite his growing temper. "What were you arrested for?"

"Breaking and entering, but—"

Ethan cut him off. "And did you find it?"

"No, but—"

"And April busted in on you?"

"She pulled a thirty-eight on me before I had a chance—"

"And dear, sweet April—I trust someone interesting was with her?"

"No, she was alone." Price gave up making excuses.

Ethan nearly slammed the phone down, but Nate was his friend, albeit his screwed-up friend. "Just stay there until my attorney comes with bail money."

"Yeah, waiting right here—that's pretty much what I had in mind." The swagger was back.

Ethan hung up and paced the floor. He punched in his lawyer's number, then disconnected. He decided to let Nate stew there for a while. He wouldn't be able to mess anything else up if he were in jail.

Or get himself killed like Freddie.

That only left Cora. The lump in his stomach he'd had all afternoon swelled into a rock. He tried her number. Busy. At least that was a good sign. She was home. Ethan grabbed his keys, kissed Jeanette on the top of her gray head, and headed out the door.

"HELLO?" CORA CAUGHT the phone on the sixth ring. Never fails when you take a shower, somebody calls. She wished against all reason that it was Ethan. There were a few things she wanted to ask him. And a few more she wanted to say. Mostly she just wanted to hear the sound of his voice, but the person on the other end spoke with no charming French accent.

"Cora? So you're home. Good. It's Bowen."

"What's up, Andy?" Cora balanced the phone between her ear and shoulder while she struggled into underwear and jeans.

"Did some digging on your boyfriend, since I can't count on my partner to give up any facts about him." He waited, as though expecting a denial.

"What did you find out?" she asked, trying to hook her bra in the back.

"I found out who owns Provincial Trust—the insurance company that holds the policy on Ada Rothman."

"And who would that be?" she asked, already suspecting the answer.

"Your rich boyfriend does. Etienne Galen, the third, Americanized to Ethan, I suppose."

"Huh. I'll be darned," she said casually, while her mind raced at a mile a minute. "I guess that gets him off the hook for her murder, since it wouldn't make sense to bump off someone you hold a double indemnity policy on."

"Yeah, I thought of that, but not so fast. He probably doesn't want to pay out that policy ever, and that's why he's trying so hard to make it look like April did it. A person can't profit financially from their crime, so Provincial Trust would be off the hook for the ten million if they proved April killed her mother."

"What do you mean he's trying so hard to make it look like April did it?"

"His private investigator, Nate Price, was arrested this afternoon, in case you haven't heard. I think he was trying to plant evidence in April Rothman's apartment."

So Nate is a private investigator, she thought. *I've spent too many years taking what people say at face value.*

"You mean Nate's not really a chauffeur?" she asked, playing along with mock innocence.

"Come on, Cora. Wake up. You're not this dingy. What has this guy done to your mind? Sucked it out with his tongue?"

"Shut up, Andy. You're crude."

"And you are naïve, at the very least. Price was arrested in April's apartment. She pulled a gun on him, no less. Try this little theory on for size, partner. Freddie bumps off old lady Rothman because he thinks she stands in his way of getting next to April. Then Price plants some evidence implicating April as the mastermind, both to clear dearly departed Freddie's name, and to get his other friend off the hook for a lot of cash." The pleasure in Bowen's tone telegraphed through the line. "Those Tulane boys really stick together. Too bad I went to LSU. I sure don't have people looking out for me like that."

A shadow moved across Cora's front window right before she heard the insistent knocking at her front door.

"I got to go, Andy. Someone's here. I'll call you back." She struggled to get her shirt over her head, not wanting to look silly talking on the phone in her underwear.

"Cora, wait, there's more."

"Cora?" A voice called her name from the other side of the door. She recognized the delicious inflection just as her head stuck in the tight neckline of the shirt. Ethan pushed open the door and walked in as her head cleared the shirt. She clicked off the phone and set it down.

"Hi, Ethan. I was just going to call you," she said, walking toward him.

He hugged her briefly, wrapping his arms loosely around her waist and kissing her forehead. "Who was on the phone?" he asked.

"Oh, Andy Bowen. He's been doing some digging for the story since I haven't been."

"Since you haven't been? I thought you gave up this silly notion of investigative reporting." His tone was cool, his face rigid and expressionless.

"I didn't want to investigate this story, Ethan, because of our involvement, and Bowen knows that. He was bringing me up to date on what he's found out." She felt oddly defensive and didn't appreciate it one bit.

"But you have been investigating the story, Cora. I don't think you've been completely honest about that. Haven't you been feeding information to Bowen?" He slouched against the door with his hands deep in his pockets.

"No," she answered quickly and felt a twinge of guilt for her own duplicity. "Well, not for a long time. Not since the beginning before you and I..." Her voice trailed off, as though afraid to name her emotions or feelings for him.

"So, it wasn't you who told Bowen that Freddie was out at Water Lilies that weekend?" He spoke with incongruous tenderness, considering the rest of his statement. "Because whoever did is indirectly responsible for his death, in all likelihood."

"It wasn't me, Ethan. He probably found out the same

way I did, checking the register of the inn down the road."
Her hands balled into fists.

He looked at her, his expression softening a little. "I
need to know. Is that what—" He made a hand gesture
between the two of them. "—you and I are about? You
spending time with me so you can stick your nose in my
life to get your story? Are you using me to get a damn
promotion?" The muscles in his neck bunched beneath
the surface of his skin. "I thought I could trust you. I
thought you knew you could trust me."

Cora's mouth dropped open and she closed the short
distance between them. "I didn't tell Bowen that Freddie
had been in the neighborhood the night before. He found
that out on his own." She forced her hands to relax but
her voice betrayed growing anger. "You have your nerve
accusing me of ulterior motives, of a private agenda. You
haven't exactly been up-front and honest with me, Mr.
Chairman of the Board of Provincial Trust," she spat,
glaring at him and crossing her arms over her chest.
"Why didn't you mention you're the major shareholder?
Did that little tidbit just slip your mind, or didn't you
think it was important?"

"I couldn't tell you, Cora, and I can't tell you why now.
It would compromise my investigation and place you in
danger." He scrubbed his face with his hands. Fatigue
and frustration etched deeply into his features. "I knew
you wouldn't stay out of it."

"Your investigation? What were you investigating?
The police were investigating, and it hasn't looked like
you and your friends offered much assistance. Quite the
contrary."

Pain and sorrow added their toll to his face, which
disintegrated into a haunted grimness.

"Are you sure your endeavors haven't been designed

simply to avoid Provincial Trust from paying out that policy? Ten million dollars is an enormous amount of money. I'm sure it would affect your ratings and shareholder dividends, or whatever."

"Is that what you believe, *cher*? That Freddie and Nate and I have tried to frame April Rothman to keep from paying out the policy?" His tone was soft, but anguished.

"I don't know, Ethan. I do know your family is very important to you and protecting the family fortune must be pretty crucial, too."

"They are important; that is true. And yes, I was partially motivated by reluctance to not pay out an unjustified settlement. Insurance companies pay out policies all the time. It comes from a pool we maintain, not directly from the shareholders' pockets. But my decision to keep you in the dark had nothing to do with them, and everything to do with you." He took two steps toward her, but her upraised palms forestalled any further approach.

Cora stared at him feeling slightly ashamed, yet without any notion why. Don't stop now; don't soften, Cora. Get to the bottom of this. Only then can it all go away.

"You should have told me you owned Provincial Trust. It might have helped me get over the notion you were a murderer a little quicker."

"You think me a murderer, *cher*?"

"I don't anymore, but I did in the beginning." She saw the look of hurt and betrayal. "Just for a short while, before I got to know you."

"When you slept in my bed and called out my name, did you think me a murderer then?" A slow building anger crept up his neck and darkened his face. "Did that make the passion burn hotter when you threw a little danger in?"

"No, Ethan. Don't think that. I knew you couldn't hurt

anyone by the time I crawled into your bed and waited for you to come home. But if you had been more forthcoming with what was going on, I could've gone in the right direction. Hell, I believed for a long time that Freddie helped April with the murder and that she killed him just like Antoine, to clean up any witnesses and not share the proceeds." Cora looked into his eyes to gauge his reaction. This was a risky chance, but she had to take it.

Ethan's blue eyes darkened to near black. "Was that question geared to make me throw up my hands and confess my culpability? I'm sorry to disappoint you. You might not believe this, but I only kept things from you to protect you. People are getting hurt, and I'd die before I let one of them be you." He walked toward the door, then stopped and looked back. "I don't deserve your trust, my love. You're right about that. I've done nothing to merit honest behavior in return. And for that, you'll never know how sorry I am."

HE WALKED OUT the door without so much as a backward glance. And out of her life, for all she knew. Cora felt she'd been kicked in the stomach. That wasn't exactly how she'd planned their next meeting since leaving his comfortable bedroom early this morning. She sank down on the sofa, confused, angry and sad, all rolled up into one mass of bad emotions. Ethan probably had his reasons for keeping her out of the loop. She did have a penchant for mucking things up lately. But the only reason she'd stuck her nose in was to clear his name. He had no clue how close Detective Rhodes had come to arresting him for the conspiracy to murder Ada Rothman. And what would that do to his tarnished family reputation? That would stick in people's memories long after the true killers had been caught and were marking the days on their cell walls.

She still needed to clear Ethan's name. With Nate Price in jail, he couldn't count on him to find out the facts. If Rhodes suspected Ethan of complicity to plant evidence, he could land in the cell right beside his Tulane buddy. Cora rose to her feet, revitalized with new determination.

She had to find out what Price had been looking for in April's apartment. The key to this convoluted mess rested there. If Cora could find what he was after, it might go a long way in clearing Freddie's name and provide rationalization for Nate's breaking-and-entering. Most important, it would clear Ethan of complicity.

And point the finger exactly where it belonged.

Price hadn't had much luck. But Price wasn't a reporter with *The Times*, one of the newspapers eager to print any fabricated story April chose to dish out. April would have no reason to suspect her of anything other than doing her job. If she could gain the woman's confidence, she might be able to get her hands on the piece of evidence that would save Ethan's company ten million dollars, besides clear his precious family name.

Her eyes filled with tears. As time went on, his family name grew more precious to her too, in some strange way.

She couldn't think of any other way to prove to Ethan her motives were genuine and her love real. If they were to have any future together, this all better work out tonight as planned.

Or she might not have any future at all.

TWELVE

ETHAN WASTED NO time when he left Cora's apartment. His first visit to the caretaker, Emil Vacherie, was long overdue. He'd learned from Jeanette that the man watched Cora's comings and goings from the window of his garage apartment. Vacherie's spying could be useful after all, if a sufficient sum of money was dangled like a carrot. And the sum proved less than what Ethan had imagined. After a short, but pointed conversation, Vacherie seemed willing to keep an eye on Cora *au gratis*, but accepted the stack of bills anyway. Ethan would've preferred busting his jaw rather than paying him, but then he'd have a hard time reporting in when Cora left her cottage.

On his drive out to Metairie, his second destination, he called his attorney to meet him at the police station. Ethan decided to post bail for his wayward private investigator after all. Although the idea of letting Price cool his heels where he couldn't get himself into more trouble, or worse, end up like Freddie, held great appeal, he needed Nate. He needed him to follow Cora around like a personal bodyguard to make sure she didn't blunder into danger, either chasing after her story or chasing after him. This had gone on long enough. It was time to take care of some things, but he must make sure Cora was safe first.

The bumper-to-bumper traffic on Interstate Ten gave him time to contemplate his latest misstep with Cora. He had no right to get angry with her. He had no right to accuse her of ulterior motives when he'd done everything in his power to keep her from the truth. He knew she hadn't told Bowen about Freddie's presence in the bayou the evening before. If she had been able to find that out, certainly Bowen with more experience in such matters, could have found out on his own. Even if she had let it slip, Cora had no idea of the danger she was dealing with.

He had made sure of that.

He rolled down the window to breathe in the salt air from the marshes in the south. They soothed him in a way that an air conditioner blast never could. The scent of fetid decay was finally gone—Mother Nature having cleansed the swamp in the ever-present cycle of renewal.

Cora. All she had wanted was a promotion to a better paying position with the newspaper. He was no longer angry about her ambition to become a reporter. Not being able to pay your bills each month was something his parents hadn't let him experience. Not every newspaper reporter was a tabloid wannabe, or every editor a panderer of human degradation. So what if she'd pursued him initially to get her story? Hadn't he set her up just to seduce her at the B&B? Hardly a noble aspiration, leading to a secure and lasting relationship in the future. He had thought she would be an interesting challenge, besides the most delectable female he'd seen in a long time. She proved to be more of a challenge than he'd bargained for. Cora was a dichotomy he couldn't resist—vulnerable softness on the outside with a will of steel inside. He wasn't sure when he fell in love with her or why. But a secure and permanent relationship was exactly what he had in mind if she was still speaking to him when this was over. For now, keeping her out of this mess had to be his top priority.

Exiting the freeway, he forced himself to concentrate

on his task at hand. Nate Price was in jail and needed to be released. Once out, he had to stay away from April Rothman if he hoped to evade prison for the next ten years. Despite Price's lapse in judgment breaking into Rothman's apartment, he trusted him with his life, and that's what it might come down to. And he would entrust Cora's safety with him, too, since she'd become more important than his own life. With Nate keeping an eye on Cora, he could play his last trump card to flush the murdering woman into the open.

His cell phone rang as Ethan arrived at the Metairie Police Station.

"Hello, Mr. Galen? You've been a hard man to get a hold of."

"For that, I apologize. I've been a little preoccupied lately."

"I bet so. Your friend, Mr. Price, is in a lot of hot water. The Metairie Police will not be sympathetic to his theories if Miss Rothman presses charges. Right now, I don't have any idea why she wouldn't."

"I know. I'm at the station now to bail him out. My attorney's on the way. I brought a copy of his license and gun permit, so at least the firearm charges will be dropped." Then he added uncomfortably, "I didn't put him up to this."

"I know that. By the way, the gun specifications on the arrest warrant were dropped after I suggested they check the permit-to-carry data base."

"Thank you, lieutenant. I am in your debt." He'd not been completely honest with Charley Rhodes in the past. That he would amend in the future.

"Justice will be served, sir. That's all I want."

Ethan threaded a hand through his tangled hair, exhaling a rasp. "Justice will be served when I make that bitch pay for Freddie's death."

"Don't do anything stupid, Mr. Galen. You set her up right so far. It's almost over. We've got an expert to testify that the suicide note was coerced—that it wasn't Antoine's language and phraseology on the paper." Ethan could hear Detective Rhodes take a sip of something at the other end of the line. "And you have a lot of motivation to stay out of jail, no?"

"You mean Miss Dearing?" Ethan's heart lifted just speaking her name.

"I do, *M'sieu*. She's an interesting lady. Someday I will tell you about the time she pulled a butcher knife on me."

Ethan grinned into the phone receiver as he stepped into the cool reception area of the station. "I look forward to the story." A beep in his ear signaled another call. "But if you'll excuse me, I have another call, sir."

"Stay away from her, Mr. Galen. Let me do my job." The lieutenant's end of the line went dead.

"Hello, Ethan Galen," he said to the waiting caller.

"Mr. Galen?" The twangy accent of Emil Vacherie sent an ominous spike to his gut. "This is Emil from Miz Dearing's place." He drawled out the words in slow motion.

"What is it?" Ethan demanded.

"Well, Miz Dearing had me call her a cab. I told her that maybe she should just stay put, but there's no talkin' to that woman."

Ethan's impatience rose up his throat like bile. "Where did she go, Vacherie?" He shouted into the phone, drawing a curious look from the desk sergeant.

"Metairie. She went to Metairie." Vacherie sounded piqued at being yelled at.

"To the police station in Metairie? That's where I am

now." Ethan lowered his voice, glancing around the station for a familiar face.

"No," he drawled. "The cabdriver said he took her to that big condo development they threw up last year over on—"

Emil Vacherie didn't have a chance to finish his paid-for information. The other end of the phone line had gone dead.

CORA WRACKED HER brain until her head hurt, trying to remember everything that happened at *Le P'tit* Fisherman. *If only I hadn't gotten sick, dulling my brain, besides churning my stomach. Or if only I had gone through the swinging doors into Antoine's kitchen when looking for the ladies' room. Seeing Frederick back there, sipping on a Dixie Beer, would have gone a long way clearing up that man's involvement in this.*

Ethan couldn't be involved with any murder, but had he been covering up Frederick's complicity with Antoine? Ethan was nothing if not loyal to his friends. Would he ever defend and protect her like that? Even in death Frederick has Ethan to make sure no one sullies the Bearnard name.

He won't be anxious to defend me unless I can prove my motives are loftier than getting the breaking story. A clap of thunder jolted her from the pleasant reverie of Ethan back to memories of lunch at the fish house.

Something wasn't right. Something nagged at her beneath the surface. She gulped the last of the cold coffee and sucked in deep breaths of air.

And then she remembered—why she didn't go through the swinging doors into the kitchen.

"I'll go with you, Cora. I definitely drank too much

coffee at breakfast." April Rothman had gone in search
of the ladies' room with her.

"No, not that way. It's down this hall." April had
grabbed her elbow and steered her through a narrow
hallway to the unisex restroom.

How would April have known where the john was
located?

Unless she'd been there before.

Why had it been so hard for her to see it? Why was it
easier to believe three college chums were paid hit-men
than believe a woman capable of killing her own mother?
People did horrible things to the ones they supposedly
loved every day.

Like tell them you don't believe them.

Like tell them you don't trust them.

Sweet little April was in this up to her collagen-filled
lips. She had bribed Antoine with plenty of cash, probably with the promise of more to come after he'd clunked
mama on the head and made her disappear.

"*The swamp has fooled a countless number of adventurers. It closes its gaping hole, swallowing up the
unsuspecting without a trace.*" Max Roussard's cryptic
words during the swamp tour danced across her brain.
Everyone from the bayou knew how easy it was to get
rid of a body.

Then April had forced Antoine to write the note before
she killed him. Why confess to the crime and purport
suicide if you know you're going to die anyway? Unless
April threatened his family....

Cora remembered the two little girls smiling on the
dock when they'd arrived for lunch. Antoine probably
figured April was capable of anything at that point and
wrote the note in desperation. With the note, a court date
could be set. If the coroner declared the death a suicide,

then the court referee would order Provincial Trust to pay out ten million dollars.

Quite a sum. It would certainly affect Provincial's bottom line and the Galen family's, too, but Ethan wouldn't scam anyone. Not even a viper like April. Ethan knew Antoine was a murderer and the note coerced, if not forged. He believed Freddie had been murdered, too. Too many bodies for this not to be her handiwork. All they needed was proof. Nate Price had been looking for that proof—something to tie April to Antoine.

A bank deposit slip to his account?

Cash with both their fingerprints on it?

His special-of-the-day gumbo dribbled on a different outfit than the one she wore the day of the disappearance?

Nate Price wouldn't have jeopardized his PI license, his career, and his next ten years of freedom if he weren't certain proof existed. He had gambled and lost.

She had to win. Or at least try. She had nothing else to lose. Her future with Ethan was at stake. The look of hurt and disappointment on his face shamed her even now. Because she hadn't believed him. And hadn't trusted him. She had spent too many cynical years since her breakup with Jim Dearing to believe that a man like Ethan Galen could love her. She'd spent those years distrusting herself, assuming she would be easily duped by a fast-talking manipulator again.

Instead, she had done the manipulating. Afraid to take a chance, she'd denied herself a man who'd only asked for her time, attention, and a little love. And apparently, a little was all she had to offer. She'd convinced herself a promotion to reporter would give her back self-respect and let her live happily ever after. Cora laughed at her naiveté. Without a thickened hide and a hole where a conscience should be, she didn't have the right stuff to succeed in this business. Up till now, her favorite pastime was gazing down on the world from a balcony, catching snippets of conversation while hiding from the world. But no more. No more hiding.

Someone she loved needed her help whether he had asked for it, whether he wanted it or not. She wasn't going to let him down. Ethan Galen was not James Dearing. Moreover, she wasn't the same weak-kneed woman who had married him. This Cora Dearing was about to go after what she wanted. And what she wanted was Ethan.

The answer to his problems lay with April Rothman. So that's where she planned to go.

IT WASN'T THAT difficult to obtain April's address. All she had to do was impersonate a law clerk in the office representing Nate Price for a copy of the police report to be faxed to her machine. Cora stuffed her bag with her mini-recorder, several blank tapes, her notepad, and asked Emil Vacherie, who always seemed lurking about, to hail her a taxi on Dauphine. She was on her way with little time to ponder appropriate questions since the taxi driver tore through the Quarter and sped up the ramp to Route Ten like Talladega Speedway.

Once in front of the complex of long-term rentals, she regretted not asking the taxi to wait. How long would she wait for another if the deadly Ms. Rothman allowed her to leave?

"Hello, Miss Rothman? I hope you remember me, Cora Dearing from *The Times*." Cora stood on the threshold with pad and pen in hand, wearing her friendliest smile.

"Of course, I remember you, Miss Dearing. I'm just not sure why you're here." April Rothman breathed the words in a more polished affectation than her accent from Water Lilies. Smartly dressed in black silk slacks and a white shirt, she wore her hair pulled back in a tight knot, while her earlobes flashed two-karat diamond studs at the very minimum. She appeared to have had a make-over since Cora last saw her and looked surprisingly refreshed for a woman in mourning.

"I'm here to see if you can spare *The Times* a little of your time, in light of the recent events. Yesterday must have been very unsettlingly to you." Cora hoisted the bag higher on her shoulder.

"And what events are you referring to?" April crossed her arms and leaned against the jamb, her brow furrowing curiously.

"I understand a private investigator, Nate Price, was arrested breaking into your home. That must have been quite a shock." Cora offered a sympathetic purse of her lips.

"Yeah, it was. I came home to find this Neanderthal rummaging through my drawers. His jacket was off and he wore a shoulder holster with a gun in plain sight. I had no choice but to defend myself. I keep a gun for protection. A girl can't be too careful these days." She shook her head as though the memory still frightened her.

Cora shifted her weight to her other leg and swiped her forehead with the back of her hand. "Would you mind terribly if I came in for a few minutes? It's hotter than Hades out here."

April's pleasant expression faded. "If you're looking for an explanation why that man was here and what he was looking for, why don't you ask your friend, Ethan Galen?" Scorn etched her voice, but she still offered a smile.

"Well, mainly because Mr. Galen is no longer speaking to me. He cut off our relationship once he discovered I was investigating your mother's disappearance for *The Times*. Newspaper reporters do not rate among his favorite people."

"And you do understand why he has a special interest in believing I had something to do with my mother's murder, don't you?" Indignation replaced scorn as the inflection of the moment.

"Yes, ma'am. I recently discovered his true connection to the case." Cora opted for a tone of heartfelt remorse and contrition.

The newfound attitude worked. April straightened and ran a hand down the crease of her slacks. "I suppose you may step in for a little while, Miss Dearing. I would like to provide *The Times* with the facts in light of yesterday's new developments." She stepped back, allowing Cora to enter the cool, dim apartment.

Cora heard the lock turn and the bolt thrown behind her, but her attention was already on the layout of the suite. Lovely appointments for a rental. They made her furnishings in the cottage on Ursulines look downright Sisters-of-Charity. The room was arranged into a central conversation area while bookcases, potted plants and etageres holding exquisite porcelains lined the walls. The blinds were tightly closed against the afternoon sun and the air-conditioning up so high, she shivered involuntarily. It was freezing in the room. This woman didn't worry about the electric bill.

Cora walked to the sofa but waited for April to take the wing chair before perching on the edge. For a fleeting moment, panic swept from her stomach, up her throat, and into her mouth, giving her worse acid reflux than any night in the Quarter swilling draft beer and spicy food. She was alone with a woman who in all likelihood had forced one man to blow his brains out and injected another with pure heroin, not to mention had her own mother killed. If Cora dwelled on those cozy facts, she'd have a hard time speaking at all, let alone instill enough confidence for April to trust her. With April's guard down, Cora might get a few precious minutes of snooping. Cora concentrated on the hunch that the sophisticated Miss Rothman watched too much E-TV and *Inside Edition*. She was intoxicated by her fifteen minutes of fame. Cora needed to use that arrogance to her advantage.

April reached for a cigarette from a lacquered case on the table and fished in the drawer for a light. Cora used the moment to click on the mini-recorder. No need to inform her that the interview was being taped, she had no intention of using what she learned for Andy's story anyway.

"What do you think Nate Price was looking for in your apartment? Do you have any idea?" Cora asked with notebook poised and ready.

"I don't believe he was trying to find anything. I think he was looking for the perfect spot to plant something." She finally located some matches and lit up, dragging deeply on the cigarette.

Cora's eyes rounded with feigned surprise. "What do you think he wanted to plant?" She jotted a few words and waited.

"I don't know. Something that would implicate me in my mother's death."

"So you believe your mom to be dead and no longer just missing?" Cora lowered her voice to a soft questioning tone.

April looked at her like one would gaze on a dim-witted child. "I don't think my mother is still wandering around in the bayou, Miss Dearing. If she was alive, don't you think I would have heard from her by now?"

"Cora, please. Of course, you're right. I just was hoping for the best." She jotted a few notes rapidly and tapped her ballpoint on her front teeth. She'd seen the gesture once on TV and liked it. "So if Nate Price had been able to plant phony evidence to connect you with the crime, and if you were charged with anything, then Provincial Trust wouldn't have to pay out the insurance settlement." She squirmed a little on the raw silk sofa, her bladder uncomfortably full. She had to stop drinking so much coffee right before she left home, or get in line for a transplant of larger kidneys.

"I wouldn't need to be convicted of anything, Cora," April spoke patiently as though recognizing she dealt with not-the-brightest-bulb-in-the-box. "Just the implication that I had anything to do with mother's untimely death would tie up the payment of the policy for a long time. Maybe even years." She dragged on the cigarette once more and snubbed it out in a crystal ashtray. "And I'm sure you can understand why I'm anxious to get back to New York and get this over with." She rose to her feet a bit unsteadily.

That was the clue that took Cora by surprise. April Rothman had been drinking before Cora arrived; she was half-in-the-bag. Cora watched her closely for telltale signs.

April walked through the dining area, calling over her shoulder, "I'm going to have something to drink. What would you like?"

Cora scrambled to her feet to follow. The thought of the tape recorder advancing in her bag tripped her up for a moment. Any conversation in the kitchen wouldn't be picked up by the microphone, but it would look rather obvious to drag the bag along with her. She opted to forget recording the conversation. April was beginning to relax and she didn't want to jeopardize any opportunity.

"I'll have a vodka and tonic, if you've got it." Cora pulled up the breakfast stool and planted herself.

"I do. Lemon or lime?" April had already poured something dark amber into her tumbler and reached into the cupboard for another glass. The stemware had been lined up at the front edge of the cabinet, so it looked like a greater quantity than it was. No plastic cups from the old Superdome, no to-go cups from fast food joints, like those in most people's kitchens.

"Lime, thanks." Cora studied the woman's back as she reached for ice cubes and poured the liquor. Her bra cut deeply into her flesh in the same nasty way Cora's did, no matter how many blasted exercises she did. Surely this woman couldn't be a triple murderess. She was so normal.

"You know. I didn't even want the life insurance money at first. I never wanted Mom to take out that damn policy in the first place. I think life insurance is so macabre, but she'd insisted. When it looked like—" Her voice trailed off as she took a fortifying gulp of her drink. "—she wasn't turning up, I just wanted to go home. But this Detective Rhodes insisted I stick around and assist the investigation." She downed the rest of the tumbler like a trained professional.

"I'm sure Detective Rhodes appreciates all the help you've been," Cora said. "They didn't have a lot to go on."

"That damned Ethan Galen has been mucking things up right from the start." She poured another hefty amount into her glass without bothering with ice this time.

Cora sipped her vodka and tonic; it was cold, and the lime slice refreshing, but unfortunately, the icy liquid reminded her of how badly she needed to urinate. Damn. Why did she have to have a bladder control problem now?

"Do you know what I think?" April asked, leaning slightly over the counter, getting awfully close to Cora's personal space.

Cora shook her head no and sipped more of the drink. *Nothing like getting drunk with a triple murderer—do you think she'll go for four, ladies and gentlemen?*

"I think Galen's company got in over its head, writing such a large policy on my mother. After she passed the intensive physical and qualified, he probably realized he didn't have enough time to recoup enough from the enormous premiums to lower his ratings on the policy. His company would be responsible for a much larger stake of the pool. So, he planned this whole thing. If my mom is dead and the sole beneficiary, me, is implicated in her death, then his company gets out of ever paying the policy." She jiggled the remaining cubes in her glass. "He hired that sleazy Cajun in the bayou, and that flippy Frederick to help him. And then got the good-old-boy company investigator to stir up lies and insinuations." She reached over and topped off Cora's glass with straight Vodka. "When his fabrications weren't having quite the effect he hoped, he had Price break in and plant something." She tossed her head back with a hearty laugh.

The raucous sound chilled Cora's blood worse than the frigid temperature in the room or the cold drink. She squirmed again and prayed she didn't wet her pants before she learned something concrete to help Ethan.

"Too bad I was a little quicker on the draw. Boy, you should have seen the look on Price's face when I walked in on him red-handed and pulled my gun out." This time her gleeful cackle was curtailed by the phone ringing.

Cora had noticed a cell phone on the coffee table in the living room.

"Excuse me," April murmured. "That might be important." She moved with an unsteady gait toward the insistent ringing.

Time for Cora to make her move, but not to rummage through April's drawers and closets. She knew the woman wouldn't give her enough time to find anything but trouble, just like Nate. No, she had to find the bathroom, and fast. Cora slipped off the stool and headed down the opposite hallway as soon as April staggered from the kitchen.

Several doorways beckoned in the dimly lit hall. She opted for door number two and swung it open. It was not the bathroom, but the sight awaiting was no less astounding.

Ada Rothman sat in a chair positioned under a floor lamp, reading a novel. She looked up and locked eyes with Cora, equally startled. Neither woman spoke.

Cora stared at her for several moments while the brain synapses processed the impossible information. She wasn't dead. She was sitting in her daughter's apartment. *Nobody is a murderer.*

"Mrs. Rothman?" Cora asked timidly and waited until the full impact hit her. She reacted as though the missing woman had just been located after wandering days in the swamp. *It's a miracle—she's alive and well!* "I'm really happy to see you again."

"Ah, Mrs. Dearing, isn't it? I do remember you from Water Lilies. What a pain-in-the-ass you've turned out to be, haven't you?" She set her paperback on the small table and crossed her legs, as though this were just a normal interruption of her afternoon reading. "It's really a shame you've become such a nuisance for my April."

A cold gleam replaced the surprised expression in the woman's dark eyes. Cold and deadly.

"You tiresome little twit," April said, over Cora's shoulder. "So that's why you came here—to snoop around like Price? You're even stupider than him and far less lucky. He'll only get ten years in prison for breaking and entering."

Cora half turned toward April. "Honestly, I was only looking for the bathroom. I have really got to pee." She held up her hands in surrender. Maybe the dumb-act might get her out of here. "Look, I'm glad your mom is still alive. And I'd prefer to mind my own business from here on out."

Cora tried to step past April in the doorway, but felt the cold steel of a gun in her ribcage. *Must be the 38 Ruger*, she thought. Guess we no longer have to run ballistics and wait for mama's body to turn up.

"You're in love with him, aren't you? Galen. That's why you're here. Not for any story for *The Times*. What is it about that man that people are throwing their lives away to save his company's ass?" She shook her head incredulously and pushed Cora back down the hallway into the living room, jabbing her mercilessly with the gun barrel. "I just don't see it. Yeah, he's good-looking, but looks only go so far. Not worth throwing your life away like that idiot Bearnard did." She didn't sound half so drunk, as she did before Cora's unfortunate discovery.

"Frederick wasn't an idiot. He was a good friend to Ethan, but obviously underestimated your character. Nice people have a hard time recognizing true evil when they're staring at it."

April emitted another forced laugh. "Sticks and stones, Cora. Please don't try to alter the inevitable outcome by sweet-talking me." With a none-too-gentle effort, she pushed Cora down on the sofa and perched on the edge of the chair across from her. She leaned close before speaking. "Freddie was an idiot. He followed me around for days like something out of an Inspector Clusseau movie. It was truly quite pathetic. That man couldn't do anything right." She lit a cigarette but never allowed the gun barrel to waver from perfect aim at Cora's face. "It was so easy. I let him follow me to Algiers and confronted him just when he thought he'd been so subtle. I allowed him to charm me. He really thought himself quite the lady-killer, no?" She grinned sweetly.

"I wouldn't know. I didn't know him that well." Cora's eyes darted around the darkened room. Her eyes spotted at least three bolts on the front door keeping her in.

"Take my word for it. There was nothing subtle about Freddie. I told him to get us a room in one of those crash houses because I wanted to party with him. I came in the service entrance and met him in the hallway outside the room. He figured I still was hot for his body after all these years." Her laugh sounded brittle, caustic, like nails down a chalkboard.

"You mean you did know him before?"

"Why, yes, Cora. I went to Tulane. Just for a year, but long enough to meet Frederick Bearnard. He led me on. I thought we had something special going on. I didn't notice he never took me out or brought me around to meet his real friends."

Cora saw the old, but still raw pain. The kind that made people do horrible things. It was not a sight to stimulate hope for getting out of there to write up a juicy story.

"Turns out that Freddie was nice to lots of girls, if you know what I mean." April flicked her ashes neatly in the ashtray.

Hate to forfeit a deposit for a burn hole in the carpeting.

"That's what I hate about this town. It's loaded with men like Freddie who think they can get by on looks and charm." The pain skewing her features relaxed some in her face. "I don't think old Freddie looks good anymore, do you?"

Cora ignored the question and asked one of her own. "Humor my inquiring reporter's mind, April. How did Freddie manage to OD? He wouldn't have used drugs."

"You're correct there. Freddie could drink a sailor under the table, but wouldn't touch the no-calorie high. It was easy. I told you. He thought himself a stud. I fucked him, and when he fell asleep, I stuck a needle in his tight, little ass. Easy, predictable, Freddie. He was a bit more talented than the average loser. You know, now that I think about it…there was one thing he was good at."

Cora stared at the woman, incapable of hiding her shock. "You had sex with him, then killed him. Like a spider?"

"Spare me your outraged looks, Cora. He'd still be alive if he'd just butted out. I'll let you stew on the implications of that for a minute or two."

Cora wouldn't let herself think about implications. She had to keep April talking, at least until she figured a way out of there. April lit another cigarette. Cora glanced to the patio doors. No telling what kind of locks they had since heavy blinds blocked the view.

"What about Antoine? What did he have to do with this? I'm afraid I'm a little confused. Why would he take his own life after killing your mother when your mom appears alive and well after all?" Cora glanced to her right. Ada Rothman had followed them as far as the dining room and leaned against the breakfast bar. She was also smoking a cigarette, something Cora hadn't seen either woman do at Water Lilies.

"Cora, Cora. I'm afraid you better not give up your day job yet. You just don't have the mindset for investigative work." April clucked her tongue. "But I'll take pity on you." She sat back down on the sofa. "Antoine was one…greedy…cracker." She dragged out each word succinctly. "We paid him more than he makes in five years at that dump of a restaurant just to take mother to where we parked a second car."

"I had to hide under a tarp in his boat getting bit by God-knows-what until that pig got around to me," whined Ada, not able to remain silent any longer. Now this was the woman Cora had known and loathed at Water Lilies.

"Then, he turned around and blackmailed us. Can you believe it?"

Cora clucked her tongue this time. "No honor among thieves."

April thinned her lips. "No, there isn't. He thought he could squeeze us for more—threatened to tell the cops that mom wasn't dead and the whole thing was a scam. We paid him more at first, then mother pointed out we'd never be able to relax and live in peace as long as that creep knew the truth." April nodded affectionately at Ada.

Nice to know she was fond of mommy-dearest after all. It restored her faith in womankind.

"So I had to go back to that horribly buggy swampland and pay Antoine a social call after closing time. I found his shotgun under the bar where every good cracker bartender keeps one, and found him passed out drunk in his fishing boat. It was even easier to get the drop on Antoine than on Price. And I thought country boys would be a little slicker than that."

"Why would he write a suicide note? He had to know he was going to die with a shotgun pointed at him," Cora asked. She scooted to the edge of the sofa.

April leaned forward, as though eager to answer this one. "I explained he was soon going to hell, and that he could go there alone with a clear conscience, or with the knowledge his two little girls were going along, too. He made the right, fatherly choice."

Cora gazed into the cold, cruel eyes of a madwoman. April was right. She didn't have the right mindset for investigative work into criminal minds. Nothing in her past had prepared her for this.

"Enough of this chatter, April," Ada Rothman interrupted, walking into the living room. "You're just wasting time. We need to figure out what to do with her." The woman spoke calmly, with complete assurance. She kept her eyes focused on her daughter as though Cora were just a bug to be ignored in polite company. "We can't let anyone find her until after the court declares Antoine's note valid and orders the settlement to be paid. No more bodies turning up until we get our hands on the cash and get out of this god-awful town."

Ada looked at Cora for the first time since Cora blundered into her room. "I don't want to eat red beans and rice or cornbread ever again. I want a filet mignon and a twice-baked potato."

"Sorry to keep you from your perfect meal, Mrs. Rothman," Cora said.

"Well, girlfriend, mama's right. Our new-best-friendship is about to come to an end," April said, mimicking Cora's slight southern accent. "Too bad, I really don't have many friends."

"Maybe it's your hospitality. Do you think I can have another vodka tonic?"

"I don't think so." She moved the gun barrel in a slow circle in front of Cora. "With ten million dollars, I can buy all the friends a girl needs without a shred of hospitality. And right now, you're the only thing standing in my way." The friendly smile faded from April's face leaving an expression that frightened Cora to the core.

It was bored, weary, and consummately evil.

THIRTEEN

CORA HELD UP her hands as though in surrender. "Wait, can we take a break just for a minute? I need to go to the bathroom." She rose slowly to her feet.

April looked incredulous. "You really don't get it, do you? I'm not taking you out to lunch here." She shook her head as though disappointed with Cora's slow-wittedness.

"I know that, but I've got to go. You don't want me to pee all over your lovely sofa, do you?" She took a steadying breath and tried to move her legs. They barely supported her weight and threatened to buckle at any moment. What was that old adage? *At least I'll die trying.*

"You wouldn't dare," April said.

Cora stared at her with arms crossed over her chest. "It's almost out of my hands."

The thought that fastidious April would have to stay in a condo with a urine-smelling sofa or carpeting did the trick. "All right," she snapped. "But don't think you'll be making a break for it. That window isn't big enough for a French Quarter rat to squeeze through." She gave Cora a push toward the dining room.

Luckily Cora's legs held as she started walking down the hallway to the back. April handed Ada the Ruger. "Watch her, mom. Don't let her close the bathroom door. We don't want any silly shenanigans."

Ada delivered a savage jab to the center of Cora's back with the gun barrel. These ladies weren't the social princesses like everyone assumed back in Lafourche.

"Don't worry. I can handle her. You start packing your things and whatever money we've got left. I don't want to stay here until the hearing. Everybody seems to know where we are now, thanks to Price."

From the corner of her eye, Cora saw April turn into the first room on the left. "The bathroom's in there," Ada said, pushing Cora hard through the first doorway on the right.

Maybe it was her sixty-something age, maybe a hint of decency still survived, but Ada Rothman pulled the door halfway closed. "Don't close it all the way, or I'll shoot you right here and feed you down the garbage disposal if I have to," she snapped.

When Ada's face disappeared from view, Cora flew to the tiny, louvered window. April hadn't lied about its size. It was too small to even get her head through. But not too small to see out of, and what she spotted made her breath catch and her heart pound with a vengeance.

Ethan Galen was scrambling over the privacy fence from the next condo. He dropped down onto the balcony of what Cora knew to be Ada Rothman's bedroom. He had found her. That knowledge filled her with a primal joy she'd never known before. He was risking his life, not for his company or his family, but for her. He'd tracked her here and was about to save the day.

Or at least die trying.

She longed to call out to get his attention, but clamped her hand over her mouth instead. Any communication between them would endanger Ethan's life. If he managed to get through the patio door into the bedroom, he didn't need to run into Mama or sweet April until good and ready.

"What are you doing in there?" Ada's snarly voice brought Cora back to her own present reality.

Without another option, Cora did the only thing that came to mind. She pulled up her dress, pulled down her panties, and sat on the toilet just as Ada pushed open the door to check on her.

"I'm sorry, Mrs. Rothman, but I told you I really had to go." The distinctive sound of tinkling offered supporting evidence.

Ada colored with embarrassment and pulled the door back to the half-closed position. "Well, just hurry up," she said.

No, Cora knew she couldn't hurry. She had to give Ethan as much time as he needed to get into the apartment. She just hoped it would be enough.

A loud, crashing sound at the front door jarred Cora from her thoughts of Ethan. "What the hell?" Ada muttered. "What was that?" she screamed to her daughter.

Cora heard fear in the older woman's voice. Ada opened the door again and trained her gun on Cora as though somehow responsible for the ruckus.

"Don't take your eyes off that bitch." April's words echoed down the hallway.

Cora stood and slowly fixed her clothes. "Whew! That feels better."

The pounding at the front door shook the walls of the condo. Something was battering to get in and not taking no for an answer. Each thump against the reinforced door spiked Cora's own heart in unison. The cavalry had arrived in Metairie. She just hoped they'd get through before bullets started flying.

"Get the hell away from that door, or I'll kill this newspaper woman right now!" April's words shouted from the living room rang in Cora's ears, temporarily paralyzing her. She was the newspaper woman in question.

Ethan is here. He's right in the next room. Do some-

thing to help the situation. The mantra chanting in her head galvanized her to action. She turned on the taps and pumped soap into her palms, then began to wash her hands.

"Get out here!" Ada shouted at Cora. Ada's weathered face contorted with rage and fear, since their perfect plan had turned sour.

"I have to wash my hands, Mrs. Rothman," Cora explained as though talking to a child, but focused her gaze on the older woman. When a crashing noise in the living room grabbed Ada's attention, Cora made her move. With a fluid grace not usually evident, Cora reached for the metal wastebasket next to the sink. Lowering her head behind the can, she charged Rothman's midsection like a bull in the ring infuriated by the color red. It was the only thing she could think of, but hard to do to such a nice old lady like Ada.

The maneuver worked. Cora slammed Ada Rothman against the opposite wall with a resounding whack, while the Ruger flew from her hand. "You bitch," she screamed. "April!"

Cora dropped her grip on the trashcan as soon as she made contact and brought her fist up squarely into the woman's jaw. The pain that ratcheted through her hand and up her arm indicated the blow had to hurt Rothman as much as it hurt her. She'd never struck an older woman. Heck, she couldn't remember punching anybody before, not even as a child on the playground.

Rothman crumbled against the wall and slid down, but was by no means out. Her hands wildly grasped at Cora's head, latching onto a fistful of hair as the two tumbled to the floor—Ada on the bottom. Cora tried to keep her balance, but fell on top of her.

"You knocked my front cap loose," Ada screamed.

"I'll kill you for that." She tore a handful of Cora's hair from the scalp. Cora shrieked with the sudden excruciating tear. Rothman pushed her to the side and lunged for the gun. She tried to stop her but was temporarily stunned by the pain. No one had ever pulled her hair out by the roots. It was no laughing matter.

"No, I don't think so, Mrs. Rothman."

Cora heard the calm, collected voice of Ethan Galen even though she couldn't see anything but Ada Rothman's ample backside. Ethan leaned down and picked up the Ruger, training it on the woman with cool assurance. "Are you all right, my love?" he asked with the dear French accent she loved more than anything in the world. He didn't take his eyes off Ada Rothman.

"I'm fine." Cora scrambled to her feet. "I was providing a little distraction for you," she said, pulling her dress discreetly down her thighs.

"Is that right?" he asked with a grin. He apparently enjoyed the peek at her underwear as she recovered from the sprawl, but kept watching the hallway, not wanting an unexpected surprise from April.

"That's right. I saw you from the bathroom window when you came over the fence from the other condo."

"I want to hear the whole story later, my love. But right now, I need to see what mini-bitch is up to." Ethan dragged Ada Rothman to her feet and nudged her past Cora. The woman kept fingering her front tooth where the cosmetic cap used to be. "And I want you to wait in there." Ethan pushed Cora backwards into the bathroom. "And no argument! Once we're married, you can give the orders for the rest of our lives, but not today."

Cora's mouth gaped open. "But I could—"

The deafening sound of gunshots coming from the living room forestalled any further arguments. There were shouts from a bullhorn and wild, screamed obscenities from April. Cora heard the police bellow out police identification just like in the movies and the crashing sound of breaking glass, followed by the sound of furniture being overturned.

Please hide in the bathroom with me Ethan until this whole thing is over. I can't bear the thought of anything happening to you now that I know I love you. And know you love me.

But Ethan disappeared down the hallway with the Ruger aimed at the small of Ada's back before Cora could express her fears. She heard another gunshot, then a piercing scream of pain that had to come from April.

She couldn't hide in the bathroom for another moment. A *Times* reporter needed to see what the heck was going on. And make sure Ethan was all right. Did he really say once we're married or did she imagine it, brought on by calamitous events and the shock of having part of her glorious mane ripped from her scalp?

Cora crept into a room that resembled a war zone. The front door lay splintered into pieces across the foyer floor. The sliding glass door to the balcony was shattered into millions of pieces and spewed everywhere. A large battering ram lay discarded across the once pristine overturned sofa. There were vested SWAT team members and uniformed police stomping through the debris of the living room with more arriving through the hole in the balcony door.

"Cora," Ethan said as she walked in and stepped over a table lamp. He pushed Ada Rothman toward a waiting a police officer, then hurried to wrap her in his arms. "It's over. You were very brave, *ma petite*, but you must never do anything like this again. It was very foolish of you to come here to get your story. The Rothmans are dangerous, desperate women. They could have killed you." He shook her like a rag doll and pulled her against his chest.

Cora felt his heart thud against the thin silk of his shirt. "I didn't come here to get any story," she said with muffled voice. She looked over his shoulder to see April Rothman sprawled face down on the ruined carpeting. Her hands were restrained at her sides by a police officer while a medical technician worked on her back. A large red patch on her blouse widened and darkened while Cora watched. She'd been shot in the shoulder. She looked back at Ethan. "I didn't come here to get any story," she repeated, keeping her voice level and controlled. "I came here to find what Nate had been looking for or find something to tie April to Freddie's murder. I thought I'd have more luck than Nate since she kinda liked me."

Ethan's eyes widened, then darkened with fury. This news was apparently worse than trying to get a scoop for the paper. He released her shoulders abruptly. "You endangered your life by coming here." He struggled to keep his tone a raspy whisper when he longed to roar at her. "The police were closing in on them with the information I'd been providing all along."

Cora straightened her spine and looked him in the eye. "Ethan, Detective Rhodes thought you were in on the plan with Antoine and Freddie. He thought you were the mastermind. I couldn't let him arrest you and further blacken your family's reputation. Even if you were cleared later, the stigma of the arrest would dog you in society forever."

Ethan looked like he'd been kicked in the stomach with a steel-toed boot. Color faded from his suntanned face. He exhaled a long weary breath of air and ran his hand through his hair.

"Well, that's not entirely the truth, Ms. Dearing."

Charles Rhodes stepped from where he'd been eaves-dropping to Ethan's side. "Mr. Galen suspected from the start that these women were the two who'd pulled an insurance scam before."

"An insurance scam?" Cora said. Things were starting to make sense.

"They defrauded an insurance acquaintance of mine to the tune of five hundred thousand," Ethan explained, tracing a path down her forearm with his fingertips. "A court in Oregon ordered the policy to be paid before investigators could prove no death had actually taken place. It was an elaborate scheme. And we believe they did it once before that, too, for fifty thousand, shortly after Mrs. Rothman got divorced. With double indemnity for violent or accidental death, this would've been the scam to set them up for life."

"We just found tickets in their luggage for Costa Rica," Rhodes interrupted. "And a hundred thousand in cash. That must be left from the last time she met her untimely death."

The three paused for a moment as April was carried from the apartment on a stretcher and Ada was led out in handcuffs. She was complaining loudly about the cuffs being too tight and cutting into her wrists. Some things never changed.

"So, you knew from the start Mrs. Rothman wasn't dead?" Cora asked Ethan, narrowing her eyes.

"I suspected it, my love." He bent close to her face and kissed her forehead tenderly. "I decided to follow them out to Water Lilies after Price found out that's where they were headed. I wanted to get a look at them, besides keep tabs on their movements." His mouth trailed kisses down the bridge of her nose.

Cora gently pushed him back. "That's when you had Freddie plant the idea of my going there, too?"

"*Oui*, Madame. But I never thought they'd actually pull it off in the bayou. Since they knew no one there, and the swamp isn't a friendly place for the unfamiliar, I really thought they were just taking a getaway weekend."

"And you thought I'd make a pleasant diversion while you're there." Cora balled her hand into a fist and pushed it into his solar plexus. "Someone to pass the time with while you were on stakeout."

Charles Rhodes discreetly turned his attention to the officers gathering and bagging evidence from the destroyed room. "I think I'll see if the boys need my help," he murmured.

"*Oui*, Madame." He trapped her fist in his two large hands and brought it to his mouth for a kiss. "Never imagining that I would fall in love with a raven-haired newspaper woman. Yikes, how am I going to explain that to *grandmère* before the wedding?"

"You're putting the cart before the horse, Mr. Galen. I didn't agree to marry anyone, least of all a conniving, scheming, despoiler of women at romantic B&B's."

"Ah, but you will agree to marry me, or I'll follow you around like a love-starved dog for the rest of your life." The grip on her wrist tightened as he drew her closer to his body. "I love you, Cora. Forgive me for not being honest with you from the beginning. But knowing your penchant for—" He struggled to select the right words. "—being knowledgeable about all situations, I thought it best that you not know of our suspicions. The last thing we needed was the scam story to appear in *The Times*. The two women would've packed up and left New Orleans, only to set up their scheme someplace else. We had to stop them. It went far beyond the money involved; they killed two men this time. First Antoine, then Freddie."

Cora saw the pain in Ethan's eyes with the mention of Freddie's name, but she had to press him. She had to know the whole story. "So, Antoine was in it with them?"

"Yes, he was paid to transport Ada out of the bayou, but he got greedy. He was blackmailing them for more money. Detective Rhodes found the proof out in La-fourche Parish that April had paid him cash on two different occasions." His hands slipped down to Cora's waist and he stretched his long fingers across her back. "We know the suicide note was coerced. We have tire tracks close enough to the camp and other forensic evidence proving that April was out there the night he died. She's in a lot deeper than insurance fraud this time."

"Wait a minute." Cora hurried over to her bag, partly buried under broken glass and retrieved her mini-cassette recorder. The machine was still running. She clicked it off and handed it to Ethan. "Here's all the proof you need that she killed Freddie." Cora didn't want to remind Ethan of his friend's murder, but now was the time to get the details cleared up once and for all.

Ethan exhaled a pent-up breath as he took the machine, slipping it into his pocket. "Thank you. I'll listen to it with Detective Rhodes later."

"Freddie had no part in this. He had been following April to help with the investigation," she said.

Ethan backed Cora up to a counter stool. When she sat, he nudged her knees open to stand between them with sweet closeness. "I know. He wanted to help me, and he thought Price got to have all the fun." Ethan shook his head and raked his hair back from his forehead. "Freddie thought this all an amusing game since he'd known April during his sophomore year of college. That tidbit I just found out." He ground his teeth and reached for an un-opened bottle of water on the counter. "He never told me about April. He thought he'd be able to get close enough to pin Antoine's murder on her. But she got to him first."

"Frederick pretty much did what he wanted. You can't blame yourself, Ethan."

Ethan's haunted gaze returned to Cora's face. "Losing Freddie to this pair was bad enough. I couldn't bear to lose you. When she killed Antoine and then Freddie, I feared for your safety. Ordering you off seemed to have the opposite result." He lifted her chin to stare into her eyes. "I wanted Detective Rhodes to cast suspicion on me so you'd stay away until this thing was over. If you thought me a murderer, *cher*, I would not be quite the catch to take home to Columbia to meet your mama."

"I'm still not sure about that, Mr. Galen," she teased, but tightened her thighs around his legs.

"Torment me, punish me anyway you see fit for my deception, but don't shut me out. I couldn't bear it. I love you, Cora." The last poignant words were whispered next to her ear, but nevertheless, Detective Rhodes who still lingered nearby, overheard them.

"That's what I like to hear, a happy ending after all. Boy gets girl and we get our crooks," Rhodes said, finishing his notes on a legal pad.

"Detective, you're a worse eavesdropper than me," Cora said.

"Yes, ma'am. That is the truth, but I get paid to do it."

Cora wasn't about to be put off so easily. "And you purposely deceived me about Ethan. You had me believing he was part of a murder plot, when there hadn't even been a murder." She struggled to keep her voice down, since several police officers seemed more interested in their conversation than bagging evidence in the room.

Rhodes shrugged into his sport coat. "Ah, that was for your own good. I agreed with Mr. Galen."

"And you knew who'd been leaving me flowers, didn't you?"

"Not originally. I had to do a little investigating on that one." He looked a little uneasy as several officers exchanged curious looks and held up a pleading hand. "Enough for now. I'll need both of you to come to the station to give statements for the file, but tomorrow will be soon enough. Tonight, you both have a bit more explaining to do. To each other." He winked at Cora, nodded to Ethan, and started toward the door.

"One more thing, Detective. In your discussion with the prosecutor regarding the Rothmans, do you think you might convince him to drop the charges against Nate Price?" Ethan asked. "I can't have that guy in jail for ten years. I'm going to need him to be my best man." He flashed Cora the smile she couldn't resist. "And thereafter, when I take over the day-to-day running of Provincial Trust, I'll need his expertise. It's time I get a serious day job since I'm about to become a married man."

"I'll do what I can. I'm sure April can be induced to drop the complaint against him, in return for regular extermination of her jail cell. We know how those two feel about crawly things." Rhodes waved his hand in the air at them and walked out the door.

"My car's parked down there." Ethan pointed at the gaping hole in the patio door leading to the balcony.

"But I prefer to exit the old-fashioned way—out the front and down the steps," she said, slipping off the stool. She stepped gingerly over the broken porcelain figurines. "How about I take the streetcar home and meet you somewhere later. I'd like a good, long shower." She pulled her cotton dress free from her backside.

"No, you can shower at my house." He picked up her hand and led her through the broken doorframe. The sunshine blinded them as they stepped outside the building, while the heat and humidity hit Cora like a slap after the iciness of the apartment.

"I'm not letting you out of my sight for a few days. Not until the Rothman vipers are behind bars. And not until the story appears in *The Times*," he said, squeezing her palm tightly in his grip. "I need to know if your affection for me was real or staged to get the scoop and a promotion at the paper."

Cora burst out laughing. "Ethan, I'm more likely to get fired than promoted. I'm not sure when I last checked in at the office." Then she sobered immediately. She'd heard the uncertainty in his voice and wanted to put any misconception to rest right now. She pulled him to a stop in the parking lot and faced him directly. "I haven't been interested in the story for a long time now. I wanted to find out who the killer was to clear you." She shook her head thinking about the true nature of April and Ada's crime. "I thought I could use my access as a journalist to gain their confidence, to find something to help you." Then she added in a small voice, "I know some reporters sensationalize stories to the point of creating fiction, but I'm not one of them. I never have been."

"*La vérité, m'amie.* I don't doubt you, but I love hearing it in your own words." He kissed her tenderly as though she were a newborn babe, pulled back, and kissed her again with the passion of a grown man, a man who hadn't held her for two days. His arms locked behind her back as he deepened the kiss into something very wicked indeed.

"Hey, could you two save that stuff till we're back at

the ranch and relaxing in air-conditioning? I'm dyin' out here. It must be a hundred and five."

The voice of Nate Price broke the delicious intimate moment. Ethan and Cora separated long enough to turn hostile eyes on him. He was leaning against Ethan's Jag, which sat in the full Louisiana sunshine. Not a bit of shade in sight. His shirt had dark sweat rings by the arms, while his face was streaked with perspiration.

"I thought you were in jail."

"I should have left you in jail." Ethan and Cora spoke simultaneously.

"He didn't even leave the keys so I could run the AC. He just ordered me to stay by the car," Nate complained, crossing his arms over his chest. He looked like a small boy who'd been punished unjustly.

Ethan guided Cora toward the car with his hand on her back. "The judge ordered him to stay away from the Rothmans," he explained, "or be held in contempt of court. He's out on bail; he's not a free man yet. Otherwise I'll have to get my phone disconnected. Nate whined more in jail than I even think Ada Rothman will." Ethan threw Nate the car keys.

Nate plucked them from the air. "Did I forget my manners? Thanks for springing me, good buddy. Jail really is a lousy place to meet women." He unlocked the door and started to get in the passenger side of the two-seater car.

"No, you're driving, good buddy. I'll hold Cora on my lap." Ethan hit the button to lower the convertible top. "Either that, or you can take the streetcar back. Your choice."

"Boss, you know I'm still your chauffeur no matter what wheels you've got." He opened the passenger door with a flourish for Ethan and Cora.

"We're not all going to fit in there," Cora said, as Ethan got in then reached for her hand.

"We will, *ma petite*. You'll see."

She shook her head and clambered into the small car after him. She positioned herself carefully on his lap, but couldn't find a safe spot. The connection between their bodies was exquisite. Each time she shifted, trying to find a more comfortable position, she found instead more stimulating contact than before. Cora wrapped one arm around Ethan's shoulder and hugged his midsection with the other.

"You see? We fit like peas in a pod." Ethan gripped a hand around her waist and kept her knees away from the gearshift with the other.

"You once referred to me as a bird. Now I'm nothing more than a uniform-sized green vegetable," she said as Nate peeled out of the parking lot.

It should have been an uncomfortable ride. It should've been mildly embarrassing with Nate Price in such close proximity to their wiggling. But with the wind blowing her hair across Ethan's face, and his heady male scent assailing her senses, Cora relaxed for the first time in weeks. She watched suburban Metairie fly by as they raced down the freeway in utter contentment.

"What do you say, my favorite reporter?" Ethan drew her head down to his shoulder and whispered in her ear. "Do you love me?"

"I think I do."

"And will you marry me?"

"We'll see. But I think I just might."

FOURTEEN

"JEANETTE! JEANETTE, WHERE ARE YOU?"

Ethan's thunderous voice pierced the stillness of the courtyard garden. The incredibly serene fall morning in the quiet Garden District came to an abrupt end. Cora set down her coffee cup and blushed deeply upon meeting the eye of Ethan's housekeeper. She would never get used to the idea of having a housekeeper for one thing. Her own mother never hired help even for spring cleaning, opting instead to prod Cora along until they made the house shine. Then again, they'd never lived in a fourteen-room mansion built over two hundred years ago. Jeanette had moved with them to the Chestnut Street house upon their return from a honeymoon. They'd agreed to housesit *grandmère's* palatial digs while she toured Europe with two other widows. Where they would live after that, Ethan declared, would be up to Cora—buy a house in the Quarter, or the Garden District, or in the country, or live in his suite of rooms above the gallery on Rue Royal. But the longer she stayed in the elegant home that breathed with fascinating history, the more she wanted to stay here, at least for awhile, and get to know his grandmother. She had been utterly charming at the wedding, offering her home on a permanent basis before the ink dried on their marriage license.

"Jeanette," Ethan called down from the back gallery.

"I am here, my ass-pain," Jeanette said, refilling Cora's cup.

"Oh, there you are." He gentled his thunderous look when he spotted his bride staring up as though he were a madman. "Good morning, my dear. I trust you're enjoying your coffee. I'll join you in a minute for breakfast." His sweet tone sounded like an enormous effort had been expended. "Mrs. Peteriere, may I speak with you upstairs for a moment, if it wouldn't be too much trouble?" Ethan asked, and disappeared behind the French doors into their bedroom.

Cora looked at Jeanette, who was trying, but failing to suppress a grin. "What is going on?" she asked.

"Nothing to worry about, Madam Galen," Jeanette said, slicing melons and strawberries on a cutting board in her lap.

Cora had asked her several times to call her by her given name, to which Jeanette always replied "When the time is right, I will. Right now, you need to be called Madam Galen."

Jeanette glanced up to the second-floor windows and smiled broadly this time. "He just discovered I cleaned out his wardrobe while he was at the office yesterday." She chortled with glee.

"What did you throw out that has him in such a dither?" Cora relaxed somewhat and sipped her coffee.

"Nothing important. Just that horrible *Tulane* shirt that lost its sleeves and any semblance of decency years ago."

Cora's eyes widened in disbelief. Although Ethan left for the offices of Provincial Trust dressed in the finest suits his local tailor could find, Saturday mornings with his wife, flying kites on the levee or roller blading in Woldenberg Park were reserved for his favorite shirt from his alma mater. Cora usually switched between the *French Quarter: Home of the serious drunk* shirt and the *I love South Carolina* shirt that had been a wedding gift from her six-year-old niece. "You threw out the *Tulane* shirt?" Cora held her breath unwittingly.

"Yes, am I not truly horrible?" Jeanette rose from her chair and set the board of perfectly sliced fruit on the table. "I best go have this out with him. If he doesn't send me packing to my son in Baltimore this time, then I can relax and rest easy. I will be around to meddle in another generation of Galen lives." She gave Cora a conspiratorial wink. "I just couldn't stand to launder that rag one more time. After all, he's respectable now and needs to dress like it, even on Saturdays." She graced Cora with a long generous smile and headed up the stairs to face her employer, the man she watched grow from infancy.

"Good luck. Let me know where I should send your last paycheck," Cora teased.

"Just leave it on the kitchen counter as always," she answered and disappeared inside. "Don't you worry, *ma petite.*"

Cora finished her coffee and picked up *The Times* as the last fragrance of fading lilies wafted from the back garden. She was dying to see where they'd positioned her latest feature story on "The Quality of Life in the Mississippi Basin." She'd been getting better placement lately since threatening Jim Matthews she'd jump ship to a competitive newspaper. She didn't find her story. Her eyes fastened instead on an article on the front page of the metro section.

French Quarter heiress and eight other women arrested in campus brawl. A smaller typeset proclaimed: Sorority to lose its charter.

Cora glanced toward the French doors of the gallery. Ethan was nowhere to be seen. With an ominous sense of dread rising up her throat, she skimmed the rest of the article.

*"Chloe Galen, daughter of Clotilde and the late Eti-
enne Galen, was among several sorority sisters and members of an unidentified fraternity arrested on the grounds
of the Chi Omega house on the Oxford campus of Ole
Miss. Police responded to disturbance complaints in the
wee hours of Saturday morning where they found a brawl
underway between members of two rival fraternities on
the back grounds. Miss Galen was arrested after inter-
vening with officers quelling the disturbance. Several
other young women were arrested on the same charge
and for underage drinking. The men had been attending a
party in the backyard of Chi Omega house. Police found
two kegs of beer and various open bottles of liquor. Chi
Omega had been placed under strict sanction last fall
following similar disturbances at the house. Under the
sanction, no alcohol could be on premises at any time.*

*"Ole Miss Dean of Campus Affairs issued a statement
indicating she would proceed with charter revocation
due to 'blatant disregard of campus policy."*

A knot tightened in Cora's gut as she finished the article like a child peeking at a scary movie from behind a
pillow—afraid to look, but helpless to look away.

*"The dean added that she would petition the board
for expulsion of Miss Galen for 'continued inappropriate
behavior.' This was Miss Galen's second arrest within
a year for public intoxication and underage drinking.
More serious charges of intimidating a police officer
were dropped in return for fifty hours of community service this past fall, wherefore she tutored at-risk students
at the local junior high several afternoons a week and
collected litter in the community park. Mrs. Galen, a
local scion of society and chairwoman of several Quarter charitable foundations, could not be reached for comment on her daughter's behavior."*

Cora set the paper down with a trembling hand. Sadness washed over her for the spirited young woman she'd met in the weeks before the wedding. Chloe had embraced her as though she'd known her for her entire life. She took it upon herself to coordinate the flowers, music, and photography for the lavish, overwhelming affair for five hundred guests. As bridal attendant, she had charmingly demurred to Cora's sister in the selection of bridesmaids' dresses, wearing the turquoise chiffon frou-frou disaster without a single complaint or lift of a disdainful brow.

Cora found her to be bright, capable, and generous, without a hint of the well-born snobbery she feared would set them apart. The young woman obviously adored Ethan and her other brother, Hunter, yet managed to expound her own opinions in the lively discussions around *grandmère's* table. Cora had liked her immediately. There was nothing not to like as far as she was concerned. If the girl had a wild, fun-loving streak, so what? At least she hadn't killed anybody. At least, not to Cora's knowledge.

She jolted back to awareness as her husband of several fabulous months slid into the opposite chair. "Ethan. There you are. Your omelet is getting cold." She poured a cup of coffee and slid it to him.

"Ah, I've lost my appetite." His expression remained stormy; lines around his eyes had deepened into a web of worry.

"Don't you fret about that shirt," she soothed. "I'll stop by the bookstore at Tulane this afternoon and buy another. I'll rip off the sleeves and pound it on levee rocks myself. I'll have it looking like a rag by dinner." She grinned at him, carefully folding *The Times* closed.

Ethan's smile filled his face, banishing the grim fatigue. He covered her hand with his larger one. "My darling wife. You are nothing a man could ever deserve. That shirt needed to be burned. Jeanette was right."

Cora blinked in disbelief. "Who are you and what have you done with my husband?" Ethan's eyes flicked over the folded paper, so Cora casually moved it to her lap.

Grimacing, Ethan said in a strangled voice. "Don't trouble yourself with the shirt or hiding *The Times* from me, although you're sweet to try. Our attorney called while I was dressing. I'm going up to Oxford to pick up Chloe and her things this afternoon. She's coming home to the Quarter." He didn't sound pleased. "She's coming home in disgrace."

"Oh, Ethan, she's just young. She'll find herself sooner or later." Cora knew that sounded lame but was at a loss for anything better. "Don't be too hard on her. Remember what they say about flies and honey, and not using vinegar."

Ethan laughed, pushing away his plate of untouched eggs. "I'm not sure I understand the analogy, but love the fact you're anxious to defend my wayward sister no matter when, no matter what she's done. We Galens are lucky indeed you decided to join our debased family." He lifted his mug in toast and downed his coffee in two swallows.

"The Galens are not debased. Any family would look dubious under the microscope of the press. Monday morning, I'm going to unplug the computer of the hack that wrote that article. He'll be sorry."

Ethan trapped both her hands between his. "You'll do nothing of the sort, my love. I won't have you arrested for journalistic espionage and have you spend even one night away from me." He bought her fingers up to his mouth. "Anyway, nothing the reporter wrote is untrue, according to my attorney. It's not the paper's fault that

Chloe manages to furnish such juicy morsels." He sucked on each of her fingertips in succession.

"They pick on her because your family is prominent and influential," Cora insisted.

"All the more reason for Chloe to grow up and behave accordingly." He bit lightly on her pinky. "But no more. That's all in the past." He released her hands with an audible sigh. "She is coming home, getting a job, and regaining her dignity. She has no other choice." Relief shaded his words. "All she has to do is look to her sister-in-law for a perfect model of Southern womanhood."

Cora giggled and threw her napkin at him. "Please, Ethan. Don't set me up as a paragon of virtue. I never had Chloe's opportunities or imagination or might have turned out the same way." She grinned at her husband with unabashed affection while he stared back with haunted, loving eyes.

They sat delighting in each other's company as only newlyweds can. Birds competed noisily for their attention as a few Live Oak leaves fluttered to the stones in the relentless passage of one season to the next.

"*Laissez le reste de ma vie avoir lieu comme ce moment,*" he murmured in a soft voice.

"I remember those words, Ethan. You said them to me in the garden after dinner but never told me what they meant. You will tell me what they mean now or suffer serious and painful consequences," she threatened, brandishing her fruit fork.

"I said, 'Let the remainder of my life be as this moment.' I love you, Cora."

Cora Dearing Galen, in a rare, almost unprecedented moment, was speechless.

* * * * *

REQUEST YOUR FREE BOOKS!
2 FREE NOVELS PLUS 2 FREE GIFTS!

 HARLEQUIN®

INTRIGUE

BREATHTAKING ROMANTIC SUSPENSE

HI15

REQUEST YOUR FREE BOOKS!
2 FREE NOVELS PLUS 2 FREE GIFTS!

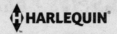

ROMANTIC suspense

Sparked by danger, fueled by passion

YES! Please send me 2 FREE Harlequin® Romantic Suspense novels and my 2 FREE gifts (gifts are worth about $10). After receiving them, if I don't wish to receive any more books, I can return the shipping statement marked "cancel." If I don't cancel, I will receive 4 brand-new novels every month and be billed just $4.74 per book in the U.S. or $5.49 per book in Canada. That's a savings of at least 12% off the cover price! It's quite a bargain! Shipping and handling is just 50¢ per book in the U.S. and 75¢ per book in Canada.* I understand that accepting the 2 free books and gifts places me under no obligation to buy anything. I can always return a shipment and cancel at any time. Even if I never buy another book, the two free books and gifts are mine to keep forever.

240/340 HDN GH3P

Name	(PLEASE PRINT)

Address	Apt. #

City	State/Prov.	Zip/Postal Code

Signature (if under 18, a parent or guardian must sign)

Mail to the **Reader Service:**
IN U.S.A.: P.O. Box 1867, Buffalo, NY 14240-1867
IN CANADA: P.O. Box 609, Fort Erie, Ontario L2A 5X3

Want to try two free books from another line?
Call 1-800-873-8635 or visit www.ReaderService.com.

* Terms and prices subject to change without notice. Prices do not include applicable taxes. Sales tax applicable in N.Y. Canadian residents will be charged applicable taxes. Offer not valid in Quebec. This offer is limited to one order per household. Not valid for current subscribers to Harlequin Romantic Suspense books. All orders subject to credit approval. Credit or debit balances in a customer's account(s) may be offset by any other outstanding balance owed by or to the customer. Please allow 4 to 6 weeks for delivery. Offer available while quantities last.

Your Privacy—The Reader Service is committed to protecting your privacy. Our Privacy Policy is available online at www.ReaderService.com or upon request from the Reader Service.

We make a portion of our mailing list available to reputable third parties that offer products we believe may interest you. If you prefer that we not exchange your name with third parties, or if you wish to clarify or modify your communication preferences, please visit us at www.ReaderService.com/consumerschoice or write to us at Reader Service Preference Service, P.O. Box 9062, Buffalo, NY 14240-9062. Include your complete name and address.

HRS15

REQUEST YOUR FREE BOOKS!

2 FREE NOVELS
FROM THE SUSPENSE COLLECTION
PLUS 2 FREE GIFTS!

YES! Please send me 2 FREE novels from the Suspense Collection and my 2 FREE gifts (gifts are worth about $10). After receiving them, if I don't wish to receive any more books, I can return the shipping statement marked "cancel." If I don't cancel, I will receive 4 brand-new novels every month and be billed just $6.49 per book in the U.S. or $6.99 per book in Canada. That's a savings of at least 19% off the cover price. It's quite a bargain! Shipping and handling is just 50¢ per book in the U.S. and 75¢ per book in Canada.* I understand that accepting the 2 free books and gifts places me under no obligation to buy anything. I can always return a shipment and cancel at any time. Even if I never buy another book, the two free books and gifts are mine to keep forever.

191/391 MDN GH4Z

Name _____ (PLEASE PRINT) _____

Address _____ Apt. # _____

City _____ State/Prov. _____ Zip/Postal Code _____

Signature (if under 18, a parent or guardian must sign)

Mail to the **Reader Service:**
IN U.S.A.: P.O. Box 1867, Buffalo, NY 14240-1867
IN CANADA: P.O. Box 609, Fort Erie, Ontario L2A 5X3

Want to try two free books from another line?
Call 1-800-873-8635 or visit www.ReaderService.com.

* Terms and prices subject to change without notice. Prices do not include applicable taxes. Sales tax applicable in N.Y. Canadian residents will be charged applicable taxes. Offer not valid in Quebec. This offer is limited to one order per household. Not valid for current subscribers to the Suspense Collection or the Romance/Suspense Collection. All orders subject to credit approval. Credit or debit balances in a customer's account(s) may be offset by any other outstanding balance owed by or to the customer. Please allow 4 to 6 weeks for delivery. Offer available while quantities last.

Your Privacy—The Reader Service is committed to protecting your privacy. Our Privacy Policy is available online at www.ReaderService.com or upon request from the Reader Service.

We make a portion of our mailing list available to reputable third parties that offer products we believe may interest you. If you prefer that we not exchange your name with third parties, or if you wish to clarify or modify your communication preferences, please visit us at www.ReaderService.com/consumerschoice or write to us at Reader Service Preference Service, P.O. Box 9062, Buffalo, NY 14240-9062. Include your complete name and address.

READERSERVICE.COM

Manage your account online!

- Review your order history
- Manage your payments
- Update your address

> *We've designed the*
> *Reader Service website*
> *just for you.*

Enjoy all the features!

- Discover new series available to you, and read excerpts from any series.
- Respond to mailings and special monthly offers.
- Connect with favorite authors at the blog.
- Browse the Bonus Bucks catalog and online-only exculsives.
- Share your feedback.

Visit us at:

ReaderService.com

RS15